Voice Lessons

Voice Lessons

A novel by Marcy Telles

Dedication

This book is dedicated to

- ❖ My daughter, my first and best critic. She is always gracious, honest, and helpful in her comments, unfailingly loving, and completely supportive of my writing. While the character of Ruth might be inspired by her, nothing I could write could come close to capturing how amazing she is in real life. Not to mention the grandchildren!
- ❖ My friends, who put up with me.
- ❖ My husband, who puts up with me 24/7.
- ❖ And to all those, known and unknown, who have held aloft the light of truth amid the darkness of human ignorance.

Prologue: September, 1964 – April, 1965

Wham! The ball hit Phoebe squarely on her 12-year-old rump, which collapsed in surprise under her. She sat for a moment, trying to regain her breath and what passed for her dignity.

"Sor-ree" said an unfamiliar voice behind her.

"You certainly are," mumbled Phoebe under her breath. She was used to being made the butt of jokes, but this seemed a bit literal, even for her somewhat crudely oriented classmates.

A hand dangled suddenly in front of her face and, looking up, Phoebe found it attached to a person she'd never seen before. Having spent her entire life in this neighborhood and knowing pretty much everyone in her class, a new face was enough of a novelty to capture her fractured attention.

"Hi," said the person. "I'm new here."

Well, terrific, thought Phoebe. God has sent another person to torture me. Thanks, God.

It was not easy to be a small, unorthodontured, bookish sort of person (who had not had a nose job) in a big New York junior high school where everyone was in a permanent state of competition. Each Friday, the girls made lists of who was most popular, which they passed around and reviewed with a serious concern they never employed in their academic pursuits. The boys strutted around like Jewish roosters, going "steady" with a different girl every week. Every one of them was brilliant at getting straight As without actually learning anything.

Well, Phoebe wasn't a complete non-contender. In fact, she won all the competitions to which she was assigned—most weekend nights spent alone, fewest friends, best attendance at the library. Her main role in the self-absorbed world of her classmates was to be a sort of poster child for who not to be. Thanks to Phoebe, every other 8th grade girl could console herself by being absolutely certain she was not the least popular girl in school.

The hand still hung in front of Phoebe's face, but it was beginning to waver.

"Oh, come on," said the same unfamiliar voice. "It was an honest mistake. Don't hold a grudge."

So, against her better judgment, Phoebe grasped the hand and it pulled her up.

"I'm Abby," said the stranger.

"Phoebe," said Phoebe, rubbing her rump.

Abby giggled. "I really got you that time," she said. "I'm going to live in fear until you decide to take your revenge."

Phoebe thought that if Abby ever lived in fear—which already seemed unlikely—she'd spend a long time there waiting tor Phoebe's revenge. For with one glance at Abby's smile, Phoebe was smitten.

* * *

And thus began the first truly happy time in Phoebe's life. Abby's family moved fairly frequently. Her father was a university professor and had been awarded lecturing chairs at colleges all over the East coast. She'd been exposed to every sort of school. She'd been looking forward to the move to New York, figuring it would offer the most interesting experience yet, but was disappointed to find herself in a suburban Jewish neighborhood in a forgotten corner of Queens rather than exciting Manhattan. But she was an optimistic person, and determined to make the best of things.

Surveying the scene in the "intellectually gifted" classes at the local junior high that morning, Abby had immediately singled out Phoebe as the most interesting person there. No one else seemed to pay attention to Phoebe, so Abby figured she had a chance to make a best friend right away. She had found this to be the key to enjoying her time in a new city. As she watched Phoebe, her heart broke to see how unhappy the girl was. She was at least as pretty as the popular girls—more so, because her face had some character and she didn't plaster makeup all over it. She was intelligent, and not just smart. She asked good questions in class, no matter how often the other kids made fun of her for it. So that morning, Abby had decided to make her move.

Gym class seemed like the best place to make contact. Most class time was heavily regimented, and lunchtime was a zoo. So as she pulled Phoebe to her feet, she started talking fast, inwardly laughing at herself because she sounded like a car salesman on a local TV ad.

"What are you doing after school?"

"Um. Going home?"

"Let's go into the city instead."

"Into the city?" Phoebe was dumbfounded.

"Yeah. It's easy. You can tell your mom you're going to my house."

"Where do you live?"

"About two blocks away—you?"

"About that."

"Great—we'll go to your house, I'll meet your mom, and we can drop off our books."

Phoebe thought her mother would faint when she introduced Abby as her new friend. Although their family was pretty non-religious, Mrs. Hirsch sent a silent prayer of thanks up to the general direction of the clouds. Phoebe had a friend! Of course she could go to Abby's house!

Abby was completely enchanted with Manhattan, and frankly, so was Phoebe. Despite growing up half an hour from midtown, she'd never spent any time in the city. They settled into a pattern—three times a week, they'd explore the city and on every other afternoon they'd race through their homework and study for tests at one house or the other. Before Phoebe knew it, Abby had found a few other outcasts and they'd formed a Scrabble club. They bicycled from house to house, scarfing down snacks, playing Scrabble, and chattering away about books and music and art. As far as Phoebe was concerned, it was heaven.

One day in late April, Abby casually brought up the Spring Fling—a school dance that Phoebe and the other two girls considered as alien an activity as ice hockey on the beach. When Abby started asking what they planned to wear at the dance, Phoebe almost choked on her Mallomar.

"You want to go to a dance?!" It was like saying that you wanted to reenact the Spanish Inquisition and were just trying to figure out who would bring the whips and chains. Julie and Beth—their two Scrabble friends—looked equally uncomfortable.

"It's our dance too," Abby said. "Why should those dopes have all the fun?"

"They're welcome to it," Phoebe said.

"Don't you like to dance?" Abby looked puzzled.

Phoebe had never really thought about it one way or the other. Like most of the girls in her class, she'd taken ballet lessons when she was six and had been told in no uncertain terms that she had no natural talent in that area.

"I don't think of myself as much of a dancer," she said finally, trying not to sound too negative. Abby hated negative.

"Why?"

"I just don't think I'm very good at it."

"What difference does that make?" Abby sounded dumbfounded. "Are you good at watching television? Riding a bike? Taking a bubble bath?"

"You don't have to be good at those things," Phoebe said. "You just do them because, well, because you enjoy them. Nobody cares what you look like when you ride your bike."

"Yeah. Well, dancing is just like that. You don't do it for other people or because you're good at it—you just do it. It feels good."

Phoebe was not sure exactly how Abby managed it, but two weeks later the four of them—the Scrabble Sisters, as Phoebe called them in her head—were standing awkwardly against the gym wall at the Spring Fling. They'd turned each of their closets inside out, with Abby voting for or vetoing their outfits. A quartet of less-than-talented ninth-grade boys was playing a Beatles song. Phoebe, Beth, and Julie looked like they'd been abducted by aliens, but Abby was moving rhythmically to the beat and smiling.

"C'mon," she said, grabbing Phoebe's sweaty hand. "Let's dance!"

"People will see us," Phoebe said, frantically trying to pull her hand away.

Abby laughed—that wonderful, joyful, carefree Abby laugh that Phoebe had learned to love so much.

"These people don't see anything but themselves," she assured Phoebe. "You might as well dance. Dance like nobody's watching—because they're not."

So they did.

Chapter 1: October, 1969

Phoebe sat on the floor of the filthy phone booth in the dorm lounge. She couldn't use the phone in her room because Carol, her room-mate, was having a conjugal visit from her high-school sweetheart. Only two months into freshman year and they couldn't bear to be apart. Phoebe had already barged in on them once, and the two shaggy heads poking up from Carol's homemade patchwork quilt reminded her of nothing so much as a pair of mating hobbits.

On the other end of the phone, Phoebe's best friend Abby was enthusing about life at Antioch College. Phoebe had not quite forgiven Abby for leaving a week after graduation. Antioch's trimester system rotated students from campus to internships every four months and Abby had been eager to leap in. Antioch was all she'd hoped it would be. With her beloved older sister already there, it offered both security and wild adventure. She was auditioning for a dance troupe. She had met this amazing guy. She was lining up a rotation at a community legal advice clinic in San Francisco.

Phoebe let all this enthusiasm slide through her ears as she leaned against the glass of the phone booth and gazed around the lounge. It was standard-issue state college decor, with a level of architectural indifference that involved a lot of concrete, linoleum, and cinder block.

Phoebe's sole criterion for a college was that it be as far from her family as possible. It was clear that she'd been a disappointment to them from the get-go, and she thought it kindest to all involved to disappear into the wider world as quickly as possible. Her parents' involvement at this point was minimal—her tuition was paid by a scholarship. A small monthly check for room and board was all that was required of them.

She let out a small sigh as she thought about her college application process. While her friends and classmates vied for Ivy League schools and scholarships, she spent most of her time crossing days off the calendar.

She found a state college—easy to get into and tucked into a distant corner of the state—and was admitted without suspense or ceremony. Her parents drove her up and helped her carry her things to her room. They said their stiff goodbyes, and that was that. The only person in Phoebe's life who felt that more was required of Phoebe was Abby, who seemed genuinely to believe in Phoebe's intelligence and ability, and was constantly stymied by her apparent lack of ambition or self-esteem.

At some point, Phoebe realized that the flood of words buzzing from the phone had ceased. After a moment of silence, she heard Abby's puzzled voice again.

"Are you still there?"

"Sure. Sure. It all sounds amazing," Phoebe managed.

"Oh, Fee," Abby said, her voice sympathetic. "Give it a chance. There's no shame in going to a state college. And maybe you can transfer to the university next year."

The very thought of the university made Phoebe shudder. Buffalo had both a state college and a state university, with the latter being far more prestigious. But she had been to the university campus a few times and the sheer volume of the place—size, noise, population—had given her the willies.

"Not sure that would help," she told Abby. "The college has a better art program anyway."

She had applied to school as an art education major because there wasn't anything she was passionately interested in, and most of her favorite high school teachers taught art. She liked the idea of being an artist and hanging out with artists. She loved the smell and color of the materials, and could wander through art supply stores for hours. She realized she had very little in the way of talent, but from what she could tell this was not a gating factor. The "education" part of art education had been a good strategic point with her parents. They saw little sign of any artistic talent that they could recognize and it was clear that they worried whether anyone would marry her. If those who can't, teach, they reasoned, then she was a natural for a teaching career.

"I am not convinced about the art thing," Abby said. "It's not that you aren't a good artist, but God, you are an amazing writer. You should be an English major. That letter you wrote me about Woodstock totally blew my mind. I showed it to everyone."

"Ugh," Phoebe said. Hanging out with English majors seemed way less cool than hanging out with artists. "And it was Woodstock that was amazing—not my letter." Woodstock *had* been amazing, but it would have been a hundred times better if Abby had been there with her. She shoved her fingers through her short black hair, wishing for the millionth time that it was long and wavy like Abby's.

"You have the most incredible ears," Abby laughed, and Phoebe, startled, moved her fingers down to her ears to see if they were some odd shape or something. But Abby cleared up the confusion. "Your ears can filter out even the smallest compliment. Hey—I have to go. Jude is taking me to some dance concert and I think Rafe might go." Judith was Abby's sister, and Rafe was the mysterious boyfriend candidate. "Just hang in there, Phoebe. If it's unbearable, get a bus ticket and come for a visit. You'd love it here. It's not that far away."

"Okay," Phoebe said.

"And write me some more letters!"

"Sure," Phoebe mumbled, and they said their goodbyes.

She stood up and opened the folding door of the phone booth. The dorm lounge was empty—there was something about it that did not encourage lounging. She started for the front door, thinking to get a cup of coffee at the Student Union, when she heard music coming from the stairwell.

It sounded like a guitar and maybe someone singing. There was something that felt out of kilter about it, and she realized that the voice was female but the guitar sounded…male? How could a guitar be male or female? Well, it sounded like what a guy would play if you gave him a guitar. A girl would strum folk songs. This music was blues, with some kind of twangy sound to it and a lot of finger picking. Okay, so maybe a guy *and* a girl. Not exactly a deep mystery but still, she was curious.

She opened the stairwell door, expecting to see a duo. But sitting on the landing was a single person who was definitely a girl. Her hair was a mass of frizzy curls, and her small round face looked like a flower bud inside a frill of over-enthusiastic foliage. She was dressed entirely in purple, except for her jeans, which she had managed to largely cover in purple patches.

She was singing softly, but she was playing quite loud. She had what looked like a lipstick tube on her left middle finger, which was moving madly up and down the guitar neck. Her right hand was playing a pretty interesting lead part. She looked up and grinned. It was a totally engaging grin, and Phoebe found herself returning it in kind.

"What *is* that?" Phoebe asked, pointing at the lipstick tube.

"Well," drawled the guitarist, "It's a slide. To play slide guitar. People mostly make them out of bottle-necks, but you have to grind down the broken end of the bottle and I wasn't sure how to do that. To tell you the truth, just the idea of breaking the bottle kind of freaked me out. Somebody told me you could use a lipstick case, which sounded safer, and it seems to works pretty good. I gave the lipstick to my roommate. I'm not the lipstick type."

Phoebe took all this in and decided to focus on the music part. "It sounds amazing," she said.

"Well, thank you," said the guitarist. "I'm Robin. Do you sing by any chance?"

"I…well, I mean, not usually for other people but, yeah, I like to sing," Phoebe said. Although she had a guitar of her own (didn't everyone?), she did not think of herself as a singer of any description. But everybody sang to some degree, right? And there was something about Robin that made Phoebe want to spend more time with her.

"So, let's find something to sing," Robin said.

Phoebe knew a lot of folk songs because Abby's sister Judith brought stacks of record albums with her every time she came home. Jude was a folk fanatic. Phoebe named a few songs she remembered from a record she particularly liked and Robin knew all of them. They started with those, and then Robin taught her some blues songs. They started working on harmonies, and Phoebe was surprised to find that the harmony parts came easy to her. They made the two voices into something else, a new voice that was all its own. There were notes that were begging to be included, like unpopular girls outside a cool party, and when you added them at just the right places, the whole song transformed—like a party with all the people you really wanted to party with, but maybe hadn't realized you did. At first she felt self-conscious. But she thought she heard the echo of a long-ago voice. "Sing like nobody's listening." Good advice.

It didn't seem like they'd been there very long, but when someone stumbled into the stairwell, Phoebe could see that it was dark outside.

"Holy shit," she said. "What time is it?"

Robin consulted a large purple wristwatch. "Holy shit," she agreed. "Dinner's almost over. C'mon, let's see if we can grab something before they close."

They quickly stashed the guitar in Robin's room and raced over to the cafeteria, laughing at nothing. The October air was already growing cold, but in that exciting way that meant that new things were starting. In the mostly empty cafeteria, they ate as though they'd run a steeplechase, instead of just sitting and singing. They chattered on to each other non-stop, and it felt like they would never run out of things to say. Phoebe hadn't felt like this since Abby moved into her neighborhood and became her first real friend. She realized she had assumed that she would only get one, but maybe she had hit the jackpot and been awarded a second friend. Or perhaps Abby had some sort of mystical power and had conjured Robin up for her out of her own compassion and Phoebe's despair.

When she got back to her room, Phoebe knocked cautiously but Carol and her boyfriend were gone. She sat down at the little desk and turned on the lamp, the shade of which Carol had decorated with yellow cellophane and tissue paper. Phoebe shook her head, thinking that if she, Phoebe, were a true art major she would have done something like this herself, but frankly such things never occurred to her. She started a letter to Abby, telling her about Robin and the music, and a very quiet voice in her head observed the contrast between her indifference toward the lampshade and the urge to write when something interesting happened.

Chapter 2: Late March, 1970

Robin looked up from a battered table at the back of the little restaurant and gave Phoebe one of her big grins. Spread out on the table were a few crumpled bills and teetering towers of change.

"We did great!" she squealed. "I think it's maybe twenty dollars!"

Phoebe was startled. That was the most they'd made so far. Sid, the restaurant owner, walked over and smiled when he saw the piles of quarters and dimes.

"Hey, not too shabby," he said. Naturally, he didn't pay them anything for performing, although he did give them dinner and non-alcoholic drinks. Both young ladies were over 18, but it didn't feel right to him to give them wine or even beer. He had daughters of his own.

"So," Robin said, looking up at him with her most appealing smile. "Are we on for next Saturday?"

"Not Friday?" said Sid.

"We don't want your customers getting tired of us!" Robin laughed, but Phoebe looked at her quizzically. She'd never known Robin to turn down a gig.

"Okay," Sid said, thinking he'd have to give one of the other girl singers a shot. Kids brought in other kids and they all ordered something. It was a no-brainer for him. If they were willing to sit there and sing for an entire evening with nothing but a lousy ten bucks each to show for it, who was he to complain? But he preferred these two. They were sweet girls—always polite, always on time. And they weren't bad either. Even the older customers seemed to like them. Hey, what's not to like about two pretty co-eds singing folk songs?

Sid went behind the bar and got a plastic bag for Robin. She scooped all the loot into it.

"One for the road?" Sid asked, holding up a couple of cokes. Robin glanced at Phoebe, who shook her head.

"Nah," Robin said. "I think we'll just scurry. It was fun, but it's a long ride back to campus."

"Lucky the buses run this late," Sid said, moving on to his closing chores—wiping down tables and such.

Robin knew how to talk to grown-ups in a way that Phoebe admired. Phoebe herself would probably have let on that they would be hitch-hiking back to school, but Robin knew that would upset Sid so she made it sound like they were taking the bus. Robin was a lot smarter than she let on sometimes. The better Phoebe knew her, the more impressed she was.

They packed up the guitars and headed out, making their way to the big street that ran toward the campus. Just walking through the restaurant door felt like being instantly encased in a shell of ice. Piles of snow remained along the curb, left over from the most recent storm, which was pretty darned recent.

Phoebe wondered when March was going to start turning into a lamb—she'd even settle for a warmer lion. She had not taken weather into account when she chose Buffalo as her college town. Could it really be that much worse than Long Island, where she'd grown up? The answer appeared to be a resounding yes. As far as she could tell, it could be that much worse than any place within the continental United States. There were actual underground tunnels between the older classroom buildings on campus so school could continue during blizzard season. The dorms, sadly, were beyond the tunnels, and when she carried two large sketch pads under her arms on her way to an early-morning drawing class, she felt sure the winds would lift her onto a nearby rooftop and no one would find her until the spring. If spring even existed in Buffalo.

"I got us another gig," Robin told her, as they set their guitars down on a dry patch of ground at the nearest intersection. The wind was whipping through the downtown streets and Robin's teeth were chattering, so it took Phoebe a moment to understand what she'd said.

"When?" Phoebe asked. Although it wasn't like she had any pressing social engagements likely to conflict.

"Next Friday," Robin said.

"So that's what that was about. And? Where is it?"

Robin grinned and did a little happy dance. "We're opening for the campus coffeehouse!"

"Wait—isn't that Tim Birch?" Phoebe loved Tim Birch.

"Yes!" Robin had the oddest way of saying "yes." It sounded like "Yay-as," with at least two, and sometimes three syllables.

Phoebe could feel an attack of terror coming on.

"Are we good enough for this?"

"We are totally good enough. And he is the nicest possible guy."

"How would you even know that?" Phoebe wondered, without quite realizing she was saying it out loud.

"Oh, let's just say I've met him once or twice," Robin said mysteriously, and then leapt forward as a car approached. It was pretty late (for Buffalo) and traffic had been almost non-existent. Robin waved madly and jumped up and down. To Phoebe's tremendous relief, the car slowed and stopped just a few feet beyond them. Snatching up their guitars, they trundled themselves into the car and took off, and that was the end of the conversation for the moment. Robin chattered on to the driver, while Phoebe sat quietly, thinking about the Tim Birch gig.

One thing about Tim Birch was that he collected songs from up-and-coming songwriters. He'd been one of the first to record Joni Mitchell's songs, and had run into Jackson Browne when Browne was just sixteen (and already writing the best songs around). So far, she and Robin did traditional material or songs written by their folk heroes, but very few songs of their own. Phoebe had made a few hesitant forays into the area of songwriting, but was still self-conscious and protective of her work. Robin was, as always, wildly enthusiastic. She loved Phoebe's songs. She could supply all and any ambition and support that Phoebe lacked. She had insisted they work one or two of Phoebe's new songs into their repertoire, and they had practiced those a little, but Phoebe always found some reason not to perform them.

Phoebe discounted Robin's opinions as the biased ravings of a devoted friend. But here was a real chance—someone who could tell her whether the songs were even slightly promising. She knew she'd have to steel herself for criticism, but criticism was what she needed. She couldn't trust Robin's take, but equally she didn't trust anyone else enough to play the songs for them. But, look at it this way—she wasn't likely to run into Mr. Birch again anytime soon. If he hated the songs, he'd just put them right out of his mind. He probably heard hundreds of wince-worthy songs on his tours.

As Robin chattered on, Phoebe sat in the back seat marveling at the turn things had taken. Only a few months ago she would have described herself as an art person—okay, an art teacher in training, but still—nothing musical would have entered the picture. Now, all her free time seemed to be devoted to music. Lots of people played guitar and sang songs and listened to records, but Robin had taken over Phoebe's entire psyche like a force of nature, transforming he entire self-image into one of a musician. Here she was, wondering if a respected recording artist like Tim Birch would be interested in her songs. You couldn't even call her music sophomoric, Phoebe reflected. She was still just a freshman.

And Phoebe had absolutely no musical training, unless you counted a half-dozen guitar lessons with some college kid during that last summer at home. She had picked up a lot of new chords and fingerings from Robin, but still considered herself a mediocre guitarist at best.

She was still mulling all this over as they approached the college. When the extremely accommodating driver dropped them off right in front of their dorm—Robin could sweet-talk almost anyone into almost anything—Phoebe said a quick goodnight and hustled up to her room. Carol was gone for the weekend—her turn to travel to see her hobbit lover. Shaking her head at the lunacy of it all, Phoebe pulled out the notebook where she stored her songs and started leafing through it. She might not be a musical powerhouse, but she did have a feeling for lyrics. It was the words she was interested in. She read through her songs and found one or two that she thought had promise, and she began to play them softly, changing a word here or there as she did.

The next evening, at their usual rendezvous in the stairwell, Phoebe brought up the idea of the original songs and Robin was thrilled. "Finally!" she crowed. "How many months have I been trying to get you to play those songs for actual people?"

"Yeah," Phoebe mumbled. "And now I wish we had. The idea of playing them in public for the first time when Tim Birch is here..."

"Practice makes perfect," Robin said. "We'll polish them up this week and get some people to preview them for us on Thursday. That'll make you a little less nervous."

Robin herself did not appear to get nervous when she performed. If anything, she was just the opposite. She prattled to the crowd, played solos she'd never played before, even took requests for songs they hadn't practiced. There were times when Phoebe would have liked to melt into the crowd to enjoy Robin's exuberance instead of sitting in the spotlight, trying to look like she felt as confident as her friend.

Thursday came, and they set up a little concert area in the dorm lounge—possibly the first time anyone had used it since they'd arrived on campus in September. There were a dozen mismatched chairs grouped around a stage area that consisted of two stools they'd abducted from the cafeteria.

Phoebe knew all the people in the "audience," since she and Robin had mostly all the same friends. The only surprise was the appearance of an older gentleman, who sat in the shadows in the back. But no amount of shadowing could keep Phoebe from recognizing her English Lit professor.

"What is Posen doing here?" she whispered fiercely to Robin.

"He loves your work. I thought he should hear your songs. It's all part of the same thing."

Phoebe's "work" was a handful of homework essays. Robin had found a few of them in Phoebe's room one time and read the review comments out loud in a dramatic voice. It was true that the comments were positive, but Phoebe figured Mr. Posen was eager to encourage any freshman who actually turned in an assignment on time. She started to try to figure out whether playing songs for her teacher would help or hurt her grade, but she was too wound up about playing them at all to get any kind of angle on it.

Robin grinned at the little clutch of friends in the improvised dorm-lounge coffeehouse and took up her role as mistress of ceremonies.

"Hello, friends!" She beamed out at them. "We are opening for none other than Mr. Tim Birch tomorrow night and we are thinking of trying out some new, *original* material! And when I say original, what I mean is never-before-heard songs written by our own Phoebe Hirsch!"

Phoebe tried to smile, but her face felt like it had turned to granite. Sensing Phoebe's nervousness, which might well have been radiating off her like heat, Robin hastily added, "We'll do one or two of our old favorites just to warm up."

Phoebe looked at her gratefully. "Sing like nobody's listening," she told herself fiercely. They launched into a blues song they had made free with, until it sounded nothing like its original self. Then a short ballad with haunting harmonies, and then their own version of a pop song. Phoebe could feel her chest relaxing, and she nodded to Robin to indicate that she was ready.

"And now, an original song by Phoebe," Robin said, belatedly realizing she had no idea which one it would be.

It was a song about winter, and the kind of hopelessness that permeated the atmosphere on a gray Monday morning after the glitter of Christmas and the abandon of New Year's. Phoebe had incorporated some of Robin's adventurous minor chords and after the first chorus, she was touched to hear Robin join in, improvising a supportive guitar part.

The surprised, pleased, and impressed response was impossible to misinterpret. Her friends seemed to be genuinely amazed that Phoebe could create something like that. She smiled a little and said, "Well, thanks. And now for something completely different."

She launched into a classic eight-bar blues chord progression and sang a song about the cluelessness of a pathetic freshman—herself—and her valiant efforts to hide it. She had thought it kind of cute when she wrote it, but her friends thought it was hilarious.

She looked out at the little crowd and saw that her professor was still there, in the back. She decided to take a chance on the last song.

"One more," she told the audience.

The last song was funny too, but far more biting. She wrote about all the things you learn in college that they don't teach in a classroom. It covered come-ons by upperclassmen, drugs, drinking, and room-mates who had sex while you pretended you were asleep. The audience—mostly freshmen like her—roared with laughter, but she saw, out of the corner of her eye, her professor rising and quietly leaving. Perhaps she had taken things a little too far for him.

Phoebe had only two classes on Friday and she skipped both of them to prepare for the coffeehouse that night. She had decided to work on all three of her original songs, in case Robin wanted to include them. Robin came by at lunch-time and they planned their set as carefully as if they were being featured on the Ed Sullivan show, rather than a college coffeehouse in Buffalo. They spent the afternoon practicing their usual material, working out kinks in the guitar parts and harmonies. At 6:00, Robin said, "Time for the sound check," making the phrase sound like a religious ritual she had been awaiting all her life.

They were pretty good friends with Marilyn, who ran the coffeehouse program, and so were treated with kindness but little ceremony. They had never sung with microphones before, and used every second they could to get used to that. You had to listen to the little black monitor speakers at the front of the stage, and not to the room at large, which was a totally different experience. And you had to remember that every time you turned your head, the sound changed for the audience. Robin was more thrown by this than Phoebe was, but she got the hang of it by the time Mr. Birch showed up for his own sound check.

He was easy-going and friendly and seemed surprised and pleased to see Robin. Phoebe couldn't hear their conversation, but it was clear they'd met before. She figured that was probably a good thing and let it go.

It was terrible waiting for the show to begin. The audience drifted in slowly, chatting and laughing, taking their seats with all the haste of a parade of 80-year-olds with walkers crossing a country road. After what seemed like several lifetimes, the lights went down and Marilyn welcomed everyone and introduced "our very own songbirds: Robin and Phoebe!"

The response was sort of lukewarm, but Phoebe was too freaked out to notice. They launched into their set, with the original songs waiting until they felt they had the audience on their side. Out of the corner of her eye, Phoebe saw Tim Birch take a seat at the back. Interestingly, she noticed that the tall man next to him was her Lit teacher. Either he took sadistic glee in watching her fail, or else that last song hadn't completely turned him off. Maybe he was just a second-chance kind of guy.

After their big crowd-pleaser—a raunchy folk blues with a great guitar solo—Robin announced that they would play a few of Phoebe's songs. Phoebe felt as though her heart saluted her sadly and jumped right out of her chest. "So young to die," she thought. But she took a deep breath and launched into the clueless freshman song.

Direct hit! The crowd loved it. Some instinct told her to switch gears and she played the winter song. She could hear Robin's quiet accompaniment behind her, and it felt like a loving embrace. Greatly daring, she looked out at the audience and saw every face turned up to her, drinking in the words, some heads nodding unconsciously as the images struck home. There was respectful applause.

"One more?" she asked the audience, and they called out their agreement. By now, she felt they were like a little family. So she launched into "They Don't Teach That in Class," and the laughter just about lifted her out of her seat. She turned toward Robin, who was glowing with love and approval, and they closed with a sing-along.

"I want more of that," Phoebe thought. And, for the first time she could remember, she felt that she could be someone real, someone who mattered, someone besides the disappointing nobody she'd always assumed herself to be.

Chapter 3: March, 1970, continued

There was a brief intermission, and Phoebe made her way to the little meeting room that served as the artists' green room. She stowed her guitar in its case and collapsed into a chair, closing her eyes, her head spinning. She heard Robin come in, chattering away to someone. A deep voice answered her. Tim Birch?

"And here she is," said the male voice. With an effort, Phoebe opened her eyes.

A pair of intense blue eyes under a shock of dark hair were smiling down at her. "I like your work, young lady."

Phoebe's heart decided to return to her chest. "Honestly?" she blurted out, before thinking that this was perhaps the lamest possible response.

"Honestly," he assured her. "How many more songs do you have?"

"Not a lot," she admitted. "Just some unfinished stuff."

"Well, finish it. There's a lot people looking for good material right now — myself included. How long would it take you to put together a tape of, say, six songs for me?"

Robin jumped in. "We could do that in a month or two, I bet. I'll help with the recording part."

Tim looked at Phoebe with a questioning eyebrow.

"I, well, I think I could do that," she said, wondering what on earth was compelling her to say this.

"Do it," Birch said. "It could change your life. I'm serious."

The door banged open and Marilyn poked her head in. "We're just about ready for you, Tim" she said. "Nice set, ladies!"

"Be right there," Birch said, striding over to his guitar case. "See you later?" he said to Robin.

"You betcha!" she replied, and Phoebe felt a little breeze of something nameless make its way around the room.

Phoebe looked at Robin questioningly, but Robin was fussing with her purse, pulling out a comb and dragging it through her unruly curls. Without looking at Phoebe directly, she said, "Let's go watch Tim's set. We did great, Fee! I bet he'll say something nice about us."

And he did, specifically praising Phoebe's songs and Robin's guitar playing. When the set was over, Robin seemed to have mysteriously disappeared and Tim was mobbed by happy fans, so Phoebe went back to the green room, collected her guitar, and headed for the door. A voice stopped her.

"Congratulations, Miss Hirsch," said her Lit professor.

"Thanks, Mr. Posen," Phoebe said. "Thanks for coming out to hear us."

"Well, your little friend invited me to the 'preview,' and I confess I found it quite intriguing. You have some real talent."

"Thanks!" Phoebe said for the third time, thinking that anyone with actual writing talent would have thought of something else to say by now.

"Of course, I'm not much of a music person," Mr. Posen said, managing to give the impression that this was a good thing. "But I do recognize good writing when I hear it. Have you considered doing other, er, forms of writing?"

"Such as?" Phoebe asked.

"Well, I'm starting up a campus magazine—humor and current events, that sort of thing. I think you have a real gift for humor. I wondered if you would write a little column for us."

Phoebe, thinking of the project for writing and recording six songs she'd just agreed to, on top of maintaining her classwork, let out an inadvertent groan.

"I'm not sure I have the time," she began.

"Oh, there isn't much pressure involved. The magazine is still in the planning stage, and we'll be lucky if we publish once a month, so there wouldn't be a lot of commitment required. I don't expect to get the first edition out until next fall, to be frank. Just give it a bit of thought. You could choose any subject you like."

Phoebe allowed herself a moment of fantasizing a column on the freshman experience and smiled a little to herself. If she were honest, she actually had a lot of material already, if she could get Abby to send back a few of the letters she'd written. Mr. Posen saw the smile and felt encouraged.

"Songwriting is wonderful, of course," he said. "But it's a bit limiting, isn't it? With a column, you wouldn't need to rhyme everything, and you could go into much more detail…"

"Let me think about it," Phoebe said. "I'm really flattered that you'd even ask. To be honest, I was afraid I'd offended you with that last song."

"Oh, I'm not easily offended," said Mr. Posen, who had written his share of satire back in the day. Not that his day had been all that long ago. He was resigned to the fact that all professors looked ancient to the freshman class. The handful of incoming women who did not find their professors ancient tried to involve those professors in highly questionable relationships. On the whole, Mr. Posen preferred to be ancient.

"Well, I'll see what I can come up with," Phoebe told him, and picked up her guitar case to signal that she was ready to go. He smiled. "Congratulations again," he said warmly. "This evening was quite a triumph for you. Enjoy it." And off he went.

It was all pretty heady stuff. Phoebe wished she had someone to celebrate with, but Robin had disappeared and the audience had pretty much dispersed. She headed back to her room and consoled herself by writing a long letter to Abby.

In the morning, she stopped by Robin's room but there was no one there. Phoebe went to her classes, feeling as though she was visiting an alternative universe. In one world, people wanted her to write songs and columns. In the other world, people felt that her pen-and-ink renderings of feathers and green peppers were lacking in substance. Abby's frequent advice to change her major to English played like a distant radio station in the back of her head, but she didn't feel an urgent need to change anything just yet. School itself felt artificial, as though it had switched places overnight with a world out of her wildest fantasies.

She looked for Robin at lunch, and after her last afternoon class. Finally, she gave up and went to the Student Union for a snack. Just as she had gotten embroiled in a political argument in the Rathskellar, Robin came bouncing in and plopped into the chair next to hers.

"Where have you been?" Phoebe asked her. "You vanished into thin air last night."

Phoebe's political adversary, sensing a distraction, gave a little salute and wandered off to look for another argument. Robin sighed.

"Well, not quite into thin air." She smiled mysteriously.

"I have so much to talk to you about," Phoebe said, then stopped, sensing she probably had things to listen to first. "Okay, what?"

"Tim," Robin purred, making the single name into half a paragraph.

"Isn't he married?"

"Sure. But. You know."

"I know it's not gonna be any good for you," Phoebe retorted.

"Oh, believe me, it was very good for me," Robin laughed.

"Yeah, but when will you even see him again?"

"You never know. There's all those folk festivals in the summer."

Phoebe played back her own interactions with Tim Birch from the previous evening and wondered just how serious he'd been about her songs. Maybe it was just a little sugar for his little sugar, she thought. Just a cheap, easy way to keep Robin on his string. Jeez, and now she was going to kill herself to get him that tape? What was the point?

She could feel the hot air balloon of last night's experience slowly deflating. When she called her parents later that day, the balloon deflated further. True to form, they flipped quickly through a narrow set of emotional responses and chose 'mildly alarmed.'

"I think you need a bit of perspective," her father told her. "You seem to feel that college is some kind of sleep-away camp. I'm sorry Phoebe, but you know you have a tendency to daydream your life away and your mother and I are concerned that you will spend your time singing folk songs. We expect you to go to class, do your work, and graduate on time. It's a full-time job for most young college students just to manage that much, especially during the difficult transition of freshman year. I'm glad you're enjoying yourself, of course I am, but this musical hobby of yours seems like it could be a real distraction."

"The thing I worry about, dear," said her mother, "is that being a big fish in such a small pond can be very misleading. Let's face it, if you were truly that talented, you'd have gotten into a much more, er, prestigious school."

Apparently Phoebe's mother had discovered that her bridge-playing friends regarded their children's schools as so many trading cards, and a state college was just not worth as many points as a private school. She seemed to feel that Phoebe had compromised her parents' social standing without warning her mother of the consequences.

Phoebe offered her professor's magazine idea as an alternative victory, but neither of her parents was much impressed by that either.

"You're not thinking of becoming an English major?" said her father in horror. "What sort of job do you think you could get with that sort of degree? Stick with your teaching major, Phoebe. Trust me, it is a much safer plan."

Phoebe gave up. She told them she had a class to run to, and got off the phone. She rummaged through her desk for the latest letter from Abby and found the phone number for her in San Francisco.

"Your parents are morons," Abby told her flatly, after hearing Phoebe's account of the ecstasy of the concert and the agony of the phone call.

"Yes, but they are my parents." Phoebe said in a small voice. "Sadly, I cannot trade them in on this year's model."

"Listen," Abby said. "I'll send you back your letters for humor-column inspiration, but you have to send me the essays you come up with. Deal?"

"Sure," Abby agreed. "After I write six songs and flunk all my classes." She had not told Abby about Robin's relationship with Tim Birch, feeling vaguely that this would be disloyal. But now she couldn't get Abby's take on whether the request for the tape had been genuine or not. She'd have to work that out on her own.

"Oh, yeah, and I want a copy of the tape." Abby added, and Phoebe noted how the essays had taken priority, with the songs an afterthought.

"And, now I have to tell you *my* news!" Abby said, her voice growing excited. Phoebe wondered how Abby's life could even get any more exciting, and was taking bets as to whether the news involved the boyfriend, the dance company, or the next work rotation.

As it turned out, it involved two out of the three.

"Rafe came out to San Francisco for a visit and he introduced me to these amazing people," Abby began. "They're called Sufis. They're a spiritual group, but they do all this singing and dancing and stuff. So I've been going to their meetings and I am totally into it."

Phoebe felt immediately uncomfortable. Abby had never been religious—or spiritual, whatever the difference was. Abby's dad was a non-practicing Jew and her mother a devout and politically active Catholic, but they had given each child the choice of religion—or non-religion—when they turned thirteen. Abby had chosen to be a Quaker, but she almost never went to services or worshipped in any way. Quakers had seemed cool to Phoebe—non-violence and silence and all. The Sufis sounded like a cult.

"How do you mean, totally into it?" Phoebe asked cautiously.

"I mean I go to these classes they have and I'm learning how to meditate and I just feel like I'm changing inside, I'm becoming this *mindful* person. I'm connecting with something bigger than myself, something truly meaningful. Deep."

Phoebe was now completely alarmed.

"That doesn't sound like you at all!" she said. "Are they brainwashing you or something?"

"No, no, not at all," Abby laughed. "They're just insanely cool people. You would love them."

Phoebe doubted this. "Where is this going?" she asked.

"Well," Abby said, taking a deep breath. "This guy Murshid Khalid, he's the head of the Sufi Society? So he decided he wants to start an intentional community. Right now, he holds these seminars and camps and things, and people just adore coming to them, but then they have to go back to their old, boring lives, separated from all the inspiration and love and spirituality and stuff. So he wants to make a place where people can weave their spiritual practice into their everyday lives, and vice versa. Like spirituality all the time, whether you're meditating or making dinner, or fixing a car or whatever. So they started looking for the land and they figure by next spring people will start moving there."

"Where?"

"Well, obviously they don't know yet. They just started looking. But I get the feeling it's going to be someplace on the East Coast. I mean, it's just way too expensive out here. Unless you go to Oregon, where it rains all the time…"

Phoebe was horrified enough to interrupt—something she rarely did to Abby. "And you're going to move there?"

"No—well, not permanently—at least not right away. No, I'm going to make it into a work rotation—starting a new community. I mean, how many times do you get the opportunity to design a whole community?"

Phoebe allowed that this could be interesting.

"More than interesting," Abby said. "I mean, all we do is protest, protest, protest, right?"

Phoebe, who was not particularly political, did not comment, and Abby went on.

"So this is a chance to say how things *should* be, instead of complaining about how they are."

Phoebe had no response to this. She couldn't get past the idea that she was losing Abby, that Abby was becoming somebody else. What possible value would Phoebe have in this spiritual world? Maybe she'd been right in the first place, and she only got to have one friend. Now that she had Robin, she was going to have to give up Abby.

Abby chattered on a little longer, and finally Phoebe told her she had to go. She couldn't lie to Abby and make up a class she was going to. But she couldn't stay on the line without saying something she might regret. She tried to cheer herself with the thought that the next rotation was six months away and maybe the whole community idea would evaporate by then, but somehow she felt it wouldn't.

She lay down on her bed and stared at the ceiling. She was losing Abby. Life without Abby was impossible to imagine. She loved Robin, and she hoped they'd be friends forever, but Robin wasn't Abby, and Phoebe wasn't sure she was Phoebe if Abby wasn't there.

Chapter 4: June, 1970 – July, 1971

As it turned out, Buffalo did have a spring season. It lasted for approximately three days in early June. Those were the three days when you could wear a leather jacket instead of a parka, and everyone on Elmwood Avenue seemed to be carrying little bunches of daffodils.

After that, it was straight-out Buffalo summer, which was a film negative of Buffalo winter. For freezing, substitute sweating. For icy winds, substitute humidity indistinguishable from outright liquid. For crazy hyperactivity, substitute languid catatonia.

Phoebe and Robin had decided to stay in Buffalo all summer so they could develop and record Phoebe's songs and maybe—just maybe—make it to a folk festival or two. Phoebe had been right in insisting that they could never make a reasonable demo in a month, and Robin had communicated this to Tim. She leveraged this shortcoming into thinly veiled requests for invitations to festivals so they could play the songs for him—and so that he and Robin could spend more time together.

The dorms were unavailable during the summer. They were used as housing for the freshman orientation sessions that ran from June through August. Ever-resourceful in support of love and music, Robin wangled a summer sublet from an upperclassman. She and Phoebe moved their meager belongings into the nearby apartment, feeling bohemian and sophisticated. In their eagerness to keep the apartment for the following school year, the upperclassmen paid a bit of the summer rent and Robin assured Phoebe that they'd gotten a great deal—after all, the place came furnished. The furniture was a combination of Goodwill chic and sidewalk cast-offs, but it made everything easier, and that's all they cared about.

Phoebe, for her part, negotiated a part-time job working at the freshman orientation sessions. These three-day workshops required little more than a knowledge of the class registration system and a willingness to hold the hair of freshman girls as they vomited their Harvey Wallbangers into dorm toilets. On the basis of this, she informed her parents that she had a paid job for the summer and had to remain at school. At the word "paid," they decided Phoebe was being practical and forward-looking at last, and that this experience might help her land a job later—although Phoebe could not see how, unless she changed her major to freshman orientation. They even agreed to continue her monthly allowance through the summer, as a reward for her industriousness.

So far, writing, rehearsing, and recording the tape for Tim had consumed them for the better part of May and about half of June, but now it was finished and had been sent off. A week went by. Two. So far no word from him. Every afternoon at 3:00, Phoebe made her ritual journey downstairs to the mailbox.

"Anything?" Robin called from the kitchen.

On this particular late-June day, Phoebe flipped through the day's mail which didn't take long. She was about to shout her usual "Not today," when, to her surprise, she found a letter addressed to the two of them.

"Yes!" she yelped, and dashed back to the kitchen waving a small envelope. She handed it to Robin, who tore it open without ceremony.

"It's from Tim," she grinned.

"And?"

"He…likes the songs…" Robin continued, at a maddeningly slow pace. "Oh!"

"Oh what?" Phoebe demanded.

"He wants us to come up to Toronto for the festival. He'll comp us. And he wants us to play a few of your songs before his set!"

The Toronto Folk Festival was only a few weeks away and they had studiously avoided discussing it. Their finances did not stretch to festival admission, and they had not dared to let themselves hope that anything like this would develop.

"Do you have an orientation session that weekend?" Robin asked.

"No. I kept it open. You know, just in case."

"Far out," Robin said, continuing to read. "Oh!"

"Again, oh?" Phoebe wailed, wishing she'd held onto the letter herself.

"He thinks he can get us into the Philly festival as well. We might even get paid for that one, or at least comped. There's some kind of panel discussion/demo thing on songwriting and he thinks he can get you on that, and there's another one on slide guitar, and he thinks he can get me on that one."

Phoebe collapsed into a kitchen chair. Robin folded the letter back into its envelope. "The rest is just stuff for me," she murmured. She sighed happily and looked up. "Hey! Let's celebrate!"

Phoebe sat numbly in the sunny kitchen while Robin called some friends and made arrangements to meet at a neighborhood bar. The one good thing about Buffalo in the summer was the bars, which turned into sidewalk cafes as soon as a normal person could sit outside wearing anything lighter than a snowsuit. Everyone gathered at their favorite watering hole for dinner—with their dogs, children, etc. Every bar had its culinary specialty—a particular salad or an inventive burger—and you could wander down Elmwood Avenue any summer evening, seeing different sets of friends at each bar, breaking into song, arguing politics, or dancing to a jukebox, depending on your preference or mood.

Phoebe listened to a few of Robin's giggling and excited phone calls and then let a slow smile break out over her face. She got up and shook herself all over like a wet dog, making Robin burst into laughter. In her room, she changed into a sundress, and then danced back out to the living room. Pulling out some Motown records, she stacked them on the record-player spindle and the two girls danced until they fell into the shredded armchairs that passed for furniture in their borrowed digs. Then they linked arms and headed for the bars.

The rest of the summer was a happy blur. They played some local coffeehouses, hitch-hiked up to Toronto, got stoned and played music after hours with performers and fellow folk fanatics, and then they hitch-hiked down to Philadelphia and did it some more. Phoebe stayed up til all hours writing songs and humor columns, and tried to stay awake the following days as she guided impossibly young freshmen through their three-day escape from mom and dad. It seemed like a single breath between receiving Tim's letter and the start of fall classes.

They ended up staying in their sublet digs, as some of the previous renters had changed their plans over the summer. Phoebe was delighted. She had grown attached to the sunny kitchen and the shabby living room. She bought a mattress and a cheap dresser to replace the ones that moved out, and added a few plants to make it feel like home. Or maybe just to make it feel like summer.

The summer had been a revelation. With Robin's unflagging confidence and enthusiasm surrounding her 24 hours a day, Phoebe had allowed herself to fantasize a life she had never even imagined before. She'd found the festivals terrifying but amazing. In a kind of fog, Phoebe wandered around to the various stages, hearing every type of folk music she could imagine, from her own established heroes to new voices she fell in love with at first listen. People recognized her—well, not a lot of people, but a few—after their set with Tim. And the crowning moment—Tim announcing from the stage that he'd be recording one of Phoebe's new songs on his next album—was something she played over and over again in her head.

The glow of all that music and comradery enveloped her in her own little cloud, but Phoebe's inherent cynicism and self-doubt could not help but whisper some not-so-sweet nothings in her ear. At the festivals, as she moved from stage to stage, she wandered into private conversations about recording contracts and touring arrangements that revealed a much seamier side to this business than she had expected. There were petty rivalries and an endless spiraling history of broken marriages and affairs. The girl singer who turned every male head had a snapshot of a baby in her wallet. The headstrong male protest singer had a shouting match with his manager over his billing in a benefit concert against the war. Everyone was an idealist and wanted to change the world, but each one was equally determined to achieve fame and fortune at the same time.

It was fascinating, frustrating, inspiring and crazy—and now it was all over. Phoebe couldn't help feeling she'd somehow imagined the entire thing. Returning to school, she felt like Alice trying to slither back through the looking-glass. She was returning from her first day's classes when she encountered Mr. Posen.

"Miss Hirsch," he said heartily. "And how was your summer?"

Phoebe was speechless for a moment, wondering how to sum up the events of the last three months. "Um," she said. "Great?"

"Good, good." She realized he wouldn't have really heard anything she said in any case. 'Great'' was probably sufficient.

"Got any material for me?" he asked, looking as though he expected the answer to be no.

"I do, actually," Phoebe told him. "I'll bring a few drafts over to your office tomorrow."

"Well, that's wonderful," her professor said in a surprised voice. "I'll look forward to that."

Phoebe wondered how other people dealt with the unending series of low expectations they encountered. "Are we all that disappointing?" she wondered silently. "Or would that just be me?"

The next day, she dropped a sheaf of typed essays on Mr. Posen's chair and waited while he began reading the first one.

Welcome to college! If you thought high school was unpleasant, here's the good news: college will make you look back on high school with love and nostalgia. Oh, to be hounded by teachers for your last assignment! Ah, the days of feeling trapped with the same people you've known your entire life! Now, no one cares whether you do your homework, and you don't know a soul aside from your dorm roommate, who's busy arranging conjugal visits with her hometown sweetheart. Oh, did you forget to have a hometown sweetheart? Well, if you're a female you can count on having an upperclass sweetheart—at least until he meets a more naïve freshman he can impress with even less effort. If you're a male, sorry, but it's going to be that sad prom experience all over again for you until next year's freshman girls arrive.

"Hmm," said Mr. Posen, looking over the rims of his glasses. "Must we terrify the freshmen so early in the game?

"Too harsh?" Phoebe asked.

"Perhaps a bit." He picked up the next one.

And now for this week's weather report. Awful and getting awfuller. No need to check the forecast for next week because it's pretty much going to be the same from now until late May.

All you dorm-dwellers and out-of-towners, we know you cherish a secret sense of superiority over the commuter gang. After all, you're not living with your parents—at least during school terms. You mostly come from somewhere near "the city," because we all know there's only one real city. But here's the thing—you are total wimps when it comes to the weather, and the locals know it.

Those adorable little sweaters and corduroy jeans looked fabulous in the Bloomingdale's dressing room, but the wind just whistles up your legs and slices right through those sweaters, and the icky-looking puffy down jackets you sneered at are appearing in your dreams. Yes, we know what you want for Christmas. And a flannel ear-flap hat wouldn't go amiss either, am I right?

"Hmm," said Mr. Posen, but with a distinctly upward pitch.

"Better?" Phoebe asked.

"Definitely better." He looked up and smiled. He had a surprisingly warm smile and, if Phoebe wasn't mistaken, a small dimple.

"You have a voice, Phoebe." So it was Phoebe now, she thought.

"It's not that common to find around here. You have to learn to recognize it and trust it. It's not enough to get the easy laugh—you've got to get the laugh that takes an extra second, but sticks in the reader's mind, that she finds herself repeating later to a friend."

Phoebe wasn't sure how to know what her anonymous reader would find of lasting value—it wasn't a concern she'd even considered. She'd applied Abby's old maxim, which she guessed in this case would be "write like nobody's going to read it," but somehow it didn't fit as nicely as it had with dancing and singing. And now Mr. Posen was specifically telling her otherwise. Hmm. Conflicting mentors.

She must have looked worried, because Mr. Posen broke into her thoughts with an unconvincingly unconcerned air. "Go ahead," he told her. "I'll get to the rest later. It looks like I've got enough here for the first couple of issues."

"Good," Phoebe said, and was surprised to find that she meant it. She gathered up her books and went off to write to Abby about it.

Chapter 5: September 1971 – January, 1972

The fall semester began in surprising glory. The trees outdid themselves with autumn color and the air remained practically balmy through September. Phoebe had just begun to settle into it when the first issue of the student magazine came out.

Phoebe nearly missed it. She and Robin had been working on some arrangements of her new songs, and the process had pushed almost everything else out of her head.

She was driving Robin crazy by tweaking the lyrics over and over. She was on her way from Drawing II to Ceramics, trying out different versions of the latest song in her head, when one of her housemates—Francine—ran up to her, flapping a copy of "Buff State in the Buff."

"Phoebe!" Francine shouted. "This is fantastic!"

"What is it?" Phoebe asked, staring at the flapping pages as though Francine had gotten hold of a bird by its spine.

"Your column of course," Francine said, staring at Phoebe in confusion. "It is totally hilarious."

"Oh, for heaven's sake," Phoebe said, grabbing the magazine. "Has that come out already?"

"I had no idea you could write like that," Francine went on. "I mean, I thought you were more of a songwriter."

"I am," Phoebe said. "I mean, I do that too."

"I am so jealous," Francine said. "I mean, I am a speech therapy major, for heaven's sake. I can barely write a term paper, and here you are an art major who writes songs and funny columns and everything."

"Well, at least you know what you're going to be when you grow up," Phoebe sighed. "It feels like everyone and her sister writes songs and poetry but you know none of us is going to make a living at it."

"True," Francine said with no hint of intentional cruelty. "But you are definitely having more fun than I am at the moment. And who knows—you could beat the odds." But she laughed when she said it, and then, giving a quick wave, ran off to her speech therapy class, where she was doing just fine. A suburban ranch house complete with husband and part-time speech therapy job was written on her future like a big red B-minus on a term paper, and it was a grade she was quite content with.

Phoebe knew she should feel a sense of accomplishment and pride, but a big part of her wished she was a speech therapy major. She wondered if there would ever be a time in her life when she could answer the question, "So, what do you do" with a single straightforward noun. Deciding to skip Ceramics—at which she frankly stank—she slouched over to Mr. Posen's office.

When she knocked and walked in, he looked up from his desk and began a smile, but dropped it when he saw her face.

"What?" he asked. "I thought it was really good. I've gotten some very positive comments on it already."

"The magazine?"

"Your column in particular," he said.

"Maybe I should switch my major to speech therapy," Phoebe growled.

"What? Where is *that* coming from?"

"Never mind."

Phoebe kicked at a piece of crumpled paper on the office floor, feeling like an overtired toddler in the supermarket, on the verge of a tantrum.

"Phoebe," Mr. Posen began. He was quiet for a moment. "Look, it's early days for you. I know it feels like you're flailing in a sea of possibility and uncertainty, but that's not necessarily a bad place to be. You have quite a lot of time to figure out how to take all the talents you have and harness them to something that looks like a career. It's a process. It's a question of going through the next door—the one that beckons to you right now. If you make some arbitrary decision based on what you think you might want in some future incarnation of yourself, chances are it will never lead to a place where you'll be happy."

This was, by far, the longest speech Phoebe had ever heard Mr. Posen make. He was much more of a listener than a lecturer. She wanted to continue to sulk, but she had to admit that his words had an effect. She liked the image of the doors. She could see herself in a long corridor of unlabeled doors, each one leading to the next in a particular path, but no indication of which path was the one she ought to follow. She could get a tiny glimpse—like Alice looking through the keyhole at the garden in Wonderland. For a moment, she could see a place where her apparently conflicting mentors overlapped: if you wanted to find the right door, you had to write for yourself—almost as if nobody was reading it.

She must have had an intense look on her face because she glanced up to see Mr. Posen examining her quizzically and wondered how long she had been wandering down that corridor of doors to the future.

"Right. Okay," she said slowly, and got up. "Okay. For a while, anyway." And, leaving Mr. Posen with a look of bewilderment on his kind face, she went off to Ceramics, where she spent a good forty-five minutes at a kick wheel making an alleged pot that brought actual tears of pain to her teacher's eyes. She had heard that he drank a bit and she had a feeling she was responsible for more than a few bottles of rotgut.

It felt to Phoebe as if the movie of her life froze into a snapshot at that moment and the next moment the film restarted and midterms had arrived. The second issue of "Buff State in the Buff" came out, and snow started to fall. Perhaps she was in a time warp, where time crept by in her classes and then swept through like an avalanche when she was writing. She had disciplined herself to stop questioning every decision—and non-decision—she was making, but it left her feeling a sense of ongoing chaos. She often found herself compulsively sweeping her room, just to feel as if she could control something, even if it was only dust.

She was doing exactly that when Robin planted herself in the doorway, munching an apple.

"I got a letter from Tim," she said, smiling around the apple.

"How's his wife?" Phoebe mumbled.

"Now, now," Robin laughed. "That's between the two of them."

"And so are you," Phoebe retorted.

"Anyway…"

Phoebe gave up. "Yes?"

"His new album is coming out next week!"

This was indeed news because the new album had one of Phoebe's songs on it.

"Holy shit!" Phoebe said, dropping the broom and sinking onto her bed.

"Indeed."

Phoebe was silent, and Robin let her be for a moment. Finally, she looked up at her still-munching friend.

"We should figure some stuff out."

"Yes."

"I mean—it's possible—just barely, but it is possible…"

"That other people might want these songs?"

"Well…"

"It's more than possible. Look at all those other singer-songwriters."

"But they're…"

"Performing."

"Right."

"But how would we…?"

"Well, that's a problem to solve. But it's not like we can't solve it."

Phoebe realized that the last three minutes of pseudo-conversation was the lengthiest discussion she and Robin had had about their situation, and that the undiscussed aspects of their incipient musical career were filling up the room like some invisible but potentially poisonous gas, replacing the oxygen with something nameless and scary. After all, Robin was not a singer-songwriter, exactly. She was an amazing musician. She was the Mimi Farina to Phoebe's Richard, the Sylvia to Phoebe's Ian. "And why am I always the guy?" she wondered.

But mostly she wondered how to make things fair. Robin was the driving force, the ambition, and, in Phoebe's opinion, the real talent. Like most people who write, Phoebe figured anyone could do it if they just took the time.

Robin sat down on the bed. Uh oh, Phoebe thought.

"Look," Robin began. "It's not like you are single-mindedly pursuing a college degree that you care passionately about and that you hope will define your life and career forever more."

This description was so far from reality that Phoebe had to smile. "No," she said. "I mean, not exactly."

"And neither am I," Robin said.

"Clearly."

"So. Why shouldn't we take a little time off from school?"

Because my parents would kill me after cutting me off without a cent, Phoebe thought but did not say.

"Well," she said instead. "There's the money thing."

"So, suppose we could solve the money thing."

"That's a lot of supposing."

"Suppose I have a plan," Robin said.

Phoebe sighed. When did Robin *not* have a plan?

* * *

Phoebe was sitting in Delaware Park, staring at the sculptures outside the Albright-Knox Museum. It occurred to her vaguely that the sculptures were harder to see than they had been, and she glanced at her watch. She had been sitting here for three hours. The sun was setting.

She got up, stiff and shivering a bit. A beer was what she needed. Maybe some French fries. She started walking toward campus, her hands stuffed deep in her pockets and her head down. As she got to the main quad, a hand landed on her shoulder.

"I've been looking everywhere for you." Mr. Posen was looking at her with a worried expression. "You look like you've had a shock. What's going on? Have you had bad news? Is everything all right?"

Phoebe sighed. "I am not all right," she said. "I haven't had anything that actually qualifies as news, since it's all stuff I knew before, but something is going on—I'm just not sure what it is yet."

She could swear that her teacher rolled his eyes at this, but when she focused on his face all she could see was concern.

"Yes. Well. Be that as it may," he said, and then got hold of himself. "Look. I *do* have some news."

He handed her a sheet of paper. It seemed to be a flyer—the sort of thing plastered on department bulletin boards all over campus advertising summer programs or study abroad. It didn't seem like anything all that momentous. Phoebe wanted to hand it back, not wanting some trivial thing to deal with when she was wrestling with her future, but Mr. Posen pressed it back into her hands and stood back a bit.

"Take a look," he said gently.

She forced her eyes to focus on the flyer. It was a contest of some kind. A writing competition. The first prize was a summer internship at a New York magazine.

"Oh, come on," Phoebe said.

"You don't think you have a chance?"

"Well, maybe a chance, but honestly—it's like Publisher's Sweepstakes. There must be thousands of students entering this thing. And they probably have someone all picked out for it already."

"Now that I know is untrue," Mr. Posen told her. "A former student of mine works on the magazine. It's legit."

Phoebe looked at him with a half-smile. "You have an in?"

"No, no," he actually blushed. "Nothing like that. I'm just telling you that it is a real contest and I think you have a shot."

"Can we get a beer?" Phoebe said, wondering how her relationship to this rather formal man had progressed to the beer stage.

"Sure," said Mr. Posen, wondering the same thing.

So over a beer or two she explained her dilemma.

"I owe this to Robin," she said for the third or fourth time. "She can't do it without me—I mean, chances are she can't do it *with* me either, but at least I'll know that I did all I could."

"But if she can't do it without you and it isn't your dream—what good is it? To you or her?"

Phoebe felt muddled about that. On the one hand, she thought Robin was genuinely talented and could, in the crazy folk world, make it. But you needed a way to get started and Robin had convinced her that it was the two of them that created that opportunity—one slide guitarist wasn't enough. It was the songs, the arrangements, the voices. That would get them the gigs and maybe even a record deal. After that, Robin would make her own way if Phoebe didn't want to continue. But Robin always felt sure Phoebe would want to continue once they were a success—who wouldn't? Phoebe had started to think that was how she felt, too, but somehow the actual feeling of it eluded her.

"Look, how about this," Mr. Posen said. "Go ahead and take a leave of absence for a semester—why not? Let Robin make whatever plans she can for performing or whatever. But meanwhile, write the essay and send it in. If you don't win the contest, you haven't lost anything and neither has Robin. If you do win…"

"Oh no!" Phoebe said in mock horror. "Oh no, I've won the contest!"

"Exactly," said Mr. Posen, with an air of "my work here is done."

* * *

And the crazy thing was, working on the essay made the whole thing with Robin bearable.

They arranged to take the spring semester off, with a view to setting up gigs for the summer and the following fall. Phoebe decided that the easiest way to deal with her parents was simply not to tell them anything at all. She spoke to them so rarely now that it wasn't even necessary to lie—they never asked about her classes, or much of anything else. They continued sending her monthly stipend, and—with the surprising arrival of a royalty check for her contribution to Tim's album—she managed to get by.

Robin went at her plan the way she did everything in her life—head on, full out, all in. She contacted every performer she'd ever met, got the name of every agent in the business, made copies of demo tapes, lined up potential gigs on a calendar illustrated with kittens. When she ran out of gigs to pursue, she subjected Phoebe to long practice sessions and worked out complex guitar arrangements that she taught Phoebe with a surprising amount of patience.

Phoebe felt a little like Eliza Doolittle to Robin's Henry Higgins. It was not an altogether pleasing feeling. So, when it all got too frustrating, Phoebe would lock herself in her room and write.

Sometimes she wrote long letters to Abby, but she rarely sent them. Abby had fallen further under the spell of the Sufis and tended to respond to all problems with Arabic catch phrases or advice to meditate. As a result of these non-responses, Phoebe's letters eventually morphed into essays. She had hoped to write something funny for the essay contest. But the essays were not all that funny. Phoebe wasn't feeling all that funny. The fact was, she was mostly confused. A career as a singer-songwriter had seemed like a no-brainer at first—it had always been a source of recognition, success, pleasure. But continued exposure to the actual world of singing and songwriting revealed things Phoebe would rather not have known.

She realized that she, like countless others, had taken the folk movement at its word. The songs were about real feelings and real people, a backlash against the empty pop lyrics that came before. Or they were about changing the world with love and a pure, righteous anger. It was that purity that she had loved, that willingness to walk away from the cynical, self-involved, self-promoting world she had always hated.

She wanted so badly to believe that there was something more out there, something good and kind and different—something beyond suburbs and social ambitions, beyond a lucrative career that you tried to fit your real self in around the edges. But now, with Robin beavering away at "making it" in the folk world, it felt like there wasn't much difference between succeeding in some mainstream career, like advertising or teaching, and this new, idealistic alternative. Under the patchwork skirts and the passionate voices were the same egos vying for success. In a way, it was even worse than the original set of choices. It felt like betrayal.

Every Thursday afternoon, she dropped off another essay draft at Mr. Posen's office, and every Friday morning he returned it with a sad little face drawn in the corner. She tried riffing on college life, tried political humor, tried feminist humor, tried pretty much everything except finger puppets. She just wasn't feeling funny.

Meanwhile, things with Robin were tense. For every gig Robin lined up, another one fell through or became less profitable. A concert/workshop became an opportunity to open for someone else. An inquiry about one of Phoebe's songs went nowhere. Robin decided that they needed to be more present on the folk scene, so once a month they hitch-hiked down to New York and tried to make friends with other aspiring folk people. At first, Phoebe enjoyed these trips. The folk scene was rich and varied and it was fascinating to meet people who were so passionately devoted to some corner of it—Shape Note singing or Hawaiian slack key guitar. But after a while, she couldn't help but see the sad side of it. The traditionalists who argued bitterly over the 32nd verse of some dead-queen ballad, or the songwriter who swore that Joni Mitchell had stolen all her ideas. Even the protest singers, who seemed most devoted to social change, were competing on some level.

One night, sitting at the bar at the back of a dive in the Village and listening to some not-very-in-tune woman from West Virginia, Phoebe was daydreaming about some lyrics she was working on when Robin's voice penetrated her awareness. Robin was talking about recording contracts with another musician and for a moment, Phoebe thought Robin was possessed by a capitalist demon.

"Ten percent is ridiculous if the royalties are only 8 percent to begin with," Robin was saying, in a voice that sounded so worldly that Phoebe could not believe it belonged to the same person she had met, covered in purple patches and listening to old blues musicians with tears in her eyes. Where had this new person come from?

Without thinking, she turned to Robin and said, "Face it, it's never going to be about the money. You'd have a better chance betting on the stock market, if profit is what you're after."

"The stock market?!" Robin looked at Phoebe as though she had suggested that Robin invest in tract homes on the planet Mars. "What on earth are you talking about?"

"When did this all get to be about percentages and royalties?" Phoebe asked her.

"It is not about that," Robin said, unconvincingly.

"Really? I haven't heard you talk about anything else in weeks."

"Well, that's just…Sure, you're off in La La land, dreaming up lyrics while I try to make sure we have some kind of future and that's all you can say to me—that I'm all about the money?"

"Well aren't you?"

"Look, the money makes the music possible," Robin said, and Phoebe thought "She was ready with that."

Phoebe got up from her barstool and stood for a moment, staring at her friend. Her world had narrowed, she realized. It was her and Robin, and most everything else had been pushed aside. And now neither of them was getting what she wanted.

"Robin," she said slowly. "You're right. I'm ungrateful. And irresponsible. I've let you shoulder all of that stuff. And it's poisoning you. It's taking your music away from you. We need to change that. I…"

"Oh, don't tell me what to do with my music," Robin blazed at her. "Who do you think is the talent here?"

Phoebe nodded slowly. She looked around the room at the other conversations, probably much like this one, and thought to herself that what Robin said might well be true but that the talent Robin was talking about was one she didn't much care for. Robin turned away and Phoebe told her stiff little purple back that she needed some air.

She walked around the Village like a small out-of-town ghost, her hands shoved in her pockets. She passed by coffeehouse after coffeehouse, their doors open, music spilling out with a bit of light. She took in the tired faces of the waitresses counting their tips, the hungry faces of the performers longing for applause, the cynical expressions of the owners hoping this fad would last just a little longer.

The emotions of the past few months swept over her, nameless and confused. It seemed suddenly obvious that there was a way to deal with those feelings, and she had somehow been ignoring it all this time. Ducking into a café, she dug a notebook out of her purse and started writing. Writing like nobody was reading it.

Throwing caution to the wind, she skewered the traditionalists, with their inscrutable ballads about incest among long-dead royalty and the protest singers, for whom nothing was pure or high-minded enough, and the singer-songwriters with their endless introspection. And underneath it all, few aspirations beyond getting a recording contract.

Backstage at a Sing Out benefit, the folk musicians were discussing the important issues of the day. The war, you say? The women's movement mayhap? Or the coming environmental apocalypse? Oh, please.

"I would never go with Warner-Reprise," confided a young man in carefully patched denim. "They refuse to divest their holdings in South Africa."

"Well. That and the fact that they haven't offered you a contract. Not even after the tenth demo you sent them," remarked a young woman in a patchwork skirt.

"And you're making a living wage on Folkways?" the young man sneered.

"If it's good enough for Pete Seeger, it's good enough for me," she retorted, and watched with satisfaction as he turned beet red.

"She doesn't need a living wage from her records," a young man whispered to his neighbor, putting down his pennywhistle for a moment (to the great relief of those nearby). "Her great grand-dad started Monsanto. She doesn't exactly advertise that, of course, but she's basically a trust-fund victim."

"I heard that," said the patchwork skirt owner. (On closer examination, the skirt appeared to come from Bergdorf's).

"Well, I should hope so," he replied. "There were rumors that you were losing your hearing. Or at least your sense of pitch. Personally, I find it hard to respect your music as an art form. I mean, basically your contribution is memorizing endless verses to ballads that were politically relevant 600 years ago."

"Ah yes, and the mastery of the pennywhistle is the highest form of culture, I suppose. Your crap is ephemeral. If you can even spell that. Face it: after centuries of war, it is these ballads that survive, that remind us of what it means to be human. I am but the humble servant of generations of troubadours who didn't have the benefit of high fidelity..."

"No, dear," the pennywhistler threw over his shoulder as he and a banjo player retired to a distant corner. "The humble servants are the ones who polish your shoes at home."

"Well, Warner-Reprise is working for *me*," yawned a lithe blonde in a low-cut peasant blouse. "They understand me. My broken heart. My poetry. And did you know I slept with Leonard Cohen?"

"As who has not," muttered an attractive young man hovering nearby. "Damn Canadians. And if that skinny bastard from Minnesota hadn't outright stolen my best work from that singer-songwriter project album, it would be working for me too."

"Yeah!" came a shout from the back of the room. "I almost got it," where a painfully young suburban kid with acne was playing a 4-bar blues riff for the thirty-ninth time. Somewhere, a black blues musician was holding his head in pain.

A waitress came by and pointedly asked if Phoebe wanted anything else. Startled, Phoebe ordered a coffee and re-entered reality. She stared at her notebook, unable to recognize her own handwriting for a moment, and glanced around, hoping no one had been reading over her shoulder. Frankly, she hadn't realized how much the various sides of the folk scene had warred within her, and she wasn't sure if it was funny exactly, but it was true in some way that was new to her. She caught herself reaching for the corner of the page, prepared to crumple it and toss it before anyone saw it. But she stopped. Sitting back, she began editing it in her mind, making it a bit lighter here, a bit sharper there. When she looked up again, there was a cold cup of coffee at her elbow, the café was closing, and she realized she had no idea where to find Robin or how to get home.

Chapter 6: January 1972 – March, 1972

Glancing at her watch, Phoebe discovered that it was 2:00 a.m. The last bus, she knew, had left for Buffalo at 1:45, and Robin was probably on it. The next bus was at 6. Four hours to kill.

Standing on the sidewalk outside the shuttered café, she rummaged through her bag, wondering just how much cash she had and whether she had anything to read. There were Automats just a little ways uptown that were open all night. Pulling out random items, she found herself clutching the writing-contest flyer Mr. Posen had given her. The magazine's address was not that far away.

It wouldn't do any harm just to walk past it, she thought. See where the contest winner would be spending the following year. The deserted street she was on didn't feel threatening exactly, but somehow she felt better having a destination, even if it was only a place to walk past on the way to Port Authority.

The address was in the West Village, a little north and west of where she was right now. In a few minutes, she found herself on a tree-lined street with wrought iron railings around window boxes filled with little evergreens. She half-expected some B-list Fifties musical comedy stars to come dancing down the sidewalk. The magazine offices appeared to occupy a handsome little three-story brownstone. Staring up at its windows, she thought she could see light seeping out of a back room on the second floor.

A small gate led to a side yard where the trash cans were kept. Stepping carefully around them (New York was famous for its rats), she found that she could make her way to the back of the building, where a tiny brick courtyard held a few weathered outdoor chairs and a sad-looking umbrella. She looked up at the floor where she'd seen the light and, sure enough, there was someone up there, pounding away on a typewriter. Before she could think it through, she scooped up some pebbles from the courtyard and flung them at the window.

They made a satisfying spray of sound and the typist looked up, startled. She threw one more. She watched the figure—a man, she could see now—move cautiously to the window and look out. She waved gaily. He looked puzzled, but opened the window and leaned out.

"Did you want something? Do I know you?"

"I do, and you don't," she replied. "Do you have a minute? I have some questions."

If he had looked puzzled before he looked completely mystified now, but he nodded and pointed downward toward a door. Closing the window, he disappeared. When the door opened, Phoebe could see he was only a few years older than she was.

"Hi," she said. "Can I come in?"

* * *

On the 6 a.m. bus, Phoebe dozed on and off, her dreams melting into the conversation of the previous night and the conversation writing the script for her dreams.

The young man she had interrupted at his typewriter was named Kent, and he was, in fact, the previous student of Mr. Posen's that she'd heard about. They bonded over stories of their professor, whom both of them adored. Kent hastened to tell Phoebe that he had no influence over the contest and could not be of any help there. This came as a relief to Phoebe, who didn't relish the idea of being accused of courting favors. At this point, he was a lowly copy editor, but he had aspirations. He showed Phoebe some of his work and talked about the magazine in terms so glowing that it might have represented the afterlife of his personal religion. Phoebe found herself comparing the zeal of this writer with the folksingers she was skewering and found many points in common. But there was something about the young man's enthusiasm that was catching, and he made her laugh out loud more than once. By the time the sun came up, she could imagine herself so clearly in this world that she could almost see a little ghostly version of herself, out of the corner of her eye, at a battered table in the corner, scribbling away and laughing to herself like a crazy person. When she compared this vision to the one of herself and Robin on stage at a folk festival, there was no contest.

Or rather, there was. And now she had to win it.

* * *

"This is…."

"Edgy?"

"That would be one word for it."

"Yes," Phoebe said. "But is it funny?"

Mr. Posen looked at her for a long moment.

"That's your question?" he asked.

"Well, I'm competing as a humor writer," Phoebe said, with exaggerated patience. "Funny is the operative word, I'd think."

"Phoebe," Mr. Posen sighed. "I think I've created a monster."

"Um. That would be me?"

"In a word."

"Because it's edgy."

"Because the people you are closest to..."

"Robin."

"Yes. Because Robin will probably never speak to you again."

"Yeah," Phoebe stared out the window, trying to look nonchalant. "Probably." She was thinking that writing like nobody would read it was not as easy as it sounded.

"Is this essay really worth that? There are lots of other things you could write about."

"But this is real. This is something I can see that most people can't see. This is something that allows people to laugh at something they wanted to laugh at but that felt too sacred for laughter."

"Profound. Or..."

"Or?"

"Or an excuse for indulging in some holier-than-thou behavior of your own."

"Well, there's that," Phoebe said. But Mr. Posen suspected that this essay was going to be on its way to New

York in the very near future, no matter what he said. So he didn't say anything. He wasn't entirely sure how he felt about that. Apparently, not a hundred percent positive.

* * *

It wasn't all that long before the campus newspaper ran a story on the contest, congratulating Phoebe on a prestigious achievement. Unfortunately, they also ran her winning essay. Phoebe came home that afternoon to find her mattress on the sidewalk.

Phoebe's key still worked—Robin was great at the grand gesture but a little loose on details—so she let herself in. Nobody home. Looking around her mattress-less room, she realized how few possessions she had, and she quickly packed them up in a few boxes she'd snagged from the local grocery store. Addressing them to the magazine office, she hauled them, one by one, down to the post office in the wheelbarrow that the landlord kept in the back yard. On her final return trip, she ran into Robin.

"Nice," Robin said with a raised eyebrow, summing up the essay, the empty room, and the wheelbarrow with economical sarcasm.

"Sorry," Phoebe said.

"Or not."

"You're right. I'm not." Phoebe wandered into the living room and sank into one of the threadbare chairs. The mattress thing had shifted her mood from uneasy to defiant. But as she sat there, she could feel the needle moving back toward uneasy. She was just beginning to realize what "burning your bridges" could mean. She was already wondering whether she could backpedal somehow, undo the damage, when Robin walked in. She looked as defeated as Phoebe felt.

"I guess it never was your dream," Robin said. "It's just—you were so good at it."

"You're plenty good," Phoebe said. "And you want it. You'll make it happen."

Robin shrugged. "Maybe."

"I don't expect you to forgive me."

"Good thing."

"Or anyone else either—I'm sure there are lots of other people mad at me too."

"Understatement."

Phoebe cast about for something else to say, but there wasn't anything. The set of Robin's shoulders told her in no uncertain terms that there was no turning back. There were no guarantees that this new path was going to work out, and she was setting out on it alone. She realized how important Robin's unshakeable confidence and faith in her had been, and that there would probably be no one in her new world who would come close to supporting her in that way. A cold ball of terror began to form in her stomach and she stood up suddenly, willing it to go away.

"Good luck," Robin said to the floor.

"Thanks," Phoebe said to the air. And then she left.

* * *

On the bus, she read the congratulatory letter from the magazine approximately three hundred times. Each time it gave her an address, date, and time for a meeting, but no further information. Hauling her suitcase through the subways, she wondered where she would stay and how she would afford a year in New York. If the contest involved too much fine print, she might find herself back in Buffalo by nightfall. Not that she had a place to stay there, either.

Dragging the suitcase up the front steps of the brownstone, she cast her eyes skyward and mumbled something that might pass for a prayer. She rang the doorbell and tried to catch her breath. It was Kent who came to answer and she gave him a relieved smile. In this new life, he qualified as an old friend.

He opened the door with a flourish and welcomed her in.

"The top brass are waiting in the big conference room," he told her.

"The one where we played wastebasket-ball?"

"That's the one. You can leave the suitcase here—we'll get it later."

Phoebe wondered where they would take it, but that was still in the future and she had enough to deal with in the now.

She climbed the stairs, gazing around with new, proprietary eyes. This was her place of work now, her magazine. Through partly open oak doors, she could see young people bent over desks, reading from pages that were still in their typewriter platens. The sound of typing formed a kind of percussive background music, punctuated by occasional snorts of laughter. It all seemed perfectly wonderful to Phoebe, sweeter than any folk music she'd ever heard, more beautiful than any painting she'd studied.

The people in the conference room were older than the writers and none of them were laughing, although several smiled at her as she walked in. The man at the head of the table waved her to a seat. There was a moment of shuffled settling down as everyone took his place, and Kent waited for a moment, apparently hoping for an invitation. After a long moment, he figured out that he was not going to be included, so he squeezed Phoebe's shoulder and left the room. The door made a solid thunk as it closed and the room was suddenly much quieter.

"Well," said the man in charge. "Our heartiest congratulations on winning what was a very competitive contest. And welcome to our little world."

Phoebe felt the eyes of the group on her and she managed a smile.

"Thank you. I'm proud and happy to be here."

"I want to fill you in as quickly as possible on what you'll be doing here and what we expect from you," the man continued. "First, let me introduce our executive staff."

The man in charge was named Hudson Everson. Phoebe reflected that every wealthy man she'd ever met had a last name for a first name. Apparently, Hudson was no exception. Everything about him said money, from his signet ring to his Brooks Brothers suit to the fact that he could indulge himself in being editor-in-chief of a literary magazine.

The other executive staff members were all men. Phoebe was sure she'd heard some female voices on her way upstairs, but apparently the top level of the magazine business was as dominated by men as any other. Most of the executive staff had titles that included the word "editor," but one or two seemed to be on the business side of things.

"Our magazine, as you doubtless know, is published monthly. For the first three months of your internship, you will act as editor on three or four humor columns. You will edit for content and organization as well as for grammar and tone. I suggest you spend this week reading some recent past issues to get a feeling for our style.

Phoebe nodded.

"After that, you will be responsible for reviewing unsolicited manuscripts. Each issue includes a few such pieces. You can select three to six unsolicited pieces per issue, if you deem them up to our standards, and your supervisor will recommend which ones, if any, will be considered for publication. I, of course, make the final decision on that." He smiled paternally.

Phoebe nodded again, wondering who her supervisor would be.

"And finally, once your three-month trial period is over, we'd like you to submit a few articles of your own. I should tell you that it is unusual for an intern to have more than one article published in the entire course of an internship, but technically there is no limit."

Hudson glanced around the room at the others. "Have I forgotten anything?"

One of the business types smiled. "Compensation?"

"Ah!" Hudson said, "Yes. Of course." He turned back to Phoebe, who was thinking that naturally this would be the last consideration for someone like Hudson.

"The magazine will provide you with room and board. We have a small apartment on the third floor that you can use and we will stock it with groceries and so on. In addition, you will have a stipend of a hundred dollars a month."

Phoebe felt as though she had been holding her breath since she rang the doorbell and that it now left her body in a long whoosh. If a fairy godmother dressed in Disney raiment had winked at her through the window, she would not have been the least surprised. Apparently, she had gone through the right door in Mr. Posen's corridor because—at least for a year—dreams she didn't even know she had had come true.

* * *

Kent was waiting for her outside the conference room. As it turned out, he was assigned to be her supervisor. Both of them were pleased about this. Kent had survived his internship and been granted a staff position, but he was still the lowest of the low men on the totem pole. Being someone's—anyone's—supervisor seemed like a step up. And for Phoebe, it meant working with someone she already felt somewhat comfortable with.

Kent helped her drag the suitcase up to the third floor, where she found her boxes already waiting for her. She looked through the tiny kitchen and found some soup and crackers and put together a makeshift lunch. Kent was eager to fill her in on all the office gossip and his takes on who was who. Kent was a good storyteller and, even without meeting them, Phoebe found images of the writers forming in her mind.

There was Sterling, the 'senior' humor writer, who was on the far side of thirty and played up his elder status with a kind of pathetic desperation. Sterling smoked a pipe and called the other male writers "old man" and the female writers "my dear." He seemed to aspire to be a character in a black-and-white English art film, with a decidedly left-wing bent.

There was Damian, the 'bad boy,' who lived in the East Village and came to work on a motorcycle. Damian moonlighted at the New School, seducing Upper East Side matrons who yawned through his modern lit classes and then vied with each other to take him out for coffee to discuss the "fascinating ideas" he'd presented.

And then there was Garth. Garth had published a novel that was thought to be a kind of comic roman a clef. It had been reviewed favorably by the more obscure literary journals and pretty much ignored by anyone remotely mainstream, which made Garth an instant hero among similarly opaque artists. His column continued in the same vein—its primary appeal seemed to be keeping his fellow hipsters guessing as to the true identity of its subjects. The jokes—if you could call them jokes –were so intellectualized as to be little puzzles with a tiny bubble of laughter as the reward if you figured them out.

"That about covers the guys," Kent wrapped up, and was about to start in on the female writers when he glanced at his watch. He let out a yelp of dismay, and scampered off to a meeting, looking for all the world like the White Rabbit.

Phoebe pulled out her notebook and started making feverish notes on everything he'd told her. Kent might be a bit naïve, but he had a good eye for office scandal and she was certain it would come in useful. It might even form the basis for a satirical piece if she changed the names to protect the guilty.

* * *

Phoebe sat at her little desk, battling her fears with her favorite weapons: organization and strategy. She decided that her best approach was to display some muscle but to temper it with informed intelligence and humble appreciation. The muscle wasn't going to come easy, but she could see that she had no choice. If she didn't make a case for herself, no one here was likely to make it for her.

She chose Sterling as her first test subject, because he seemed the most vulnerable.

The first column of his that she found in her in-box was political. It was clearly anti-war, but skewered the liberal end of the spectrum, much like a Phil Ochs song she knew. She compared him favorably to Mr. Ochs and complimented his excellent use of language. But then she suggested sharpening a few of his barbs to be a bit more controversial. She gave only one example, not wanting to one-up him in any way, and made sure that it was something he could improve on, but also made it clear that the piece could be stronger.

She got a reasonably good response from Sterling—pretty much what she expected. He was avuncular—some might say fatherly—but she noticed that he took her suggestions and that the piece was better for it. When she heard Kent tell Sterling that the piece was "terrific," she figured she'd scored a minor victory. She overheard Sterling humming "Love me, I'm a Liberal," and thought, "Good start. Onward and upward."

Damian's column was half gossip and half literary criticism with a comic sneer. Looking back at past issues, she noticed that it was the third time he'd discussed Thomas Pynchon. She knew a bit about Pynchon, but mostly from Richard Fariña's point of view. Fariña, a legendary folk music figure who'd died spectacularly in a motorcycle accident, was also a novelist very much in the Pynchon mold. As she would have predicted, Damian never referred to Fariña —probably didn't know he existed.

She figured Damian would need to be convinced that she knew what she was talking about, and that this would not be easy to pull off. Sure, she read a lot of modern literature, but she didn't teach at the New School, for heaven's sake. She decided she needed some help.

She found an empty room with a phone and called Mr. Posen's office when she knew he was "in" to his students. He was more of a classics kind of guy, but he kept up with literary developments.

"Who's hot in modern lit right now?" she said, with little preamble.

"Pynchon," he said immediately, and then, after a pause, added a few more names.

"Who's not quite hot, but looks like they might become hot soon?"

"Well, Joan Didion is looking good."

"Excellent. Damian ignores women writers completely. The last thing I remember of hers is *Slouching Toward Bethlehem*—what a fabulous book. Anything more recent?"

"She just came out with *Play it as it Lays* and it's getting a lot of attention."

"Great. That's good enough for now."

"Wait! How's it going? How are you?"

"I am ecstatic, overworked, terrified, and exactly where I want to be."

"Perfect. Call whenever you need to. Or want to."

"Be sure that I will. Take care. And thanks!"

Phoebe wrote three drafts of comments before she felt even mildly satisfied. Even then, she forced herself to sleep on it while she worked on Garth's column.

Garth was Phoebe's bête noir. No one—not even the hippest of the hip—could reliably identify all the targets of Garth's in-crowd digs. Phoebe suspected that many of these lit-scene targets were part of the homosexual community, a world that was closed to all but its own members. She didn't have a handy phone number in that department. But on the other hand, she had Kent and she had her suspicions there.

She slipped out during the editorial meeting—to which she was not yet invited—and bought a few treats for lunch using the magazine's account at the local grocery. Then she left a folded note on Kent's desk inviting him to join her.

She poured Kent a glass of wine and passed him a plate of brie and crackers while she warmed up the remains of a noodle dish she'd made the night before. At first he sipped virtuously at his glass of Perrier, but she noticed that the level in his wine glass was mysteriously lowering and she didn't think it was the prophet Elijah who was responsible.

When she topped up his glass for the third time and they'd been munching and chatting for a while, she decided it was safe to start talking about Garth.

"So, do you guys have staff parties, like for Christmas or birthdays or whatever?"

"Oh, definitely. Hudson just loves that kind of thing. He likes to think we're a big family—maybe it helps him rationalize the low salaries."

Phoebe laughed appreciatively, topping off his wineglass again.

"Do people bring guests, or is it mostly just the staff itself?"

"It depends. For birthdays, the honoree might bring a girlfriend – or boyfriend as the case may be." He giggled a little and Phoebe saw her chance.

"I'm guessing that there are some boys who tend to arrive with their...boyfriends?"

"Now and then," Kent said. "I mean Hudson is open-minded, but let's face it—his generation..."

"Oh, sure," Phoebe said. "You'd have to be pretty bold, I would guess."

"Yeah. I mean, basically it's really only Garth who can pull it off. And even he introduces them as 'my old college roommate,' or 'my dear friend.' That kind of thing."

"Yeah. Glad to have confirmation on that. I mean, he's an attractive guy, but I kind of got that feeling…"

"Oh, absolutely. You don't want to go barking up that tree."

"Even if I was his type, I'm not sure I'd have the courage."

"Yeah." Kent was silent for a moment, his face a sad blank. It wasn't hard to imagine Kent trying that tree and finding no shelter there. Garth's loss, she thought. Kent is a hell of a nice guy. But Garth, she suspected, found nice guys a bore.

"It makes his columns that much more mysterious. And intriguing. I'm guessing a lot of the nicknames are a bit more familiar if you are part of that world."

"Frankly, even if you are 'part of that world,' his references are still pretty opaque. The only one I know at all is the guy he calls the Masked Freak."

"You know who that is?"

"I'm pretty sure. There's a guy who hangs out at the clubs sometimes who's a total comic book fanatic. Every Halloween, you can count on him showing up in a new superhero costume of his own design. There's always a cape involved, and often a mask."

"Who is this guy? Is he a writer?"

"Well—kind of. He works for DC. The comic book place. He's a colorist, actually, but he has aspirations to write and illustrate his own series."

"Wow. I thought Garth's interests would be more…literary somehow."

"Well, they are, generally. But the Masked Freak is a hunk, I have to say."

"Hmm. That could trump literary."

Kent got that blank look again. "Yeah. It certainly could."

They finished up and Kent, once again yelping at his watch, went off to another of his interminable meetings. Phoebe vowed to avoid all meetings if she were ever hired. They were a great way to keep a writer from writing.

She started her review of Garth's column with gushing compliments on his insights and humble confessions of her own abysmal ignorance of the writing scene. But she added a few remarks about the Masked Freak that she thought might pique his interest.

"The Masked Freak is so intriguing! Looking back on past columns, I see he is a recurring figure. For some reason— maybe his nom de plume—I get visions of comic book superheroes when you talk about him. I'd love to see you riff on comic book stories—the way they take themselves so seriously with occasionally hilarious results."

She took her work on Garth's and Damian's columns up to her apartment—to keep it from prying eyes and to give it further benefit from her own. By three the following morning, she had drafts of comments she was willing to submit.

Chapter 7: March 1972 – May, 1972

At the end of her first month as an intern, the score was Phoebe 2, obnoxious writers 1, which she tried to tell herself was okay for her first time out. But since the 1 was Garth, who had so much more influence than the other writers, any real-world scoring would leave them at an uneasy tie.

Sterling adopted her as a kind of little sister, giving her earnest lessons on being a professional writer that Phoebe carefully ignored while Sterling himself used Phoebe's edits to actually become one.

Damian, it turned out, was intrigued by Richard Fariña, as who was not. He dashed out to the local record store to get some of Richard's records—Fariña had written and performed Dylanesque songs with his young wife, who also happened to be Joan Baez' sister, before leaving her a widow on her twenty-first birthday.

Damian perched confidingly on Phoebe's little desk, milking her for stories about the tragic young couple and vowing to make Fariña the subject of his next column. Phoebe found herself relaxing and enjoying his company. She invited him up to her little apartment for lunch later that week, making a mental note to include Kent—both as a chaperone and to give him a leg up on socializing with the established writers. Poor Kent was too shy to initiate anything like that on his own. And the jury was still out on Damian—Phoebe wasn't sure who would be the chaperone and who the innocent young thing.

She looked back at her reluctance to mingle with writers with bemused puzzlement. What had made her think that visual artists would be more fun or more interesting? Wasn't it obvious that people who use words are more interesting to talk to? Granted, art supplies are more fun than typewriters, but clearly she hadn't thought the whole thing through. She was feeling pretty good about her situation in general—new friends, new challenges, new ideas…and that's when Garth came by, a thundercloud looking for a little sapling to destroy.

"Who told you about the Masked Freak?" he demanded, with no preamble.

"Told me? No one," she said, finishing a note on a manuscript before she deigned to look up. She made sure her own face was as clear as an April sky. She was damned if she'd let him fluster her or make her apologize for doing her job. "It's just as I said—the name you use for him reminds me of comic book heroes. I thought that was what you intended. I liked it. The whole anti-intellectual slash intellectual feeling of it."

"The Masked Freak is confidential information," he growled.

"Then what is he doing in a magazine?" she countered. "If he's so confidential, save him for your memoirs."

Phoebe nearly looked around to see who on earth had made that comment. Did it actually come out of her own mouth? But to her surprise, it landed a punch. Garth didn't actually take a step back, but his face and posture gave that impression. Encouraged, Phoebe went on.

"I'm not sure if you saw Amy's column this week, but it is by far the funniest one I've read so far. I'm going to recommend that it take the intro position."

Phoebe had learned that the 'intro position' was a page at the front of the magazine, directly opposite the executive editor's monthly essay. Had she not been told the name for this page, she would simply have called it 'Garth's column,' since that's what appeared there month after month.

"*You're* going to *recommend* it?" Garth practically crowed with laughter. "Well, I'm sure, with your gold-plated reputation and experience, that recommendation will hold a lot of weight. And, as you apparently have failed to notice, the intro essay is traditionally my column." Garth smirked, shaking his head as though in disbelief that anyone could be quite so clueless.

"Yes, I noticed that," Phoebe replied, with no heat in her voice or expression. "But I've been going through the reader mail and quite a few people are puzzled by all your veiled references to personalities they can't identify. Or perhaps puzzled isn't quite the right word. I think 'frustrated' might be more accurate. That's partly what motivated my comic-book comment. I thought some of those readers might like a few breadcrumbs to follow. It might make them feel like they were part of your in-crowd."

Garth stared at her for a long moment. Clearly, he was not used to being challenged on a regular basis, and certainly not by interns. He didn't dignify the conversation with any further comments, but turned and stomped angrily toward Hudson's office. Phoebe, for her part, made a point of returning calmly to her edit of Amy's column, which really was quite good.

* * *

Phoebe was allowed to attend the initial editor's meeting for each upcoming issue, where the pieces for inclusion were tentatively determined. Final decisions were made in a smaller meeting, and she was far too junior a member of the staff to attend that one. She lobbied for Amy's column, and the editors listened respectfully. If they were surprised, they didn't show it. However, when the new issue came out, Garth's piece was in its usual place. Amy's piece was included, but a reader would have to wade through the entire magazine—including the pages of classified ads—to find it.

Phoebe shrugged, accepting that it would take more than one month to be taken seriously. She invited Amy up for lunch, where she told her that she'd tried. Amy was floored. No one at the magazine ever went to bat for another writer. Especially a woman writer. She invited Phoebe over to her apartment on Friday night, where a few of the women got together regularly to commiserate.

Phoebe showed up at Amy's with a bottle of wine and murmured sympathetically while she took mental notes. She already had drafts for several potential columns, and would love to do one on the plight of female humor writers. It would have to be particularly funny, of course, and totally self-deprecating, but she thought she could see a path to getting Hudson to back it.

And so things went for the next two months. If you didn't count Garth, Phoebe was making great progress. She didn't get Garth's column to budge from its usual position, but Amy's work moved closer to the front of the magazine and she got one of Kent's columns included in the third month. She and Damian shared their latest music enthusiasms—he had become quite a folk convert—and Sterling dropped by her desk for friendly chats.

She felt at home for the first time ever, in a way. She liked all her fellow writers and they seemed to like her. She was good at making their pieces better. They could trust her to be on their side, something they'd never experienced from a potential competitor before. And the letters from readers were positive—Phoebe couldn't exactly make the case that she had personally improved the magazine, but—whatever the reason—people actually sat down and wrote letters of praise—that had to mean something. She even saw a memo showing that sales were up slightly for the last issue. Whatever Garth had said to Hudson when he stomped off in high dudgeon, nothing seemed to have come of it. Even this made Phoebe feel good. She decided that Hudson was onto Garth, and wouldn't leap to do his bidding just because he had a bit of a name among the literati.

In the evenings, Phoebe worked on her own columns. Tonight, she wrapped herself in a soft bathrobe and sat in her little apartment, shuffling through her drafts. This was the beginning of her fourth month—her first opportunity to submit her own column. She narrowed it down to three choices—"Singing my Way to the Bottom" (essentially a reworking of her winning essay); "Are Women Funny?" (a sly send-up of male writers who dismissed female humorists as an oxymoron); and "What to Wear to A Tear-Gassing" (an attempt at political humor that she wasn't quite qualified to write).

She decided to show all three to Kent and let him decide which—if any—to show Hudson. Her plan was to dazzle Hudson, but not to expect anything to actually make it into the magazine for another month or two. Maybe May, she thought, as she sat down to work on a funny slant on Mother's Day. Whatever her own feminist leanings, she felt she had to start from the far more male-centric stance of the magazine's editors.

She was about to call it a night when someone knocked on the apartment door. Glancing at her watch—nearly midnight!—she hurried to the door, hoping no one was hurt (or too drunk to make it home).

Cracking the door open, she found Kent leaning against the opposite wall, looking even unhappier than usual. Phoebe wrapped her robe tighter around her and ushered him in. She poured them each a glass of wine and waited for him to unload.

"Garth," he finally said.

"You don't have to whisper," Phoebe told him. "There's nobody here but us chickens."

"The walls have ears."

"But no mouths. What's he done now?"

"Apparently he's been peppering Hudson with complaints ever since you edited his column three months ago. At first, he demanded that interns wait a full year before they submit anything."

"And?"

"Hudson said he'd consider it for the future, but that your internship provisions had been agreed on already and he couldn't change them now."

"Nice, Hudson." Phoebe grinned.

"So then Garth suggested that, since Hudson was so overloaded, an established writer should pre-screen all unsolicited manuscripts."

"And he graciously volunteered his own services?"

"Natch."

"And how did that go?"

"Hudson thanked him and handed him a big stack of unsolicited manuscripts."

Phoebe nearly lost her mouthful of wine on that one. When she had safely swallowed and managed to turn her laughter into a cough, she ventured "Job security?"

"It can't last. I don't see how he'll have time to write anything of his own! Plus, I don't think your work is considered 'unsolicited.'"

"Nice and getting nicer," Phoebe laughed. "Now he has to wade through a bunch of unpromising columns while I submit mine directly to Hudson — after all, no one has told me about this new procedure."

"How do you know they're unpromising?"

"Oh, I read them all as they arrive. Then Hudson reads them, then he gives me a subset. I was expecting it today or tomorrow, actually. There was one that was sort of okay, but I wouldn't replace any of our permanent writers' stuff with it. And neither would Hudson. He has pretty good taste for a suit."

"Do you have anything of your own to submit?"

"I was trying to decide between these three," Phoebe said, gesturing toward the desk where her drafts sat in three little two-page piles.

Kent picked them up and scanned each one quickly. "The one on women writers looks promising."

"I was leaning that way," Phoebe admitted. "Shall I just hand it over to you now and we'll call it a submission?"

Kent nodded absently and put the pages in his inside jacket pocket. "I'll give it to Hudson tomorrow." Kent paused, looking uncomfortable. "You have carbons, right?"

"Sure."

"Hang onto them."

Phoebe wondered about that, but decided she could think of several reasons that this was good advice.

* * *

Phoebe hummed to herself as she read through the columns by the women writers. She always spent extra time on these, trying to sharpen them and convince the women to take more chances and be a little more out there. Amy was getting it, but Anne and Joanie were still making dating jokes and telling the occasional homemaker/newlywed anecdote. Kent came out of Hudson's office and flashed her a discreet thumbs-up. At least he'd managed to get the column to its intended target.

But moments later, Phoebe saw Hudson himself emerge and walk directly to Garth's desk. A familiar looking set of pages changed hands and Phoebe's hum changed to a groan.

Her first reaction was to confront Hudson directly, but what would she confront him with, exactly? She couldn't prove that Garth would reject her column. She'd have to wait and see what he did with it.

* * *

The waiting was agonizing. Garth wasn't giving anything away. He smiled at her as he walked by, but never said a word. As usual, Phoebe had no inkling as to what would be included in the next issue until it actually came out. The editors kept the final content under wraps to avoid "stop the presses" arguments and emotional scenes. She'd already done final edits on all of the staff columns, but a final edit was no guarantee that a piece would be included—or excluded, for that matter.

When she learned her fate, it was worse than anything she'd imagined. The column on women was included all right. And it had pride of place—in the intro position. The only problem was, the byline read Garth Earlham.

Chapter 8: May, 1972

Phoebe told herself to wait, to cool off and come up with a strategy, but Garth was not about to allow that to happen. He wanted a scene, and he figured that if he pushed hard while Phoebe was still in shock, he was likely to get one.

He parked his capacious butt on the corner of Phoebe's desk and smirked. "I'm getting some excellent feedback on my latest column," he said in a light but challenging tone.

"You know, I ought to thank you for getting me to try something a little different."

Wow, thought Phoebe. The guy's got balls. Not even allowing herself a deep breath, she moved her red pencil along a random sentence and counted to ten.

"Glad I could help," she said, looking up at him with a cool smile. She was gratified to see that, whatever his plan for this play, she had just rewritten it. His smirk faded and he seemed to shrink back a bit. His eyes narrowed. This wasn't quite what he expected, but Phoebe could read his thoughts as if they were scrolling across his forehead: She's playing it cool but I hold all the cards here. Was she not even going to mention the fact that he'd stolen her work right out from under her? Apparently not. He decided to skate close to the edge of acknowledging it and see what she did.

"I'll be totally honest with you," he said, lying effortlessly. His brotherly, kindly air did not suit him. "You have a lot of promise.

"How kind of you to say so," Phoebe said, picking up the next manuscript in her pile. She allowed herself a patient little sigh, like a high-school teacher interrupted from correcting her papers by a student trying to get her to raise his grade.

"But you're young," Garth continued, gazing out the window and warming to this new persona he was inventing. She was just going to let him get away with it! No scenes, no screams, no icy put-downs. Unbelievable. He decided to push it a little farther, just to see what would happen.

"I can tell you have a solid head on your shoulders. I'm sure I don't have to tell you that succeeding in this crazy writing thing not just about promise and youth. It's a competitive world, and the sooner a young writer learns that, the better off she—or he—will be." He congratulated himself on the "or he." Nice touch, he thought.

Phoebe expected him to call her "young lady," next, but even Garth knew when he was going too far.

"There is a great deal in what you say," Phoebe said, playing her part in this little charade as solemnly as she could manage. "Life is for learning." She was pretty sure he didn't listen to Joni Mitchell or Crosby, Stills and Nash, and figured she could get away with a reference to the Woodstock song.

"Well," Garth practically beamed at her. "Glad to help."

"Mutual, I'm sure," Phoebe said. "And now, on to next month's issue." Again, she picked up her red pencil and the manuscript, dismissing him with an absent-minded nod and smile. He couldn't believe his luck. Giving her a little salute, he took his leave.

Other than Kent, the other writers had no idea that Garth had stolen Phoebe's work. She wrote a quick note, asking Kent not to mention it to anyone, and dropped it on his desk as she walked by. He looked up, ready to commiserate, but she shook her head once and walked on. They could talk about it at lunch, which was now a regular thing.

All morning, she could hear bits of whispered conversation about the unexpected turn Garth's column had taken. In his hands, the column about women writers had taken on a supercilious and cynical tone that was all that the women really expected of him. He'd basically turned Phoebe's jokes on their heads, with the men coming off as talented and long-suffering and the women as full of themselves and clueless.

But the women still had to admit that the column was much funnier—and far more accessible—than anything he'd written in years. The other male staff writers were floored. Where on earth had this come from? No one remarked on the absence of content from Phoebe—after all, it was nearly unheard of for an intern to publish anything in the first month of eligibility.

Phoebe managed to get through the day, but she could feel anger growing in her like a forest fire. She embraced it. The anger protected her from the other emotions she could feel churning in her gut. Her parents' low expectations echoed like a funhouse clown in her brain. What she saw now as her own arrogance in assuming she could convince anyone in the real world that she should be taken seriously as a writer ate away at her self-esteem. Her terror in finding herself in this predicament after cutting all her ties with everyone who cared about her convinced her of her own bad judgment. But most of all, her longing for Abby's unfailing support and optimism made her weak and frightened. Each of these dragons raised an ugly head, but it ducked down when faced with the pure and fiery breath of her anger. While some might see anger as a dangerous thing, even something indulgent, for Phoebe it was a lifesaver. It was her heart and soul, pressed to the wall and fighting back.

At lunch, Phoebe told Kent about her conversation with Garth. He was open-mouthed. "How did you manage to keep your temper?" he asked. "I would have exploded. I would have gone straight to Hudson. I would have…"

"Yeah," Phoebe sighed. "I was very close to doing all that. Or jumping out the window. Or moving to Nebraska. But it wouldn't have gotten me anywhere. Except possibly Nebraska."

"So…" Kent leaned back in his chair.

"So, now what, right?"

"Exactly. I mean, you can't just let it go completely. Can you?"

"No. I need a strategy." She slumped back in her chair. "I just haven't quite figured one out yet."

Kent was quiet for a bit, and then he leaned in again with an odd light in his eyes. "What if…"

Phoebe stared at Kent, the world's most unlikely savior. It was good to have a friend.

* * *

That night, Phoebe began work on Kent's strategy, which she thought was, if nothing else, a promising milestone in the development of Kent's backbone and worth doing for that reason alone. She had three weeks to submit her next candidates for publication, and Kent's suggestions had definitely lit a spark.

She decided to use a style that Garth would never touch, and couldn't imitate if he wanted to. She began composing a ballad. The Ballad of the Written-out Writer, she called it to herself—a tragic tale of someone so bankrupt of ideas that he had to steal them from helpless interns. The magazine occasionally published bits of doggerel, but nothing remotely resembling folk music. It was a niche custom-made for her. She decided to address it to "The Macho Rake," which other writers might notice was reminiscent of the Masked Freak. Even Hudson might notice that.

I'll tell you of the Macho Rake
His cover now is blown
From lady writers he did take
A story not his own
He hovered like a wicked elf
And pawed through manuscripts
And what he could not write himself
Into his pants he slipped
Oh who would think to challenge him?
When he was busy scavenging?
There was no real talent in him
Other than his plagiarism!
But here is what will do him in,
The foolish, trusting boy
The carbon copies that were hidden
He did not destroy
The lady writer has her proof
The Macho Rake she'll sue
And when the public learns the truth
His writing days are through

Phoebe slipped Kent a copy of the ballad the next day, and they focused on sharpening and lengthening it over lunch. They spent several enjoyable lunches on the project, and Phoebe could tell from Garth's face that he was puzzled and intrigued by their light mood. She warned Kent that they had to be careful not to show their hand, and they worked on looking unhappier, but it wasn't easy. The Ballad of the Written-out Writer was just so much fun to work on.

After two weeks, Phoebe was ready for the next step. Waiting until the office was dark and silent, she slipped downstairs and pushed a copy of the ballad under Hudson's door. She included a carbon copy of her previous month's column—her own, original version—so Hudson could clearly see that Garth had stolen it. She had to assume that Hudson had not had time to read it before handing it to Garth as part of the "unsolicited manuscript" collection.

She went back upstairs in a hopeful mood. Hudson would know how to handle the situation, and Phoebe was sure he would be grateful that she had not taken the matter into her own hands and created a scene. Garth was a valuable asset, but he couldn't be allowed to run roughshod over all the other writers—and he certainly couldn't be encouraged in his pursuit of plagiarism.

But when she came down the next morning, she could feel a change in the office atmosphere, and it wasn't a good change. Garth was not at his desk. Hudson's door was closed. The usual banter was absent and no one greeted her. Phoebe felt like she was walking to the gallows instead of to her humble little desk.

She shook off her concerns and waited for further developments. It was nearly an hour before anything happened, and by then she was engrossed in her work and had forgotten her worries. A shadow fell across her desk and she looked up to see a very stern-looking Hudson looking down at her.

"Please accompany me to my office, Miss Hirsch," he said. "We need to talk."

Phoebe couldn't tell if the office fell silent at that point or if her own sense of dread made it seem that way. She followed Hudson to his office, where he closed the door with an ominous thud.

"I have had a very serious complaint about your, er, behavior. I'm afraid that I cannot allow such behavior to continue, and I am seriously considering cancelling your internship. Effective immediately. I will be meeting with the executive board this afternoon to discuss it."

Phoebe's heart felt as though, once more, it had slipped its moorings and taken up refuge in a broken down fishing cottage located somewhere in her shoes.

"Is this about the draft I left under your door last night?"

Hudson looked puzzled. "Draft?"

"Yes, I…you didn't find a draft from me when you came in today?"

"What I found when I came in today was a disturbing memo from Garth. Young lady, I would never have taken you for the sort of person who would offer to trade sexual, er, favors for special consideration from the editor who selects work from our unsolicited manuscripts. To find that, as soon as I changed the policy to have Garth review these manuscripts for me, you had thrown yourself at him in such a …I don't even have the words to describe…"

Phoebe stared at him. "I have no idea what you're talking about."

"Yes, well, I would expect you to say that," Hudson said, growing red.

"But look—I can prove that this is all lies. I have a carbon copy of my column—the one that Garth stole and published under…oh, honestly, you don't really believe that he suddenly decided to write something actually funny, and on the subject of women writers, which he's never…"

Phoebe stopped mid-sentence. She sounded incoherent, even to her own ears. She could see confusion in Hudson's face and an anger that she had never imagined he was capable of.

"Well, this really is too much," he exploded. "So this was all calculated—you wrote your own version of Garth's column last night, after the magazine came out, so you could claim you'd written it in the first place? This is positively Machiavellian!"

Phoebe felt very much as though she had wandered into the Mad Hatter's tea party, but she had a strong feeling that anything she said now would only make things worse. All she could think of was how to get out of this room before her heart simply gave up beating.

"Hudson," she said slowly. "I hope someday you'll find out the truth. But until then, I wouldn't dream of troubling you further. I'll be gone by 5."

She gathered what dignity she could and walked out of his office before he could respond, closing the door carefully behind her. As she walked past Garth's desk, he opened his palm to reveal an old-fashioned key. Of course. He had probably had a key to Hudson's office for years. Maybe all the long-time writers had one. It would be just like the trusting and determinedly democratic Hudson to hand them out like Christmas candy. And Garth had no doubt checked Hudson's desk every night since the last issue appeared, waiting to see what Phoebe's move would be. When he found the column and the ballad, he'd probably used them to light Sterling's pipe.

It took all her strength to keep her face still and her posture unrevealing. She focused on each step and kept her mind a complete blank. It wasn't until she reached her apartment door that she realized she had told Hudson she'd be gone by 5 and—she had absolutely nowhere to go.

When Kent found her a few hours later, she was packing her last box.

"I just heard. This is crazy! What are you going to do?" He handed her a bottle of wine.

"I'm not sure," she said. Her cheeks were stiff with dried tears, but she had stopped crying. "I can't go back to college— Everyone there hates me."

"I'm sure that's not true," Kent said, astonished to think that Phoebe could believe that anyone could hate her. But then, he didn't really know the whole story there. For someone who seemed so breezy and open, Phoebe managed to keep her past something of a mystery. Phoebe could tell Kent had a million questions but decided not to enlighten him at the moment. She went on with the thoughts she'd been chasing around her head for the last hour or so.

"I can't stay here in New York—without the internship, I've got no way to support myself and no reason to be here."

"Home?" Kent asked, thinking he personally would rather live on the street than go back to his own parents.

Phoebe laughed. "The worst of all possible alternatives. What would my parents say? 'I told you so' in several hundred different ways? And then they would explain—for the millionth time—that I need to accept that I'm mediocre at best. Hurry on back to school, Phoebe dear, where you can learn something useful."

Phoebe collapsed on a chair, staring at the neatly packed boxes and wondering what address they would display when she finally figured out what to do with them.

"I need to go to the last place anyone would look for me."

"Which is?"

Phoebe thought about all the times she had run out of ideas and confidence and strength, and the answer was suddenly quite clear.

"Can I borrow fifteen bucks?" she asked Kent.

"That's going to solve your problem?"

"That and a phone call," Phoebe said. And she picked up the receiver and called Greyhound.

"When is the next bus to Jordan, Massachusetts?" she asked. The next bus to Abby.

Chapter 9: May 1972

Abby was the one who volunteered to repoint the bricks in the kitchen. Phoebe didn't know what repointing even was. Did you face them in a different direction? But Abby basically raised Phoebe's hand for her, and an hour later there they were, perched on little step ladders with a bucket of mortar and an odd looking tool each. Lazarus showed them how it was done and then slouched off to another task. There was so much work to do at Spirit Mountain—the Sufi community that Abby had moved to. Every day provided a new opportunity to try something Phoebe had never even known existed on the previous day. And now, after digging out a foot or so of mud from the kitchen, the next task was the bricks, which housed an old oven.

Phoebe, who was short and afraid of heights, concentrated on the lower bricks. Abby, fearless and tall, climbed to the top of the ladder and worked on the higher ones, surveying the rest of the room as she worked and making a verbal list of the things that remained to be done.

"It's a great stove," she said of the 12-burner gas monster with its yawning ovens. "But it needs to be completely cleaned out. And we'll need an industrial mixer—like the kind the bakery has."

When Abby and her boyfriend Rafe were in San Francisco, Rafe had become so intrigued by the Sufi community that he'd arranged his next work rotation around the Sufi community so he could spend more time with their spiritual leader, Murshid Khalid. For his part, Murshid Khalid had recognized in Rafe a natural leader with an ability to oversee a large project. He had enlisted Rafe to find a home for the new community and Rafe had found a spectacular site—an old Shaker village. Built by Mother Ann Lee, the head of the Shaker movement in the late seventeen hundreds, the village had at one time in its past been a summer camp; at another, an ill-fated ski resort. For the past ten years, it had been empty and abandoned. Now it was transformed again into yet another spiritual center under the name Spirit Mountain.

So far, 40 people had shown up and were basically camping in the huge buildings. Only one of the buildings had heat, but several of the guys were working on that. The community was lousy with large long-haired guys who knew how to do things like weld and repoint bricks. The testosterone was palpable.

Murshid Khalid had recruited mostly leaders—people who had their own Sufi centers in cities around the country. But many followers wanted to come, too. Phoebe had heard about dozens of phone calls and letters that arrived every day from people who were on their way. They figured to double in size by September.

But now it was still early May. Phoebe had been here less than a week, and already all she could think about was work. She spread the mortar with the little spatula thing she'd been given, but she seemed to get more on her hands and jeans than on the wall. The mortar had an odd drying effect on her skin, although it was wet enough. The skin on her fingers felt like it was shrinking away from her bones. And yet it felt good to be doing something with her hands other than typing. She felt that if she never saw another typewriter, it would be too soon. Every time she thought about the situation in New York, she shuddered and turned her mind to the nearest physical task she could find. It was cheap but effective therapy.

Lazarus returned to check on their progress. He was a beautiful man. He looked like a figure in a Russian icon, with large soulful eyes and long wavy hair. One would have to dress him differently of course. Few Russian icons wore Be Here Now t-shirts.

"Looks good ladies," he said in his hollow, otherworldly voice. He leaned over to take Phoebe's tool with a little smile of apology and smoothed a few of her sections. Handing the tool back, he gave a little salaam gesture from the general area of his heart. "Mid-day prayers in ten minutes," he said and showed them how to cover the pail of mortar so it wouldn't dry out and how best to rinse the tools.

Phoebe had to read the midday prayers from a little book while everyone else recited them from memory. The prayers had motions associated with them—hand movements and little bows of the head, which she imitated a beat late. The Meditation Hall (formerly an apple-drying barn built by summer campers) was cool and dark, and often she just let her mind wander while her voice and body went through the motions. Like everything else at Spirit Mountain, it was peaceful, and Phoebe thought she could stand a little peace.

She wrote to her parents and told them she was visiting Abby for a while. She did not provide a return address or phone number. She had left New York with a single suitcase, her boxes piled neatly in the coat closet. Kent had her contact information in case of emergency. No one else knew where she was.

After prayers and a quick lunch, a woman named Shaloma told Phoebe that she had been summoned to "see

Murshid." Phoebe was still getting used to the odd names that some of the community members had. Apparently, the names were gifts from Murshid Khalid, representing characters from sacred texts or qualities that you were supposed to work on. Shaloma's name came from the Hebrew word for hello, good-bye, and peace. Phoebe was pretty sure that Shaloma concentrated on the peace aspect. If Phoebe had that name, she would have felt more comfortable with the hello and goodbye parts. That seemed to be the story of her life at the moment.

Putting her dishes in the scullery for the clean-up crew, Phoebe thought about her appointment with the spiritual leader. The whole idea of it made her extremely uncomfortable. She had never visited Murshid Khalid in his "pod," as he called it. It was a tiny structure that looked a little like a parachute or hot-air balloon, except that it was earthbound. The guys had built it in the barn and then created makeshift rollers to move it up the hill, where it perched like an alien overlooking the old Shaker buildings. The sides were long windows, and Phoebe felt watched.

The sun was at its zenith as she trudged up the rocky little path to the pod. Through its windows, she could see the flicker of a candle, though it was bright afternoon. As she drew closer, she could smell incense—not the easy scent of vanilla or cinnamon, like the incense her old college roommates had favored, but something strange and Indian. The door to the pod stood open, and inside Murshid sat cross-legged on a small scrap of carpet. His eyes were closed and his lips were moving.

She wasn't sure how to announce her presence or whether to disturb him at all. No one tells you how these things work, she thought with some frustration. But just then he turned his head and opened his eyes. He motioned her in, but stopped her at the door and pointed at her feet. "Remove the shoes," he said, in what sounded like an accusing tone. Feeling exactly like Alice confronting the caterpillar, Phoebe slipped off her Birkenstocks and left them outside the door. He motioned to another small rug. "Sit, sit," he said, so she sat and faced him.

He closed his eyes again and she sat uncomfortably, wondering what she was meant to do. She willed herself not to fidget. Finally, she closed her own eyes and breathed in and out, trying to effect an attitude of meditation. When he spoke, she jumped, startled.

"Why are you here?" She opened her eyes. He was staring at her. She said the first thing that came into her head. "I love it here."

"Yes." He seemed to be considering this. "Yes. You love the place. And the physical work. But do you love the spiritual work?" It was her turn to consider. Finally she said, "I don't know."

To her surprise, he smiled. He reached out his hands and took hers. His hands were warm and surprisingly hard, as though he too did "physical work." She stopped feeling quite so frightened.

"Will you give it a chance?" he asked her. He looked genuinely anxious, as though eager for her to find it good.

"Yes," she said, after a moment, wondering if her innate cynicism could ever fully embrace the ritual and mysticism that pervaded his work. But she could give it a chance. After all, how many choices did she have at this point? She wondered if he guessed that she found it impossible to meditate. She found herself making lists in her head, while everyone else appeared to be transported.

"They're all faking it to a certain extent," he confided, with a little twinkle in his eye. She laughed before she could stop herself, partly because the phrase "faking it" sounded so odd in his formal Indian/British accent. He laughed too. His laugh was delightful.

"It's all right to fake it. The reality of it will come of its own accord. The thing is to try to make space for it so it—well—so it has a place to land when it arrives. That makes sense, does it not?"

"I guess," she said, wondering what "it" was.

"It's spirit," he said. "That's all. Nothing magical. Just the thing that inhabits and enlivens the universe around us. It's actually the only real thing. The rest is shadows. But since we ourselves are shadows, the shadows are what seem real to us."

Phoebe tried not to think of this as pretentious nonsense. Raised in a secular Jewish family, her religious experience, such as it was, was a lot of odd rules that her grandparents followed, some great food, and Hebrew songs whose meaning was entirely opaque. There were good associations with family at Seders and so on, but basically religion was something that other people did for reasons she had never understood. She found it vaguely embarrassing. But she liked the image of the shadows and his words had a kind of elegance, so she nodded her head.

"It might make more sense to you later," he said kindly. "You may go now."

Phoebe wasn't sure what either of them had gained from this little interview, but she got to her feet as gracefully as she could, slipped on her sandals and went back down the hill, imagining that she could feel Murshid Khalid's watchful gaze as she did.

Back in her room, she wondered frankly if she could ever "make room" for this spirit thing, but she promised herself to try. She sensed that the community itself—which she genuinely loved, and which required no explanation—would not exist without its spiritual aspect. If she wanted to stay here, she had to respect Murshid's ways and give them a try.

Normally, she skipped prayers. Lots of people skipped the noon-time ones, and even the early morning ones, since they had jobs and couldn't always make time for them, even if they worked right here at the community. But almost everyone tried to attend the evening prayers, and when she heard the bell for them this evening, she decided to go.

She slipped off her Birkenstocks and left them in the big pile of identical-looking ones just inside the Meditation Hall door. Padding down the steps to the floor, she found a spot on a bench in the back. There was soft music playing and incense burning. One candle stood on the little altar, waiting to be lit.

She recited the prayers, keeping up as best she could with the more experienced community members. It felt artificial and a bit contrived, but she concentrated on the words themselves, thinking that someone had composed these with an actual intention. The prayers were a kind of request to some being or entity—the spirit?—for light and guidance and unity. There was certainly nothing disturbing about them unless you objected to the idea of petitioning the Lord with prayer, which, as Jim Morrison had noted, was unlikely to succeed. After that, there was just the music and silent meditation, which was restful after her long day. She tried hard not to think about anything, but this, as usual, proved impossible so she decided to channel her thoughts at least. Instead of making her usual list, she called up the faces of each person she'd encountered that day and tried to think of something positive and unique about each one. This was easy, since she was fond of them all. It was also mildly entertaining. She wished each person well as she moved on to the next one.

When she got to Abby in her thoughts, she glanced over at her best friend, sitting knee-to-knee with Rafe—who was now calling himself Raphael, like the angel. The two of them knew all the prayers by heart, and all the little motions. Phoebe wished she were Abby—not for the first time. As she gazed at them, Raphael's hand on Abby's knee, she was startled to see Raphael look up and into her own eyes. For an odd moment, it felt exactly as though it was Phoebe's knee he was stroking and not Abby's at all, and she quickly turned her head to the altar, closed her eyes, and prayed for guidance with the most sincerity she had managed since she arrived here.

Chapter 10: July 1972

July arrived, hot and fragrant. Phoebe felt like she'd lived at Spirit Mountain for years. She was finishing her lunch in the dining hall and thinking about attending Abby's New Moon class for women, when Abby herself came down the stairs and waved to her. Picking up her dishes, Phoebe walked over, glancing at Abby's bare feet. She must have been interrupted while preparing for class in the library. Everyone took off their shoes in the library, and no one liked to walk through the dining hall without shoes.

"What's up?" Phoebe asked.

"You have a visitor," Abby said. "He looks nice."

Phoebe was baffled, but relieved that "nice" could not, by any stretch of the imagination, describe her parents, and "he" left Robin out of the running.

"Okay," she said slowly, following Abby up the stairs. And there in the hallway outside the library stood Kent.

The look of relief on his face was comical, and her own face split into a smile. Kent and Spirit Mountain were definitely an unlikely couple.

"Hi," Kent said shyly. "You look normal."

"Well, shucks, Kent," Phoebe laughed. "You could turn a girl's head with that fancy talk!"

Taking his arm, she led him outside to the courtyard, where a few small children were playing under the watchful eyes of the community moms.

"Passing through?" Phoebe said, thinking how unlikely that was.

"Um, well, sort of" Kent said, staring around him as though he had landed in Munchkin country and the good witch was about to land her bubble. "Is there someplace we can talk?"

They sat in the shade of a big willow tree on the lawn. Kent looked squeamish about having direct contact with dirt, but his mission seemed to drive this concern from his mind. With a few pointed questions, Phoebe learned that Garth had left the magazine under something of a cloud and that his claims of her sexual misconduct had been revealed to be complete fiction.

"So he—what? Confessed?" Phoebe loved the image of that.

"Not exactly. It was more that Hudson totally believed Garth had written that column—um, yours, you know—and then of course he was incapable of writing another one. He stalled for a month or two, telling Hudson he had a few columns that had been ready to go before he got onto this new angle, and he wanted to get them into print before he switched gears, etc., etc. But Hudson got impatient with all the excuses and demanded another column like yours. And of course, Garth couldn't write one."

Phoebe stared at Kent and burst into laughter. "Of course! He could steal my work, but he couldn't duplicate it! Did he try stealing from the other women?"

"Well, the women were onto him by then. Nobody leaves their work lying around anymore. The women knew from the get-go who had written that column—oh, and they gave you the full benefit of having written something much nicer, blaming all the nasty stuff on Garth. They hate Garth."

"Who wouldn't," Phoebe murmured.

"None of them was willing to go to Hudson—they didn't have any evidence, after all..."

Or any nerve, Phoebe thought but did not say.

"...but they figured it would come out soon enough. And it did. Maybe not soon, exactly, but..."

"How did it happen, exactly? And when?"

"Just a few days ago, actually. Your departure put the execs into a tizzy. Some of them thought Hudson had acted a bit precipitately and that there might be another side to the story, but most of them seemed so embarrassed by the whole thing that they couldn't face discussing it...or something. Anyway, they managed to take quite a bit of time to decide on a plan of action. They had finally gotten around to contacting the runner-up in the contest and he was due to arrive in a week or two, so I told Hudson your boxes were still in the apartment, and wasn't it time to send them on to you."

Kent looked a little sheepish. "I'm sorry I didn't send them before. I guess I just hoped against hope that you'd come back."

Phoebe patted his hand and smiled. "It's okay. Not a lot in those boxes that I need here, really. Anyway—finish the story—what happened?"

"So I asked if the magazine would pay the shipping, and we got to talking—about Garth, as it turned out, and why he was stalling on the column thing. I was running out of ways to say 'Gosh I don't know,' so I kept inching up the stairs... Anyway, Hudson just sort of followed me up to the apartment.

"And?"

"And he saw the stuff on your desk. He found the other carbon."

"Yeah, but he had a whole story ready for that. Apparently I wrote the column and made the carbon after I found out Garth was in charge of the unsolicited manuscripts and decided to throw myself at him. It was a theory to rival the grassy knoll."

"Yeah. Well, I don't know if you remember, but the carbon was dated."

"Carbon dating! I've heard of that. I thought it was for dinosaurs."

"Came in handy for that particular dinosaur. The date was weeks before Hudson asked Garth to take on his new responsibilities." Kent allowed himself a smile.

"Well. My good name is cleared. I guess I can take that scarlet letter off all my shirts."

"It's more than that. He gave me this letter to give you. In person. He wants you to come back."

Phoebe took the letter but didn't open it. "This'll make a nice souvenir," she said. "But I'm not coming back. Please tell him how much I appreciate the gesture. And thanks for bringing the boxes. I don't need much but I *was* running out of socks. You did bring them, right?"

Kent's face fell. "I almost didn't. I was so sure it was a waste of time. If figured once the whole misunderstanding was cleared up, you'd just have to bring all of them right back. Phoebe, you have to come back! They'll do anything for you now. You can get your columns published, you can get Amy's stuff in the magazine, you can…"

He stopped. Phoebe was looking around, and Kent followed her glance. There were guys unloading firewood in front of the massive barn across the road. There were couples lying on patchwork quilts, laughing and talking. There were little kids racing across the lawn. A group of people formed a circle under a nearby tree, holding some sort of meeting. An air of peace and goodwill seemed to envelope the whole scene. Even Kent could feel it. Phoebe breathed it in, fueling her courage.

"I can't do it anymore," Phoebe told him, after a moment. She sounded surprised, and she was. All these months, she'd avoided even considering the possibility that all would be forgiven and that she could return to the life she'd enjoyed so much for the brief time in which it was all working. But now it felt like it had all happened to someone else.

"All that desperate effort to be funny, to be clever," she said slowly, piecing it together as she spoke. "It just feels—I don't know—petty and unhelpful. I thought I was coming here to hide, but it's just the opposite. I came here and now I can…emerge? Is that the right word?"

Kent had that blank look he got when his heart was breaking and he was hoping no one would notice. Phoebe thought that he looked like a prince who had come to fight a dragon for a damsel, only to find that the damsel and the dragon had decided to share an apartment.

She looked away, knowing he was embarrassed and trying to find the words to make him more comfortable. At that moment, Raphael got up from the circle under the nearby tree and strolled over to them. Putting a hand on Phoebe's shoulder, he lowered himself to the ground in a single, graceful movement and smiled at Kent.

"I see you have a visitor," he said to Phoebe. "About time someone from your past took an interest in you."

"Raphael, this is Kent. He is a wonderful writer in New York who helped me immensely when I lived there."

Raphael smiled at Kent. "Thanks," he said. "She doesn't talk about New York much, and it's good to know there was somebody on her side there. I got the impression that was rare."

Kent smiled a bit tightly, then stared down at his shoes. Raphael squeezed Phoebe's shoulders, rose as effortlessly as he had descended, and strolled away. Phoebe couldn't help thinking the whole thing had been a bit—what?—proprietary. She wasn't sure if she was more amused at Raphael exercising ownership over her (did he imagine she was part of some sort of harem he was working on?) or at the thought of being jealous of Kent.

Kent had picked up on the proprietary air. "Is he part of the reason you don't want to come back?" he asked.

"I'm not sure," Phoebe said. She could feel herself blushing. "It's sort of complicated."

"Well, I'm not surprised," Kent said. "Apparently a lot of your life is complicated."

"What is that supposed to mean?"

"Your friend Robin stopped by," Kent said, plucking a blade of grass and shredding it. "Oh. And she gave me this to give to you."

Kent pulled another envelope out of his pocket. "She told me not to leave until you opened it."

Curious, Phoebe tore the envelope open and glanced inside. Not much. Two slips of paper. She pulled one out—it was a note, which she stuffed in her pocket despite Kent's obvious disappointment. The second slip was a check. Phoebe stared at it, then pulled the crumpled note from her pocket and smoothed it open. It was in Robin's handwriting—as if the purple ink had not been enough of a giveaway.

"Well?" Kent asked.

"I sold another song," Phoebe said.

"Another song? You mean you sold songs before?"

"Just one. Two now."

"You are just full of surprises. I gather you burned some bridges with Robin. Does anyone here know your whole story?"

"I'm not sure even I know my whole story."

"A writer should know her whole story," Kent said seriously. "Especially if she wants to emerge."

"Do you know yours?"

"I'm starting to. But I think emerging is still not an option. If you know what I mean."

"I miss you," Phoebe said, surprised to hear herself say it, but realizing it was true. "You're a good friend. You're a good person. You deserve to emerge—and then some."

"Thanks."

After an awkward moment, they got up and walked to Kent's car. It took a few trips, but they got all the boxes into Phoebe's room.

"Even if you don't want to come back right now," Kent said, glancing surreptitiously at his watch, "you can always submit a column. Just give me a quick call and I'll make sure the right people see it."

"Thanks," Phoebe said. "It seems unlikely, but then so much of my life does."

"And do stay in touch," Kent said, looking at her directly. "I mean that. I don't open up to people the way I do with you. It was nice to have a real friend. I don't want to lose that forever."

"I hope we'll always be friends," Phoebe said, and meant it, although she wasn't sure the person Kent had befriended would ever reappear. Could he be friends with the person she was becoming? She watched his car disappear back down their dirt road in a little cloud of dust.

She sat down on the back step of the main building, just outside the kitchen. She could hear the cleanup crew inside, singing along to Stevie Wonder and banging the big pots in the sink. Things at Spirit Mountain were so easy, so straightforward. Volunteer to clean the kitchen after lunch and everyone was grateful. Show up at evening prayers, and everyone was accepting. She knew everyone here had a past and that possibly some of them were as complicated as her own, but perhaps they, like she, found it a relief to leave it all behind for a while. In her own case, she had a feeling it was all going to catch up with her again at some point. She sighed.

"Big sigh," said Raphael's voice, and he sat down next to her on the little marble step.

"A lot to digest," Phoebe said. The little hairs on her arms felt like they were all standing to attention. If she focused, she could hear Abby's voice through the window of the library on the floor above, leading her class in breathing exercises. "You and Abby must be getting ready to head back to Antioch."

"Not sure that's gonna happen," Raphael said, pulling up a blade of grass and placing it between his teeth. Phoebe wondered why people did this. Then she focused on his words.

"You're thinking of dropping out?" she asked, after a moment.

"Well, you did, didn't you?"

"Yeah. I guess I didn't see either of you as the type, though. I mean, going to Antioch practically *is* dropping out, really. Every three months, you're off on another adventure. Why bother leaving?"

"Because I don't want to go someplace else. I want to be here."

Phoebe reminded herself that she felt the same way — about Spirit Mountain. Raphael somehow managed to imply that he wanted to be here, as in next to Phoebe. Maybe that was just something he did with women in general. She pushed her unease aside, and realized that he had answered for himself only.

"What about Abby?" she asked.

"I think she wants to stay too—you really should ask her."

"You haven't discussed it?"

"We're…drifting a little."

"I'm sorry to hear that," Phoebe said. But she had noticed that even established relationships had a hard time at Spirit Mountain. Murshid Khalid spoke often about finding one's soul mate, and you could see the members of each couple examining each other in that light and wondering if they had given the soul-mate search enough time and effort. Wondering if they had settled too soon. Phoebe did not find this particularly spiritual, and it made her wonder about the Murshid's own relationships. She stood up and stretched.

"Gotta go," she said, as she headed to the little office near the driveway where they received visitors and kept records. "I told Shaffee I'd help him with the bookkeeping."

This was true, although Phoebe would have said she was the very last person on any planet to be responsible for bookkeeping. Still, someone had to do it, and there seemed to be a tradition of doing the very thing you were least qualified to do, so off she went—glad to be out of range of the feelings that Raphael seemed to evoke.

* * *

That night in the dining room, Phoebe sat at a different table from her usual one and watched Raphael and Abby. Abby arrived in time for the grace before dinner and seemed her usual serene self. Raphael meandered in late, when most of the community was already seated and eating. Abby had saved a seat for him, but he looked around the room before carrying his plate to her table. Abby seemed eager to tell him about her day—at least, Phoebe assumed that's what she was talking about. Raphael smiled and nodded, but Phoebe noticed his eyes wandering. Once or twice, she thought he was looking for her, but she managed to engage in conversation with a neighbor before he could catch her eye. Maybe she was imagining it. She left a bit early, dropping her dishes in the plastic tubs in the scullery. She sat in the courtyard, chatting with various people as they waited for the evening class to begin. Finally, she saw Abby come out the doorway, and she hurried over to her.

"I need to talk," Phoebe told her.

"Can it wait until after class?" Abby asked. "We were going to do some chanting, and…"

"No."

"Okay." Ever the good friend, Abby smiled and squeezed Phoebe's hand. "C'mon up to Abby's Counseling Center and Doughnut Shop."

"I wish," Phoebe said, meaning the doughnut part.

Sure enough, there were no doughnuts in Abby's room, just Indian bedspreads and pictures of medieval saints. Abby lit some incense and a candle, and they sat on pillows on the floor.

"What's up?" Abby asked. "Having second thoughts?"

"No. I love it here. You were right, as always. Although how you could guess that I would take to something like this is more than I can understand."

"I guess I always feel that something I love this much has to be something you would love too." Abby smiled at Phoebe. There was always so much warmth in her eyes. How could Raphael even think about other women?

"How about you?" Phoebe asked her, pushing her Raphael thoughts aside and taking one of Abby's hands. "Are you heading back to school at the end of the rotation? Can you convince them to let you stay on for another couple of months?"

"Raphael is thinking of dropping out," Abby said, as if that were a direct answer. "He's been asked to take on the day-to-day running of Spirit Mountain. Sort of be the executive director. He's the perfect person for it."

"So does that mean you would stay too?" Phoebe persisted.

"I think so," Abby said.

"Would you stay even if he didn't?"

"Not sure." Abby looked troubled, or as troubled as she ever got. "Lately…I don't know. He's been a bit preoccupied with all the community stuff—keeping things going smoothly isn't quite as effortless as it looks." She managed a laugh, but it sounded like somebody else laughing.

"Can't shed our egos like snakeskins, eh?" Phoebe said.

"Exactly. No matter how much we tell ourselves that we would like to."

"I'm not usually the one giving the advice," Phoebe began, slowly. "That's your specialty. But I have to say—it's a big decision and you should make your own choice, without it depending on Raphael. I've seen the way relationships crumble around here. Even really solid ones. You could be giving up a terrific time at school for something that isn't…reliable."

"Is that what you wanted to talk about?" Trust Abby to keep her focus.

"Sort of."

Abby waited, calm and trusting. How was Phoebe supposed to tell her that she felt like Raphael was coming on to her? Raphael could so easily deny it.

"How serious are you about Raphael," she finally said.

"Not sure," Abby said. "He's so perfect in a lot of ways— really smart, able to do pretty much anything, and so sexy." She blushed.

"But?"

"But sometimes I feel like he's still looking. Like he wants to keep his options open."

"Yes," Phoebe said, relieved to see that Abby wasn't deluding herself. "I feel that too."

Abby looked startled. "He hasn't flirted with you, has he?"

Phoebe looked down at her lap, trying to look like she was thinking this over. "Not so much with me—I just see his eyes checking out the room, you know…"

"Yes. I do know," Abby said sadly. "But part of me wants to wait and see. I guess I'm hoping he just can't find anyone as wonderful as me." And then she really did laugh, her sweet Abby laugh.

Phoebe leaned over and hugged her. "He'd be crazy to think he could find anyone even half as wonderful as you are. If he thought he did, you'd know for sure that he isn't as smart as he looks."

"Thanks," Abby said, looking down at her hands as Phoebe sat back. This seemed like progress, and she should have felt relieved, but she found herself feeling oddly uncomfortable. She resolved that she would not allow Raphael to get to her. If he wanted to try out some other ladies, he'd have to look elsewhere. There was no way she would betray her best—her only—friend.

Chapter 11: August, 1972 – November, 1972

It was a week or so later when Abby showed up in Phoebe's room during evening prayers. Phoebe's own attendance was sporadic, but Abby never missed prayers, plus she had been crying. Phoebe figured things with Raphael had reached some sort of crisis and lit a candle, regretting that she had no incense. She sat down on the bed and motioned Abby to join her. They had sat on so many beds over the years, crying or laughing or making plans.

"Tell me," Phoebe said, stroking Abby's hair.

"He was with Shaloma," Abby said. "I found them. In his room. It was like he wanted me to."

"Shit."

"Shaloma was so embarrassed. She threw on her clothes and ran. She came up to me later and told me that Raphael had implied that he and I broke up and she didn't think she was doing anything wrong, and could I forgive her."

"Implied?"

"Yes. As we talked, she realized he had never actually said it in so many words, but she was sure that was what he was trying to tell her. She said it was like it was too painful for him to say out loud."

"So she was, what, comforting him?"

"I guess."

"The thing is, Shaloma is a good person. She's probably telling you the truth."

"That's the worst of it—I think she is. I told her I didn't hold her responsible and that I forgave her, of course."

"And Raphael?"

"I haven't talked to him. I can't face him."

"For heaven's sake, Abby, you didn't do anything wrong! What's not to face?"

"That it's over. That I was so wrong about him. That I could be such an idiot."

"Is it over?"

Abby began to cry again. "Oh, God, I don't know. I mean, my brain is telling me to get as far away from him as I can, but..."

"You still love him."

"I do. How can I be so stupid?"

"Again, not your fault. Abby, you are the most blameless person I know."

Abby sat up and pushed her hair out of her face. Phoebe handed her a box of tissues and she blew her nose—a loud, undignified honk. They both laughed.

"I'm thinking maybe I should leave," Abby said, suddenly serious again.

"He's the one who should leave!"

"No. The community really needs him. He's still the best choice to run things. Plus, I don't want it to all be so…public."

"You need to talk to him. Find out what this is all about. And then you need to do what's best for you—not Raphael, not Murshid, not even Spirit Mountain. You can't know what's best for everyone else. If Raphael leaves, someone will arrive—or arise—to take his place, as far as running things goes. No one is irreplaceable."

"In that case, neither am I," Abby pointed out.

"No, and neither am I, but you shouldn't make your decision based on that, either. You should do what's best for Abby, because although you are an excellent friend and advisor—albeit a bit disappointing in the doughnut department—you are the world's very best Abby."

"You're right. At least the part about how I can't fix things for everyone else." Abby stood up and smiled at her friend. "I think I'll take a walk. Maybe go down to the pond for a swim. I need to think."

"Good idea. And a little meditating might not be a bad idea."

"I can't believe you said that," Abby laughed. "Spirit Mountain is really getting to you!"

"Yeah. It is."

Phoebe stood at the window and watched her friend as she walked down the road toward the pond. She played the conversation back in her head and found that she was relieved that it was Shaloma that Abby had discovered with Raphael, and not Phoebe herself. It could so easily have been the other way around, and she allowed herself a moment of self-congratulation on resisting temptation. Then she realized that the temptation had been largely in her own mind and she laughed out loud.

"I'm glad something is funny," said Raphael from her doorway.

"Not really."

"You talked to Abby?"

"I did."

"It's just…"

"I don't want to hear it. There is nothing you could say that would help. If you want to help someone, talk to Abby."

"I can't find her."

"Try the pond."

He turned to go, then turned back. "There is another side to this story."

"Please. Just leave."

And he did.

* * *

When Phoebe woke up, it was pitch black. The faint starlight made her viscerally understand how dark the dark was. She could just make out the square of the window, barely lighter than the rest of the room.

She knew the bakers had yet to arrive because they woke her every morning, even though they tried so hard to be silent. So it must be sometime between midnight and five, because midnight was when she'd finally crawled into bed and five was when the bakers started. Her only clock was her wristwatch, and it was face down on her dresser.

The darkness was becoming less so as she stared into it. Before she realized what she was doing, she sat straight up and swung her feet to the floor.

She moved slowly to the window, afraid of tripping over the clothes she'd thrown to the floor when she literally fell into bed a few hours before. Leaning on the sill, she pressed her forehead to the glass for a moment, then slid the hundred-year old window upward in its frame and leaned out. All the smells were still new to her. There were no colors. She wondered why things turned gray at night. Raphael would know the science of it, but for her it was magical, like stepping into an old movie.

She turned and stared into the room, making out first one and then the other Birkenstock. She retrieved them from their far-flung positions and made her way into the hallway.

The old stairway had bannisters smoothed by a century and a half of calloused hands. There were shallow indentations in the center of each step. For a moment, the weight of the sheer history of this place enveloped her, offering her its wisdom if she only knew how to claim it. She closed her eyes, reaching out to that presence, and found it easier to trust her sense memory. How many times up and down these stairs?

The big double doors leading to the courtyard were closed, but nothing was ever locked here. The doors barely creaked when she eased them open and she hoped whatever sound there was would enter the dreams of the others without waking them.

She crunched across the gravel to the driveway and down the driveway to the dirt road. A sudden movement turned out to be a rabbit, which she sternly told herself, although her heart continued to jump in her chest like a companion rabbit long after she identified the sound. A slower, more subtle movement caught her eye, and that turned out to be Raphael.

Phoebe willed herself to become invisible and for a moment that appeared to work. Raphael was on the other side of the road, his back to her, staring across the herb garden at the farm. He seemed unaware that anyone was watching him. He sat down in the grass by the road and crossed his legs in a lotus position. Phoebe hoped he was preparing to meditate.

Holding her breath, she backed up slowly, one small step at a time, until she was in the courtyard again. Sitting on the stone wall, she felt the cold through her nightshirt so sharply that she gasped. A shadow fell across the gravel and Raphael was standing in front of her.

He didn't say a word but regarded her gravely, as if she were an unexpected problem to solve. Shaking his head slightly, he walked toward her and she felt a strange sense of menace, but not necessarily from him — more from the whole situation. In the end, he stood over her like a modern Colossus and stroked her cheek, an intimate but impersonal gesture. An improbable grin broke his face into more familiar lines. He walked quickly away, vanishing into the building where the bakery was.

Phoebe climbed back up to her room and placed her shoes carefully, side by side, next to the bed. She shut the window and turned back the blankets, tugging them into place as though preparing the bed for a guest. Climbing beneath the sheets, she lay on her back, watching the ceiling grow lighter. The bakery workers were arriving now, murmuring quietly to each other as she closed her eyes. The next day, when Abby tearfully told her that she had decided to break up with Raphael but remain at Spirit Mountain, Phoebe knew what would happen as clearly as if she had dreamed it into being. What was it going to be like, she wondered, to love like nobody could get hurt?

* * *

Phoebe repeatedly wondered how she could fall in love with someone who had hurt the person she loved best. Raphael never again tried to explain his behavior. Phoebe never asked him about it. She couldn't explain her own behavior, much less his.

She knew she must have some power in the relationship, but it never felt that way. She was certain that someday she'd walk in on Raphael and some other woman, and that asking for his fidelity was meaningless. The most she could manage was to extract a promise that neither of them would allow Abby to find out that they were sleeping together. For although Abby had walked away from the relationship, it would still be a betrayal to find out that Phoebe had walked into it. Why he had chosen to put them all in this thankless position was a mystery she couldn't begin to solve, and why she allowed herself to be part of it was too painful to examine.

From her frequent talks with Abby—who continued to be shaken by the breakup—she knew that Abby found some solace in her belief that Raphael was not with anyone else. At times, she told herself that her own subterfuge was a kind of gift to Abby, but in her clearer moments she knew this was nonsense. Each day she told herself she would end it, and each night she and Raphael continued to meet at improbable hours in unlikely places. They avoided each other the rest of the time. Before she knew it, it was October.

They were lying in a little nest of cast-off clothing at the top of the barn one evening during prayers. She lay on her back, looking up at the barn rafters and thinking of nothing in particular, when she felt Raphael's hand on her cheek. Immediately, she was reminded of that dreamlike encounter in the early hours of the summer morning, just after Raphael broke Abby's heart. She turned to look at him and was taken aback by the tenderness in his face.

"You know I'm in love with you," he said, trying for a matter-of-fact tone.

She couldn't trust her voice. Her head moved slightly back and forth. No. She did not know anything of the sort.

"I can tell you the exact moment it happened. I can remember it in every atom of my body."

She stared at him, still unable to speak, searching her own memory. Nothing stood out.

"It was in the Meditation Hall. Mid-day prayers. You had arrived maybe a few days earlier. I was sitting with Abby and I turned my head—and there you were."

And she did remember. His hand on Abby's knee, but his eyes on her. She thought she had imagined it.

"You were so real, and yet so magical. It was like all the other women were playing at being Magdalene or Saint Clare, and you were just…you. And you were taking it all in, but you weren't starry-eyed. You wanted to help, to be part of it, but you weren't sure what "it" was and you weren't sure you could give yourself like that."

He stopped. As Phoebe watched, a tear made its way down his face, and then another one.

"I want you to feel that for me," he said, his voice rough and uncertain, a voice she'd never heard from him before. "I want you to give yourself to me. To want to give yourself to me."

Phoebe closed her eyes, as if this would make her invisible. She had no idea what her face was revealing. She had no idea what she felt. If the floor had opened beneath them and she'd found herself falling through space, she couldn't have felt less safe. Even gravity was an open question.

"I know," he said, his voice a little more stable. "I know you can't right now. But that's what I want."

* * *

So things changed after that. There were more stolen moments, and the times together were intense, tender, charged. Phoebe began to think of ways she could talk to Abby about it, hoping one day she'd see Abby with one of the other men, that Abby would move on and be able to accept the idea of Phoebe and Raphael without pain. Raphael began talking about building their own house at the community, finding a way to make things more permanent—when 'the whole thing' became public and 'everybody' got used to it. Phoebe found ways to think about their relationship as being normal, acceptable.

It was a late afternoon just before Thanksgiving when Abby pulled her aside and whisked her away for a talk. Phoebe thought: finally! She's gotten involved with someone else and she wants to tell me about it. Abby's face was joyful, her eyes lit. They walked up to Phoebe's room, passing laughing groups hanging pine boughs and mistletoe in the hallway. From the hallway came the sound of the community's choir, practicing Christmas music. The run-up to the holiday season was in full swing, and no shopping malls were even remotely involved.

Phoebe turned on a lamp—this didn't seem like the kind of talk that required a candle—and smiled as she pulled her friend over to the bed, nestling down and awaiting good news.

"So?" she asked, her hands clasping Abby's.

"I have tidings of great joy," Abby said, laughing. "I wanted you to be the first one to know."

"You've fallen in love?"

"Well…in a manner of speaking. Back in love, I'd say."

"With?"

"With—pause for drumroll—the father of my child!" Abby's last word came out as a squeal.

"Your what?!"

"My child," Abby said happily, gazing down at her perfectly flat stomach.

"You're pregnant?!"

"Well, it won't be the first Spirit Mountain baby, after all," Abby laughed. This was true. Some of those soul mates were bearing fruit, so to speak.

Phoebe was stunned. How had she missed this? She'd been watching Abby like a hawk, hoping—praying—to see some sign that she was involved with someone. She cleared her throat.

"I didn't know you were even, um, seeing anyone."

Abby got up and walked to the window, as though she needed some distance to break all the news she'd kept bottled up inside her. "Well, we kept it pretty quiet. I mean, it's one thing to have everyone know that you've broken up, but to tell them that you're back together again is…"

"What?" It came out like a whisper, and Abby didn't seem to hear, because she just kept on talking.

"…it might be hard on people—or hard on us, for that matter. He doesn't even know—that I'm pregnant I mean. Obviously, he knows we're back together because…"

"Raphael. You're talking about Raphael." Phoebe said, her voice sounding strange and dead.

Abby turned around, looking concerned. "You sound worried. You don't approve. Oh, honey, I know it was rotten—what he did to me—but we got over that. It was just a momentary thing. It was like he couldn't believe how in love with me he was and it made him feel so out of control and he was trying to…" She stopped. "Are you okay?"

Phoebe just stared at her.

"Fee, you are as white as a sheet."

"Yeah," Phoebe said slowly. "Yeah, I don't feel right. I think maybe I need to lie down?"

"Of course! Oh, sweetie, I hope you don't have that flu that's going around." Abby bustled around, tucking Phoebe under the covers and turning off the light. "You just close your eyes and try to sleep. I'll see if I can find some miso soup in the kitchen." And she left, closing the door gently behind her.

Phoebe lay under the blankets, shaking as if she did, in fact, have the flu. Abby's news would have been difficult to take under any circumstances. But with two missed periods of her own, it was beyond hard.

Chapter 12: November, 1972 – January 1973

At the time Abby revealed her secret, Phoebe and Raphael had been following a regular routine for some time. After dinner, before the evening class began, they would each disappear. This was hardly unusual. Many community members used this hour to deal with personal things. Phoebe would meet Raphael in an empty room in a little-used building just beyond the barn. There was talk of making it into a residential house, but that hadn't happened yet. Raphael had managed to drag a bedframe and a mattress over there, and Phoebe had hidden some sheets and blankets in a closet. The one who arrived first would make up the bed and light some incense to dispel the musty smell of the unused rooms.

This time, it was Phoebe who got there first, and she went through the motions mechanically. Her mind was auditioning things to say to Raphael and dismissing them, one by one, like unpromising actors trying out for a particularly challenging play. The gist of it was to end this crazy situation, once and for all. If she was pregnant — and she didn't really know for sure — she'd deal with that on her own. The main thing was to end her relationship with Raphael before Abby told him her news. Then the way would be clear for Abby and Raphael, if that's what they wanted. Surely, even Raphael couldn't convince her — or himself — to keep up this insane double life in the face of an imminent baby. And if Abby and Raphael didn't want to stay together, well, that would be between the two of them. Let them work that out. If they were very careful, maybe Abby would never find out that anything had gone on at all.

As she repeated these thoughts, somewhat compulsively, she realized that some part of her had been ready to end the relationship for a while. It was Abby's news that had made her realize how she truly felt, beneath her infatuation. Each time she thought about Abby's baby, a physical pain shot through her, so strong it forced her to stop whatever she was doing and sit down for a moment. The realization of the depth of her betrayal of their friendship left her breathless. And then too, his betrayal. All these months, when she had believed him! Those tears! That broken-hearted plea! All those stolen moments when she had imagined…Never mind. Her thoughts could not encompass the Raphael of those nights and the Raphael who had been murmuring the same lying words of love to Abby — what? — hours before? Minutes? Her heart and mind simply couldn't stretch far enough to put all the elements into one reality. Oh, God, the sooner she put an end to all this the better.

When she finally heard Raphael's steps on the path, she sat down on the bed and took a few deep breaths. All the auditioning actors had left the stage and she was left with no plan of what to say. She raised her eyes in a kind of skeptical prayer to whatever powers were up there and, as usual, felt that their only message to her was "You're on your own, kid."

When Raphael came through the door, she knew immediately that he had spoken to Abby, but didn't know that Phoebe had as well. There was a kind of hesitancy, a kind of caution in his posture — he was dealing with a situation he hadn't anticipated. She decided not to enlighten him.

He came over and took her in his arms, and there was a kind of desperation in the way he held her — a little too tightly and a little too long. Gently pulling back, she placed a look of concern on her face and asked, "Something wrong?"

He looked away. "Tough day," was all he said.

Phoebe didn't have it in her to prolong all this. It was clearly just as painful for him as it was for her, even if it was a situation of his own making.

"I think I'm about to make it tougher," she said.

"Great." He looked at her and managed a smile. "Go ahead—what's going on? Maybe I can help."

"I've been thinking about us," she started, knowing these words were guaranteed to make him defensive and uneasy. Already, she could see his shoulders rise slightly.

"I can't do this anymore. I can't see us getting to the point of telling people, and I can't see us going on in secret. I think I just need to stop."

He looked hurt, and then dubious. "Where is this coming from? Just last night…"

"Well, when I'm with you I try to forget how hard it is, but all day I think about it. I guess I finally just got to the end of my rope. I want to be free to find someone else. Someone I can hold hands with and know that everyone approves. Someone I can marry and—maybe someday—have kids with. Someone Abby can feel happy about—who won't break her heart all over again."

Tellingly, he didn't try to convince her that he could be that person. He got up and paced. "You're going to stay here, though? At the community?"

"I'll try it. I don't know. I'd like to."

"What if I get together with someone else? How will you feel about that?"

"Well, obviously, it will be painful but it's what I expect you to do. Why shouldn't you get together with someone?"

"I can tell you it will be damned painful for me when you do," he said angrily. "God, just the thought of it."

He had his back to her and Phoebe allowed herself to roll her eyes. It was getting hard to refrain from exploding and telling him everything she knew. Time to end this scene.

"I'm sorry to hurt you, Raphael," she said, keeping her voice level with a huge effort. "I think I need to go now. This is all very hard."

She got up quickly and walked out of the room, forcing herself to keep from running. She heard the bedsprings creak as Raphael sat down, but the sigh she heard might have been one of sorrow or one of relief. It was hard to tell.

* * *

Abby and Raphael began spending more time together in public, and the community gradually caught on to the fact that the two of them were back together. There were varying reactions, but everyone was careful to tell the reconstituted couple how good it was to see them so happy. It felt like one of those self-improvement workshops where people can give you positive feedback only.

Phoebe heard the other, less positive reactions on her dinner clean-up duty, out in the courtyard, and in dining-room table conversation. Some of the women sought her out as a sounding board for their own opinions, and perhaps hoping she had more inside information—being an old friend of Abby's. They trusted her, and that just ripped her up inside. She was careful to remain neutral and to be as uninformed as they were. As Abby's best friend, she took the official position that Abby and Raphael had, with counseling, prayer, and good intentions, worked out their issues and become all the stronger for it. This was a welcome point of view. Most of the community women were "working out issues" and were grateful for a model that had a happy ever after.

Phoebe watched Abby for signs of her developing pregnancy. Her own stomach seemed rounder to her, and she felt completely exhausted every afternoon. She thought about getting a pregnancy test or consulting the community doctor, but she just couldn't face what she was pretty sure she would hear. It was a month after her breakup with Raphael when Abby showed up in her room, looking sad.

"Apparently I'm not pregnant after all," she told Phoebe.

"Disappointed?"

"A little. But I realized I'm not quite ready to be a mom."

"I wonder if anyone ever feels ready," Phoebe said, thinking that she certainly didn't.

"True. But I don't think Raphael was really ready either. I mean he was totally committed, and he told me with absolute certainty that he'd marry me and help me raise the child, and all that. But I could tell he was hoping not to have that kind of distraction when the community needs so much of his time and energy."

Phoebe thought that the words 'committed' and 'absolute certainty' were awkward choices where Raphael was concerned, but she just nodded her agreement.

"Maybe it's for the best," she said.

"As things so often are," said Abby, with a little of her old sunny optimism.

* * *

It was another few weeks before Phoebe came to terms with her own situation. One of the other community women, Aminah, who had two children of her own, approached Phoebe. Pointedly staring at Phoebe's belly, Aminah asked if she realized that she was pregnant. Phoebe burst into tears, and a long conversation ensued. Before she knew what she was saying, she had agreed to see the community doctor, feeling ashamed and irresponsible that she hadn't done so before. After all, this was a child inside her, not some extra weight she was carrying. And surely the child deserved prenatal care and attention. She wept for an hour while Aminah held her and murmured understanding words. It hadn't been that different for her, during her first pregnancy, she told Phoebe. The father was a married man, and there had been a lot to work out. She waited for Phoebe to blurt out her own story, but didn't push when she remained silent.

The doctor confirmed what Phoebe already knew, looking at her with a semi-amused expression.

"You honestly didn't know?" he asked her.

"I can really work the whole denial thing," Phoebe assured him. "I guess I knew but I wouldn't let myself know that I knew."

"That's all too complicated for me," the doctor laughed, putting away his stethoscope. "Just come by once a month for the next few months and we'll make sure everything is going along as it should. You're young and strong and I don't foresee any problems."

Phoebe thought she could foresee enough problems for any dozen random individuals to share, but she just smiled and thanked him and went back to her room. The next step was to tell Abby, and she wasn't sure exactly what to say. The whole truth seemed impossible, and anything less would involve a lie that she couldn't figure out how to pull off, even if she were willing to lie to her best friend.

Thinking back to her conversation with Aminah, Phoebe laughed a bit. Aminah's first hurdle was to tell the married father of her child. For Phoebe, Raphael took a distant second or third place. She groaned as she realized that one of the notifications would have to be to her parents. Terrific. It was really going to be a fun-filled week or two. Phoebe reflected that it was hard to be pregnant like there was no one watching, because they were. Or would be soon.

Phoebe's parents had officially disowned her when she dropped out of school to work at "some fly-by-night magazine in Greenwich Village," a second time when she moved to New York and refused to live with them, and a third time when she left a "wonderful" job (yes—the one at the fly-by-night magazine) to live at some hippie commune. So this would make four, at the very least. "I'm getting good at being disowned," she told herself. She began humming the old Leslie Gore song. "I'm not just one of your little toys," she sang, as she swept—her personal form of therapy.

A knock at her open door made her stop and look up. There was Abby. Hurdle number one walked through the door and sat down on Phoebe's bed.

* * *

Aminah, despite her promise to keep things to herself, had almost immediately spoken to Abby. She'd been careful not to tell her in so many words that Phoebe was pregnant, but Abby had figured out the hidden message in about three minutes flat and was here to find out the story. Phoebe could tell from her face that Abby had no idea who the father was, and sure enough, that was her first question.

"I can't tell you," Phoebe said.

"Why?"

"Trust me. It wouldn't help anything and several people could be seriously hurt. Hurt in a way they might not recover from. It just has to be a secret, Ab."

Abby was mustering her considerable powers of persuasion when Raphael walked in, his hands balled into fists and his face a dark thundercloud. Looking from one to the other, Phoebe walked over and closed the door, realizing even as she did it that pretty much everyone in the building would be able to hear the "discussion."

"Okay, then," she said, sitting down on the bed. "Just remember not to hit a pregnant woman. Either of you."

* * *

Half an hour later, Abby emerged from the room, stumbling numbly down the hallway. Phoebe stood by the window and, sure enough, Abby came out the courtyard doors and headed down the road to the pond—her place of refuge, even on a cold winter day.

Raphael sat with his head in his hands and Phoebe regretted their weight difference, which meant that she couldn't lift him bodily and throw him out the door. Or through the window.

"I'd like to be alone now, Raphael," Phoebe said in her iciest voice. "Pack up your sorrows and take them down the hall."

"Phoebe…"

"Raphael, there is nothing you could say to me now that I could even hear, much less sympathize with. Please just leave."

He didn't move, and Phoebe, with a sigh, picked up her coat and left the room herself, heading down the road to the pond.

The road had gone from its glorious October splendor to its bleak winter state. In the trees, squirrels and birds were busy—dealing with the vagaries of the cold, Phoebe assumed. At the pond, Abby sat cross-legged on the ground, which was cold but bare. The snow had come early, but they were enjoying a short respite before it set up its long-term winter residence. Abby's usual majestic presence was reduced to a forlorn little heap of jeans and scarves. She looked up at Phoebe and tried a smile.

"I can't find it in me to blame you," she said.

"I can," Phoebe sighed. "I can find enough in me for the both of us. Honestly, Abby. How is this not my fault?"

"I know how he is."

"Yeah, but we know how *we* are. No man is worth the kind of friendship we had."

"Have," Abby said, taking Phoebe's hand.

"Really?"

Abby was silent for a moment, but finally replied, "It's a little bruised at the moment but I think it will recover."

"I can leave here," Phoebe said, though it cost her an effort to say it.

"No." Abby squeezed Phoebe's hand and looked up at her. "You need the community. Where could you possibly go, pregnant and poor and alone?"

Phoebe knew just how true this was. She'd burned enough bridges to rival Sherman's march through Georgia, and now she wasn't going to be the only one to pay the price. She tried to imagine Hudson making good on his offer to take her back on the magazine when he spotted her swelling belly. Yeah. That's not going to happen.

Abby was still talking. "…and I think I need to get away. It isn't too late to go back to school for the next rotation. If I leave tomorrow, I can still register for classes. It'll be a good distraction."

"Are we going to be okay?" Phoebe asked, tears starting down her cheeks.

"We are always going to be okay," Abby said. "But if you don't hear from me for a little while, just pretend I'm in Nepal or something. Who knows—maybe I will be."

* * *

Abby's departure caused quite a buzz at Spirit Mountain, but the preparations for an upcoming New Year's meditation weekend overrode the gossip after a while. After the first Thanksgiving and Christmas at the young community, many well-wishers, family, and friends wanted to spend more time with the young Sufis. Phoebe threw herself into the cooking plans and Raphael was consumed with logistics.

Phoebe avoided Raphael in public. If anyone noticed, they figured it was because Raphael had broken up with Abby and, presumably, caused the departure of Phoebe's best friend. No one yet suspected that he was the father of Phoebe's child, and she didn't enlighten them. Raphael's public overtures to Phoebe were seen as the efforts of the community executive to smooth over an awkward situation. Phoebe realized that, generally, everyone was too preoccupied with his or her own personal dramas to pay all that much attention to those of others. She examined her own thoughts about the Spirit Mountain membership and realized how little she knew or cared to know about the issues in their romantic lives. Good lesson to remember.

Still, whether anyone else knew or cared, it was impossible for Phoebe to avoid Raphael altogether. And he used every opportunity to try to win her back.

"I've always wanted to be a father," he told her, over and over. "When I thought Abby was pregnant, I was so happy — I mean, happy to have a child. But I knew that you were the one I wanted to raise a child with. I've known it since the moment I met you. Only her pregnancy changed that."

Phoebe just looked at him in angry bewilderment. "There wouldn't have been a pregnancy if you hadn't been sleeping with her behind my back," she exploded. "Surely even Antioch covered that aspect of biology!"

"I know, I know," he groaned. "But it wouldn't have lasted if ..."

"It lasted quite a good long time before any child appeared on the horizon. Stop lying to me."

"But the child did appear on the horizon. Or we thought it did. And it changed everything—and it will for you too. So think about your child," Raphael said, changing tactics. "Don't you want that child to have a father?"

This stopped Phoebe because she did, in fact, want the child to have a father. And who would marry her now, with an infant to care for? Who would love and care for this child as his own other than the person who was its actual father?

But each time she went down this path she told herself that it was better to be alone—better for the child to be alone with just a mother, even—than to commit to a life with someone so inherently dishonest and immoral. It didn't help to know that, all around her, in the guise of searching for their true soulmates, every member of the community could be just as faithless and self-centered as Raphael. It seemed that, just as she was trying most sincerely to open herself to the spirit, the spirit was obscured in a fog of self-centered nonsense. When she found out that Murshid Khalid himself had two wives, and an alleged daughter by yet another woman, she couldn't help but feel vindicated in her initial skepticism. As always, the community was compassionate, forgiving, and kind, but she could feel her old friend, cynicism, raise its head and let out a short sardonic snort. The seemingly endless winter spread out before her and it was hard to find hope.

Chapter 13: May, 1973 – May, 1976

Like the worst guest at a New Year's Eve party, winter in the Berkshires came early and stayed late. In April, it snowed regularly. The snows were followed by torrential rains that made the "May flowers" of the old saying questionable—or at least very soggy. The farmers at the community shook their heads and tried to get seeds in on the occasional dry days. Everyone else huddled inside, praying for a little sunshine.

Phoebe's belly was so large by now that she looked like a little house on feet. She had somehow imagined that pregnancy would turn her into the Primavera, as it had the tall, willowy Spirit Mountain women who dressed in flowing dresses during their final months and looked like Art Nouveaux paintings. Phoebe looked like an ancient African fertility figure in a museum, with pendulous breasts and a blocky, jutting stomach.

Finally, with June just around the corner, the weather relented and the sun shone through. People sat on blankets on the damp grass, soaking up the warmth and light. Phoebe's due date came and went. Each morning she arrived for breakfast in the communal dining room to be greeted by groans, as everyone realized she still had not had her baby. The midwives had allowed her to attend a few births—hers was not the only winter pregnancy—and Phoebe lived in mortal terror of her own labor. One woman had been so stoic that she had not uttered a sound during the entire delivery. Phoebe was sure she would not be able to match this. The other one was so free and frank that she tried out every possible position to ease her pain and hurry the birth, shouting "Come on, baby!" as she did. Phoebe was pretty sure she wouldn't be able to do that either.

Raphael kept up his relentless campaign for her affections, buying her dresses to wear after the birth and books on child development. To complicate things even more, he had told everyone who would listen that he was the baby's father. Not everyone believed him, but Phoebe deeply resented the position this put her in. In an effort to make sense of the disparate bits of information they could get hold of, the Spirit Mountain community concluded that Phoebe had seduced Raphael, caused him to break up with Abby, thereby causing Abby's departure, and then—just as he had committed to her and the baby—left Raphael high, dry, and broken-hearted. Most of the community felt they'd traded Abby for Phoebe and gotten a raw deal in the process. She was a burden to Spirit Mountain itself—a single mother with no visible means of support.

Phoebe couldn't blame them. She hated putting Spirit Mountain through all that drama, but she simply couldn't bring herself to explain. Every time she had that conversation in her head, she sounded like a whining, defensive liar. So she allowed herself to be the target of the community's disapproval.

She thought bitterly of the stories she'd heard about the bliss of pregnancy, the photos of loving couples stroking the large belly holding their child. She had none of this. Every day, she felt like more of a pariah. It was as though the scarlet letter she'd joked about with Kent was now literally inscribed on her forehead. Spirit Mountain, the place that had felt like such a warm home and a new beginning, now felt like a prison.

It didn't help to watch the calendar creep past her due date by days and weeks. She spent a lot of her days alone, feeling like her labor would never begin. But of course it did. Her waters broke. Naturally, it was the middle of the night.

Awakened by her body's flood, Phoebe waddled down the hall to Fleur's room. Knocking timidly, she opened the door a crack and called out the midwife's name.

"Phoebe?" said a sleepy voice in reply.

"I think it's time," Phoebe said.

"Be right there," Fleur said, her voice stronger and more awake. "I'll just go and get Hanifa."

Phoebe stood for a moment more on the cold floor of the hallway and then shuffled back to bed to wait.

Before long, there were five women in her room, chanting, preparing clean towels, and instructing her on breathing. For the first time in months, Phoebe felt loved and cared for again, and grateful tears crept down her cheeks, gently brushed away by the nearest midwife. The room was lit by candlelight and scented with incense and the only thing missing was Abby. How Phoebe would have loved to be squeezing Abby's hand when the contractions came, looking into Abby's sympathetic eyes and feeling safe with her oldest friend. Once again, she was on her own.

Phoebe watched the sky get lighter between her contractions.

"Do you want us to go and get Raphael?" Hanifa asked, trying to keep her voice neutral.

"Please don't" Phoebe said, and then gasped as another contraction hit. "Please."

"It's his baby too," Fleur said, her voice holding a touch of judgment.

"I know but…" Phoebe used the next contraction as an excuse to avoid explaining.

Elizabeth pointed out that everyone in the community would know she was in labor as soon as breakfast started, so it was a moot point. Phoebe sighed inwardly and accepted that, when morning arrived, so would Raphael. She supposed he had a right to be there, but it was miserable for her, a constant reminder of all that had gone before.

The day wore on and still no baby. The midwives had begun taking turns catching a nap until the action began. Raphael came and went. The doctor looked in.

"Phoebe," he said sternly. "If you don't dilate soon, we will need to get you to a hospital."

"Doing the best I can," Phoebe gasped, feeling that once again she was failing at some task that anyone else would do more capably. But apparently the baby shared her horror of birth in a hospital, because half an hour later she was fully dilated and panting like a freight train.

"Don't push yet!" urged Fleur.

Phoebe tried valiantly to follow these instructions, but she felt like an elevator had broken loose in her insides and was crashing through to the basement.

"Damn," said Fleur—which shocked Phoebe so much that she was able to hold the elevator back for a few moments. "I'm afraid you've torn, Phoebe. Now try hard not to push. You need to…"

It went on like that for what felt like hours but in fact was only ten minutes or so. When Phoebe heard Fleur say "Now! Push!" she thought that sweeter words had never been spoken.

Finally, twenty-seven hours after Phoebe's first twinges, little Ruth was born, red-faced, screaming, and unbelievably beautiful. The big bell on the barn roof rang out, letting everyone know that a new soul had arrived. Each time she looked up, the doorway was filled with another well-wisher—fellow moms holding little ones on their hips, large, muddy, bearded men fresh from the farm, and flour-dusted bakers. Tuning out Raphael's crowing, Phoebe focused on her community. In each face she saw the awe and delight that new babies bring throughout the world, and she thought perhaps her face would break from smiling so hard. It even seemed possible that life could go on.

* * *

The first week she mostly slept, waking to gifts of juice or broth, nursing little Ruth and keeping her clean and dry. But as soon as she had recovered from the birth, the days flew by. Phoebe was determined to be an asset to the community.

She buckled down and worked on bookkeeping until even Shaffee nodded his approval. She took over running the little office, serving as receptionist, hostess, mail sorter — whatever she could do with one arm while she held Ruth in the other. Even those who had been the most judgmental of Phoebe's perceived misbehavior found ways to be kind. When she needed a break, there was always a willing pair of hands to take the baby for a little while. When she needed advice, there was always a mom whose little one had just gone through whatever phase Ruth was in. And as for clothes, there were boxes of hand-me-downs that always arrived clean and ironed. Phoebe wondered why anyone was foolish enough to have a baby in the lonely suburbs when she could be in baby paradise in a community.

Through it all, like a threatening drumbeat, there was Raphael, hovering over the baby and using his baby-talk voice to say all the things he wanted Phoebe to hear:

"And someday, Ruthie, we'll be a real family. You'll have a mommy and a daddy who love each other, just like the other kids do. And we'll laugh about how you have daddy's ears and mommy's smile..."

"And we'll watch reruns of 'I Love Lucy,'" Phoebe would say, in a parody of the baby-talk voice. "And we'll all vote Republican. And after that, we'll talk about all the other women that daddy tried to impregnate."

Raphael usually left around then. But he always came back.

Over time, Phoebe heard other stories of Raphael's infidelity. The first one had been a shock, of course. She was horrified by Raphael's betrayal of her and Abby, but at least it made a certain kind of sense. But when a woman named Vashti confessed that Raphael had come to her bed during Phoebe's pregnancy, Phoebe couldn't believe it.

"Is this true, or is Vashti just trying to freak me out for some reason?" she demanded of Raphael, the next time he came to "visit Ruth."

"Well, it's not like you or Abby were having anything to do with me," he said defensively, and Phoebe just stared at him. Later, when Shaloma told her a similar story—and confessed that she and Raphael were still "involved"—she didn't even bother to fact-check. She reported these revelations to Raphael as calmly as she could, thinking that perhaps he was hoping to use her shock and pain as a weapon in his campaign, maybe throw her off balance to the point of being mildly unstable, and thereby in need of a devoted husband. But he only seemed surprised at her disapproval. He didn't seem to find anything wrong with his infidelity. How he thought that either his behavior or his lack of remorse would help his case was a mystery. Who on earth would consent to be with anyone who thought this was all okay? But that's how this whole soul-mate thing worked, she thought. That's where it led. And for her, she knew, it would eventually lead to her leaving Spirit Mountain. But not quite yet, she thought. Please, God or whoever is up there, please don't make me leave yet.

* * *

She still refused to shed any light on the whole sordid story. By now, her determination in this regard was like an over-exercised muscle—she couldn't have used it even if she wanted to. It gave her a kind of strength, she supposed, but there was something deeply damaging about being unable to tell her own story. There were times when she wondered what her story actually was. She gave herself over to the new, fierce devotion she felt to Ruth, and a steely determination to survive, to find a way to be the mother Ruth deserved—and yet on some level she could not really say what that meant or how to make it happen.

She rarely heard from Abby these days. Abby had sent an exquisite cashmere blanket when Ruth was born—much too nice to use at Spirit Mountain, which Abby surely knew. There were occasional postcards—one was actually from Nepal.

Phoebe needed a way to cope with all the conflicting things life was throwing at her. She found herself writing long letters to Abby, as she had back in her college days, but now she never sent them. She kept them in a special box and comforted herself with the idea that in some foggy, far-off future, the two of them would huddle on a bed and read through them, their arms around each other, shaking their heads over their foolish past selves. The box was filling up. Phoebe sometimes thought that when there was no more room for the letters, she would make some momentous decision. But when she reached the point where she couldn't fit one more page into the box, she just got another box.

One night, when most of the community was at a Family Meeting, she found herself pulling out her old guitar. Just the feel of it in her arms was like finding an old lover after years of separation. At first she sang to Ruth—Pete Seeger songs, old rock and roll songs, blues songs that she and Robin had done. Her heart, roiled by so many different emotions, seemed to find a path to clarity when she sang, and words came to her that told her how she felt when she couldn't have explained it consciously—her terror of leaving this place that seemed so safe and yet was holding her in thrall to the person she dreaded most. At the same time, the gift she had received from her years here that allowed her to experience something so much greater than her own drama.

One night, when the pain and loneliness was at its worst, she found herself writing a new song. It gave her a sense of peace each time she sang it.

I have heard stories of slaves who wept with fear

When told by their masters their day of freedom was near

I have seen cages with gold and silver bars

But I have seen prisoners gaze at the stars

There is within us all a thirst for the stars

A search for what was and can be again

There is within us all a limitless place, a state of grace

And the light of the sun.

As she was working out new verses to this song, someone knocked at the door. Guy, a sweet southern man-child who'd moved to the community recently, was standing there. Phoebe smiled, thinking how this boy had arrived with nothing to offer for his room and board other than countless copies of his self-published book of poetry. Within a week, he'd totaled two of the community's vehicles. He was an odd combination of self-promotion, cluelessness, and a sweet sincerity that cut through all the rest. Like many of the Spirit Mountain men, he was impossible and yet endlessly forgivable. Here he was at her door, holding a guitar of his own.

"I couldn't help hearing your songs," he said bashfully — pointing to the wall that separated their two rooms. "I been writing some of my own and I thought maybe we could sing together sometime?"

"Sure," Phoebe said. "Come on in."

Over the next few weeks, they found a few other closeted singer-songwriters and formed a loose sort of singing group. They gave a little concert one evening in the library, and were asked to sing at the worship service on Sunday. To Phoebe's surprise — and yet, somehow not a surprise at all — it grew from there. Soon they were driving into a nearby town to play at a café on weekends, and were invited by another spiritual community to come and perform. By the following summer, they decided they had written enough songs to make a little recording. When they announced this in the Spirit Mountain newsletter, they received orders for it — it was not exactly like charting on Billboard, but the fact that anyone at all would send them money for a recording they hadn't even made yet was touching. Sometimes it felt good to sing like someone *was* listening, and Phoebe felt her old gratitude to songwriting and music, the things in her life that made her feel like she could do anything.

* * *

Ruth was a true community baby. She took her first steps in the dining room. She said her first word ("moon") as Phoebe was carrying her back to their room across the starlit courtyard. She had her birthday parties in the library.

At her third birthday, all the community children came (probably because there was cake). One of the older kids did magic tricks to entertain the younger ones and Phoebe handed out balloons. The mood was festive, and Phoebe could pretend for a moment that all was forgiven. Maybe it even was. She looked around the room at the parents and children with a huge lump in her throat. She had never felt more at home than she did right now, and yet she was aware that her time of departure was approaching.

Phoebe could feel the tide turning, although she couldn't put her finger on when it had begun or even what the nature of the change was. For one thing, despite Raphael's demonstrated bad behavior, the community seemed to sympathize with him.

Even Phoebe had to admit that he was a great dad. The moms at the community had mixed feelings about Raphael in general, but Phoebe could see the warmth in their eyes as he lay under a shady tree on the lawn, telling the baby stories that Ruth couldn't possibly understand but seemed to be transfixed by. He took her for long walks down the road past the pond, pointing out birds and holding flowers under her little nose. Phoebe should have been pleased. But for reasons she couldn't explain, Phoebe knew that each time the community made another excuse for Raphael, Spirit Mountain's residents were finding more fault with Phoebe herself.

In addition, Abby's absence was an increasing issue. Not even Phoebe had realized how much Abby had done to keep things running smoothly, to deal with issues of ego and anger, to make people feel appreciated and centered. One evening, wandering into the Family Room, Phoebe caught the tail end of a conversation between two women she would have described as close friends.

"I just can't get over Phoebe's betrayal. If I understand it right, she and Abby have been friends since they could walk. How could she seduce Abby's lover like that?"

"I know—I can't stop thinking about it. And then to throw him over as soon as he left Abby completely and committed himself heart and soul to Phoebe and Ruth. It just seems heartless."

Phoebe backed out of the room as silently as she could. Upstairs, watching Ruth asleep in her little crib, she couldn't even cry. Just breathing took every ounce of energy she had.

Meanwhile, Raphael was increasingly gone for weeks at a time. Decisions were delayed, projects were put off.

Whenever he returned, he devoted himself to Ruth, which kept the community somewhat tolerant toward him. But the summer after Ruth's third birthday, it became clear that even the most sterling father could not replace a hands-on director and a clear vision. With Murshid Khalid in Europe for the summer, the community had to fall back on its own resources. It churned through a slow process in an effort to figure out the right thing to do. During one of Raphael's extended, unexplained absences, an emergency meeting was held and the community chose a different executive director. To everyone's surprise, life at Spirit Mountain went on, and even improved.

With the realization that Raphael was replaceable, the community at Spirit Mountain freed themselves to see his behavior as irresponsible and erratic. In anger, he retaliated, but without his usual finesse. He informed them haughtily that since he had directed Spirit Mountain in its infancy, the community owed him its very survival. It was only reasonable that they should support him now, rather than the other way around. He expected to be treated like a VIP, with a large sunny room and no charge for his room and board.

He had talked everyone's ear off about his devotion to Phoebe and her stubborn unwillingness to create a real family, as he put it, but his ongoing affair with Shaloma was well-known to all. It was as though his determination to win Phoebe back had burned through the heroic costume he had worn so carefully all the years she'd known him, and though he didn't seem to be aware of it himself, the real face behind the mask was becoming visible to everyone. It was not a pretty sight. Unfortunately for Phoebe, she was tarred with the same brush. Every complaint against Raphael was an implied complaint against her as well.

These thoughts were tumbling around in her head as she helped organize a big conference that would take place at the community in late summer. The followers of Murshid Khalid had centers all over the country, and the leaders of these centers were meeting to discuss their issues and be inspired by Spirit Mountain and the other centers. It was rumored that Murshid Khalid himself might return for the final days of the event.

Phoebe was organizing housing and registration. As she sat in the little office, trying to make order out of chaos, someone cleared his throat and she looked up to see a strange young man with a wispy beard that made him look even younger. She wondered how long he'd been waiting for her to notice him.

He smiled shyly and introduced himself as Micah. He was from the northern part of California, a place called Marin County. He'd arrived early to experience the community and wondered if there was a room he could stay in.

Phoebe welcomed him and quickly sorted out a room and got him registered. The bell for noon prayers rang and they walked over to the Meditation Hall together. After that, showing him how the dining room worked and sitting together for the meal seemed only polite.

At the table, as Phoebe fed Ruth and herself, Micah told her about his life in California. He was going through a dark night of the soul, he told her. His wife had fallen in love with another man and they were trying to work things out, but it didn't look good. The children were really having a hard time with it. He had lost all confidence in himself, and his family —

terribly disappointed by the failure of the marriage—was continually adding to his sense of worthlessness. The only bright spots in his life were his Sufi practices and his music. Phoebe could relate to the second part at least. What sort of music did he do?

He sang in a choir, he told her, and someone at Spirit Mountain had sent him a cassette of her little singing group. He particularly liked the songs she'd written.

"Have you ever heard the Celestial Choir?" he asked her. She laughed, taking it as a joke. "Not yet," she said.

He grimaced. "I told them it was a dumb name," he said. "I think you'd really like their music though. Here's a tape of us singing some of Mathieu's music—so now we're even." Phoebe took the tape back to her room and played it over and over. The music was enchanting, delightful—sophisticated but catchy. Micah told her that Mathieu, the director of the choir, was an experienced composer.

"And he teaches music," Micah said, leaving the idea to hang in the air.

She sat in her room, playing the tape for the hundredth or so time. The music was transformative—she'd never heard anything like it. The singers sounded like they were ecstatic. "I want to do that," she said out loud, thinking back to the other times in her life when she'd said the same thing. Each time, it had brought her to a new place. It's true that eventually she'd had to move on, but each step had been important.

She thought about a life in California, singing in this phenomenal choir and studying music. In the past, this might have seemed almost possible, but now it felt like a fantasy from someone else's life. Phoebe realized that she hadn't felt in control of her own life for quite a while. Something within her rebelled at this. Other people left the community periodically. It was part of the natural rhythm of the place. Why not her?

She paused, examining the idea of leaving. It was hard to think about. She made herself face it. What if the music she really wanted was in California? Was it so completely impossible? It had some potential benefits. For one thing, it was a continent away from Raphael. A definite plus for her, but was it the best thing for Ruth? And… her thoughts hit a wall. Well, no need to do anything right away, she told herself.

But when the conference was over, she sought out Micah to say goodbye.

"I've been thinking about coming out to California."

"Great," Micah said with a laugh. "I'll look forward to seeing you out there." He was distracted, thinking of all the issues he'd be facing when he got back home. Murshid Khalid had been unable to join them, and he had been counting heavily on getting some advice from his teacher. Now he would have to figure it out himself. A sharp sob from Phoebe brought him back to the present.

"What I meant to say is," Phoebe stumbled over her words, blind to Micah's troubles and desperate with her own. "Look. I need some help. I've got…nothing. I have to get out of here—I have to! But it's so overwhelming. I would need a job. A place to stay. I wondered…"

Micah looked a bit taken aback. "Phoebe. Whoa." He was staring at her—not unkindly, but with an air of complete shock. She had seemed so normal.

Phoebe knew she should stop, but something in her told her that this could be her last and only chance. "Look," Phoebe said, willing herself to say what she needed to say, no matter how difficult it was. "I have never ever asked anyone for help. I've always taken care of myself. I am not asking this lightly. I can't do this on my own. I can't imagine why you would want to help me or how you actually *can* help me, but I am swallowing every ounce of pride in my being to tell you that I need help and something is telling me you are the help I need to ask for."

Micah was silent for a moment. "Okay," he said. "I've never had anyone ask me anything like that in my life. Ordinarily, I would just assume you were nuts. But …"

Phoebe waited. She was completely unaware of the tears streaming down her face. Micah thought about his own situation. What if this was redemption, coming in the guise of a stranger. It struck him as sort of Biblical.

"Give me two weeks," Micah said.

* * *

Back in her room, Phoebe was so overcome with emotions of various and conflicting natures that she could barely stand still. She paced the room. Ruth was asleep, so she couldn't go for a long walk. What to do with all this energy? She looked around at all the clutter. Her old faith in sweeping as therapy returned. But the floor was so completely covered with stuff that she couldn't sweep, so she decided to start by clearing a space for the broom.

She began with her papers—they took up so much room and seemed so irrelevant to her daily life. She piled up a bunch of unsorted pages and began putting them into piles, since at the moment they seemed to be organized geologically. Yes, here were the medical forms for Ruth, and then the letters from her angry parents when they learned of her pregnancy, and then…what was this? She looked at the sealed and unaddressed envelope, wondering what it could possibly be. Slitting it open, she saw the unmistakable handwriting of Hudson, her former boss at the literary magazine. Ah yes, the note Kent had delivered in what seemed like another lifetime. Well, what had Hudson had to say?

There was a polite, almost courtly letter of apology and…could it be? A check! A large check! A check that would likely pay for a plane ticket.

Phoebe laughed and looked up at the ceiling. Maybe she had finally received a response other than "You're on your own, kid." Apparently, even whoever was up there realized she could use just a little bit of help right now.

Chapter 14: August, 1976 – October, 1976

"I have something I need to tell you," Phoebe said, after handing Ruth to Raphael one afternoon. It was one of his increasingly rare visits and he was anxious to spend time with his daughter. By some miracle of timing, Micah's letter had arrived a few days earlier and Phoebe had begun laying her escape plans.

"Well?" Raphael said, buckling Ruth into the stroller and handing her a favorite stuffed rabbit.

Phoebe was nervous. It had become clearer to her how much her life was entwined with Raphael's—probably forever—because of Ruth. Still, there had to be a way.

"I got a letter from Matthieu—the composer guy."

"How do you know him?"

"I don't really. But someone gave me a tape of his choir and I wrote to him to say how great it is."

"Okay," Raphael said, distracted by Ruth's new game of speaking through the rabbit. She held it up to her mouth and made what they assumed were meant to be rabbit sounds.

"I sent him our recording," Phoebe continued, "and he's interested in teaching me."

"Well, how is he going to do that?" Raphael laughed. "Music by mail?"

"That's just it. I would need to go out there for a while. He suggested a year."

"What!" Raphael spun around. "Absolutely not! I mean, unless you want to leave Ruth here."

"No. I don't think that would work," Phoebe said calmly, refusing to rise to the bait. Raphael was a master at getting Phoebe to lose her temper, after which he could pretty much win any argument. Phoebe was training herself to stop that from happening. "There's a school sort of thing for kids

Ruth's age—it goes from infant care through elementary school. I might be able to get a job there and be near Ruth all day."

"You might? Based on what?"

"Well, someone at the leader's conference mentioned that they were looking for someone to run the office. It just came up in conversation because I run the office here and he wondered how we..."

"A guy, right?"

"A guy?"

"Who told you about the school?"

"Well, as a matter of fact..."

"I thought so," Raphael said. "He's obviously just trying to get into your pants. Who is this guy anyway?"

"No one you know." Phoebe concentrated on her breathing, on remaining calm. She was beginning to suspect that maybe all that breath stuff actually worked. She reminded herself to watch Raphael's neck and shoulders. Usually, when he was really angry, the muscles in his neck bunched up and his shoulders rose. She'd learned to spot the signs so she could change the subject, or at least move someplace where other people could see them so he wouldn't explode at her. But his muscles were relaxed. What was that about?

He turned around and she could see that his expression was calm. She relaxed a little, but remained wary.

"Maybe it's not a terrible idea," he said. Phoebe, braced for argument, tried not to show how surprised she felt but

Raphael went on, apparently unaware of her reaction. Or non-reaction.

"Look, babe, we're going to need to leave Spirit Mountain at some point, right?" He said. "So maybe you should spend some time remembering what it's like to live in the real world. California might even be a good place for us to move."

Phoebe did not comment on the idea of them moving anywhere together. In her own mind, she'd dismissed that possibility years ago. She realized for the millionth time how safe she'd felt here, with the community to protect her. It was one thing to depend on her own strength and talents to survive. But now there was Ruth. Everything was different. She concentrated on Raphael's apparent openness to her leaving Spirit Mountain. The community wasn't working for either of them. Maybe there was a way to use that.

"So, you're okay with that, then?" Phoebe said.

"What kind of time line are we talking about? I mean, you're not leaving tomorrow or anything?"

"Oh no," Phoebe said. "But soon. Maybe in the fall."

Raphael scowled, needing to exert some control. "Late fall. Maybe," he said.

"We'll see," Phoebe said calmly. "I'll let you know." And she walked away before he could say anything more. In the stroller, the rabbit growled, and then giggled.

* * *

It was late September when Phoebe woke up in her new home in Marin County and blinked at all the sunlight. She raised herself on an elbow to check on Ruth, sleeping just a few feet away in her own little bed. A small bathroom was attached to their bedroom—it was almost like having a little studio apartment. Micah had found a wonderful house—she shook her head to clear it. The morning felt like a fairytale.

Leaving Spirit Mountain had been something of an anticlimax. She'd informed the executive board of her departure and they'd accepted it without comment. Clearly, they'd been expecting something of the sort for a while. There was no farewell party. Very few of the residents even said a personal goodbye. Surprisingly, it was Shaloma who was the kindest, offering her a little parting gift of dried lavender and rosemary from the Herb Garden. She even drove Phoebe to the train station and helped her with her bags. The rest of the journey was just a blur of logistics and connections and arriving, sleepy and terrified, in the terra incognito of California.

As Ruth slept in her car seat, Micah filled her in on the developments in his own life. In the time between their meeting at the community and her arrival in California, Micah's marriage had fallen apart for good. He and his wife decided it would be best for the children if she remained in their old house and he moved out. So he'd found a house to rent nearby and populated it with some other Sufis, reserving a room for Phoebe and Ruth. She had an uncomfortable feeling that Micah might be expecting something in return for all his help, and that something might involve a romantic relationship she was neither interested in nor quite ready for. But so far, so good, so she put it out of her mind.

Phoebe slid out of bed and got Ruth's clothes ready. She stepped into the shower, leaving the bathroom door open so she could hear Ruth if she woke up. As she dried herself off, she heard the little girl stirring and moved back into the bedroom.

"Mama?"

"Yes, honey?"

"Where are we?"

"We are in our new house in California."

"Is daddy here?"

"No, sweetheart."

"Why?"

Since this was still the era of "why," Phoebe didn't respond directly. It just engendered an endless series of whys.

"Look what I picked out for you to wear today," she said instead.

Ruth examined the outfit and apparently found it to her liking. She started putting on the pink skirt over her pajama bottoms.

"Hang on, pumpkin," Phoebe laughed. "Let's get your pajamas off first."

When they emerged from their room, Micah was already having breakfast. Phoebe realized she hadn't made her own breakfast in more than four years. The communal dining room was always there, with its huge bowls of granola and sliced oranges. She fumbled through the cabinets, looking for cereal and bread. Micah came over to help.

"What's your favorite cereal?" he asked Ruth, who just stared at him. Cereal was cereal, as far as she was concerned.

Someone put a bowl of it down in front of you and you ate it. Phoebe found some Cheerios and poured them into a bowl with milk. She set it down at Ruth's place and began slicing a banana into it. Ruth picked up her spoon and began to eat, smiling shyly at Micah.

* * *

The little school that Micah's children attended was called "Brilliant Babies." She and Ruth caught a ride over there with Micah, who had a meeting with his daughter's teacher that morning. Phoebe stood outside the office, practicing her calming breaths. Returning to the "real world" was proving to be a rude awakening. Any dream she might have secretly cherished of returning to music or writing now seemed like the musings of a crazy person. She gave herself a stern talking-to.

"Look, Phoebe," she told herself. "Just surviving is going to be a challenge. You're 25, you never finished college, and you have barely any work experience."

"Yes," she admitted to her stern self. "True. Good points. But screw that. I need this job and I'm going to get it."

Before she could have further arguments with the various parts of her psyche, she marched into Brilliant Babies, holding Ruth's hand like a talisman. Armed with Rabbit, snacks, and a few picture books, Phoebe was prepared to do battle. A tall blonde woman looked up from a large reception desk and smiled.

"Are you Phoebe?" she asked.

Phoebe admitted that she was, and the two women sat down to talk.

"I'm Lilith," said the attractive blonde woman. "I started Brilliant Babies about six months ago. What I'm looking for is someone who can manage the office, deal with the parents, and do some light bookkeeping. Micah said you'd done some bookkeeping."

"Um," Phoebe said, not wanting to over-promise. "I've done some…"

"Well, the thing about bookkeeping," Lilith said, pretending not to notice Phoebe's panic, "is that everyone does it slightly differently. I'll show you our system and I think you'll find it reasonably straightforward. Have you done payroll at all?"

"No," Phoebe said, her heart sinking. But really, there was no point in lying.

"Again, I don't think it will be a problem. It's just arithmetic, really."

This was not reassuring. Phoebe, thinking back to her school days, immediately panicked completely. She glanced over at Ruth and pushed the panic aside.

"I…I think I'd be great dealing with parents?" she said quickly. "And I've managed an office back east for about a year and I'm great with details. But I have to be honest—my math is, well, not my strongest suit…"

Lilith glanced over at Ruth, playing happily with Rabbit. A tall woman walked in, her face a thundercloud.

"I need to speak to the manager," she said loudly.

"Go for it," said Lilith, disappearing into her little office through a door Phoebe had not noticed. It felt like a magic trick. Hmm. Trial by fire.

"How can I help?" Phoebe said, taking a deep breath and smiling.

When Lilith cracked her door open fifteen minutes later, the tall woman was laughing and heading for the door.

"You are a breath of fresh air, angel" she said to Phoebe. "Thanks so much. So long, little one," she added, speaking to Ruth, who waved a chubby hand and smiled at the nice lady. When the door closed behind her, Lilith emerged.

"I think I can do the bookkeeping for a while—until you catch on," she said. "But I can't do that." She gestured toward the door, where a breath of the tall woman's perfume still lingered. Phoebe laughed.

"My specialty," she said.

"I think we could make a good team," Lilith told her. "Or at least we can give it a try. My policy is to make the first six months of employment a trial period—for both parties. But if things work out, we can offer you a staff discount for Ruth in our pre-kindergarten classroom."

Phoebe drew a deep breath. Not since the evening she'd first played her own songs for an audience of twelve friends had she felt this nervous. If she didn't blow her chance, she had passed the second and third hurdle to a new life in California. She had a job, a place to live, and a great school for Ruth. It wasn't as glamorous as performing at folk festivals, nor as intellectually interesting as writing for a literary magazine. But she felt prouder of this moment than of any previous ones. She was going to be a good parent. She was going to provide for her daughter. She was going to survive.

* * *

The job proved far more challenging than any of her previous ones. Brilliant Babies was a bigger operation than she'd realized and it had somewhat crazy pretensions aimed at the yuppie parents of affluent Marin County. There were flashcards. For infants. Of famous composers. For the toddlers, the flashcards were words. Like "spaghetti" and "California." Whatever happened to *Hop on Pop*, Phoebe wondered. She had learned to turn her incipient laughter into a cough, but now she was coughing so often that Lilith was telling her to give up smoking.

Most of the clients were highly educated, high-powered women with stressful careers. Determined to have children, they were baffled by the added challenges of childrearing and desperately trying to keep all their plates spinning. It was not unusual for a young mother to enroll a 3-month-old for daycare from 7 am to 6 pm, and then inquire whether Brilliant Babies ever provided weekend care? Because she and her husband needed some alone time?

And although Phoebe was busy spinning her own plates, she couldn't help but find the humor in all of it. She could see that, beneath their snooty exteriors, the moms at this school were terrified of their own children. Some of them were certain that their little son or daughter would never master the use of a toilet. When she told them that almost no one goes off to college without mastering potty training, she could almost see their shoulders relax, and then re-tense when they realized she was joking, and then relax again when they realized that they were being ridiculous.

Some of the women—and it was always women—confided that their child, while obviously superior in every way, was, well, a bit of a discipline problem. "Hmm," murmured Phoebe the first time this occurred. "Well…" The mother leaned toward her, desperate for the secret to an end to tantrums. "He is a bit headstrong," Phoebe began. "But on the other hand, he is also about two feet tall." And then she would whisper her secret, as though anxious for the little one not to overhear. "If nothing else, you outweigh him. Pick him up and take him outside when he gets a little crazy. Change the environment. So you're at the store when he chooses his moment? So what? The supermarket clerk will hang onto your groceries for a few minutes, if that's what you're worried about. You're at the movies? You might miss a scene or two? Not to worry—he'll provide enough drama! You have to learn to parent like nobody's watching. Because frankly, they're not. They have problems of their own."

At first, Phoebe hesitated to take liberties with these super-women. But as time went on, and they responded gratefully to her down-to-earth advice, she found herself taking on the role of their confidante and advisor. She felt she was passing on the gift that the other moms at Spirit Mountain had given her. Sufism seemed to create some really great mothers.

Being of some help to these women was gratifying in some ways, but somewhat exhausting in others. Luckily Ruth loved her teachers and Phoebe loved being able to peek in at her during the day when things weren't too busy. She even strolled past the other rooms, checking in on Micah's kids, Bret and Belinda, and then sharing little tidbits with Micah over dinner.

* * *

Phoebe and Ruth settled into their new routine, but as it became easier and more predictable, Phoebe found herself wanting more for herself than just her bi-weekly music lessons and Sunday choir practice. Just when she was wondering if she'd ever have a moment that didn't involve an obligation to someone else, Micah found a teenager down the street who was willing to babysit, and after a few weeks Phoebe felt comfortable enough to leave Ruth for an evening to attend a Sufi class. She was eager to see the local spiritual community and find out if she wanted to be part of it.

At her first class, Phoebe felt like a visitor from another planet. The house they were in seemed palatial to her. The big room was crowded with blonde, tan, beautiful people wearing exotic clothing. The class was about to begin, but people were still chatting and laughing, so she turned to the woman next to her.

"Have you been coming to these classes for a long time?"

"Oh, yes. It's been over a year now."

"Ah," Phoebe didn't think a year was all that long, but then she considered how much her own life had changed in that timeframe and chided herself for being so judgmental. "What's the format, then? I'm new here."

"Well, Moses—our teacher—reads a text and then we discuss it"

"Oh, that sounds a lot like the classes we have at Spirit Mountain."

"You lived at Spirit Mountain? Back east? Wow. Far out."

"Well, I'm hoping to live here now," Phoebe said, not wanting to talk about her old home because she was afraid she would start crying. "What do you do—I mean outside of classes and stuff?"

"Oh, I work at a little clothing store in San Anselmo," said her neighbor, unconsciously fingering the beautiful scarf around her neck. "And I'm taking Kathak lessons."

Kathak was a North Indian dance form. From what Micah told her, there were about a dozen women out here who studied it. No one at Spirit Mountain had time for that sort of thing, but it sounded nice. She looked around the room at the other women, dressed in a kind of uniform consisting of gauzy, flowing dresses, and the men, trying to look relaxed and wise in their Afghani vests, and thought that the only times she'd seen anyone at the community so dressed up it had been someone's wedding.

"So—people discuss the stories, or texts, or whatever..." Phoebe said, hoping to hear more.

"Oh, here comes Moses," her companion said, as she put her palms together in a salaam gesture and, without rising from her seated position, bowed from her waist.

Moses bowed to the room and sat down in a lotus position on a little woven mat. He opened a book and read:

"There are two groups of artists. Which one can create the most beautiful room?

"A curtain was drawn down the middle of a large room and each group went to work on their side of the curtain. One painted beautiful patterns and pictures, the other cleaned and scrubbed until the walls shone like mirrors. When the curtain was removed, the shining room reflected the painted one in all its glory. Which one was the winner?"

Phoebe had heard this story before. She loved that these stories never had a clear answer. Back home, they would struggle with it together, uncovering layers of meaning.

There was a short period of silence. Phoebe looked around the room to see everyone in various states of meditation or cogitation. Or confusion. Finally, Moses spoke again.

"Who would like to comment?"

A beautiful young woman at the front of the room raised her hand and he nodded at her.

"I think it was the group creating the reflection," she said. "They knew that beauty is everywhere, as God is everywhere, and it is our role to reflect that beauty and God's majesty."

"Beautifully said," agreed Moses. "Anyone else?"

A few more people spoke up, all of them echoing the sentiments of the first woman. Phoebe was annoyed, and yet envious. She longed for a world, for a life, in which there was a single answer, but she could never actually accept it when it was offered. She felt a fit of contrariness coming on.

"I think it was the group who painted their walls," she said, without waiting to be called on.

Moses looked surprised, but smiled graciously. "Ah—a new voice. Welcome. And now tell us why you think it was the painting group," he said.

"It's true that we can find beauty in the world," Phoebe said, "but it's also true that we have the will and the creative nature to make our own. Why else would we write songs, create paintings—or learn Kathak dancing, for that matter?"

The first young woman who'd spoken looked distinctly put out. Clearly, she felt she had come up with the right answer. Probably she was studying Kathak and felt criticized. Phoebe relented, feeling sorry for her.

"I think the point of these stories is that there is no one right answer," she said. "The stories are there to plant a seed of thought in our minds that we can nurture through the week, to expand our thinking past our minds to our hearts, to help us see many points of view."

Moses nodded, a bit uncertainly. "Well said," he murmured, but Phoebe could tell that his heart wasn't in it. He suggested they sing some chants, and he began leading one.

Phoebe chanted along, but thought to herself that she wished she had the other young woman's approach. Why couldn't there be a single right answer? Every morning when she woke, she stared at Ruth and thought about how critical it was to find the right answer—to their lives, to money, to work, to child-raising. And how nice it would be if there was a single right answer that she could put into action. But her life didn't work that way. And, if she were honest, neither did her heart.

After several months of these classes, Phoebe began to find the experience empty. She had never been completely committed to the spiritual life. It was the way it wove itself into the community that she admired—the willingness of the people who lived there to place the good of the community as a whole above their own desires, and their ability to live their ideals every moment—even when it was painful or difficult.

Spirituality without community displayed all the less-than-compelling aspects of spirituality, and Phoebe found herself increasingly returning to her original sardonic attitude toward it. The traditions that had seemed genuine and ancient at the community now seemed like a kind of play-acting.

People here had the same fringed and flowered trappings as her Spirit Mountain family, and often displayed the same transported looks on their faces during meditation, but the strong bonds were missing. Plus, there were even more incestuous-seeming relationships out here. Everyone seemed to have been "involved" with everyone else at some time in the past. That soul-mate thing was alive and well on both sides of the continent.

The saving grace was the music. In her studies with Mathieu she found a deeper sense of spirituality and meaning than she did in any class. Still, while there was more—and better—music here, the Celestial Choir music was frothy and light, unlike the pleading, searching, soulful tunes she'd sung at Spirit Mountain. It was a relief and a joy in some ways, but shallow in others.

She couldn't imagine forging the kind of bonds she'd felt at Spirit Mountain with these beautiful California people who led ordinary, somewhat indulgent lives all week and were "deeply spiritual" only on the one or two nights they came to class. Spirit Mountain had constantly ground away at everyone's rough edges, polishing them to their shiniest selves. There was no escape—it went on 24 hours a day, seven days a week. Here, people only polished their outer shells, and only at their own convenience. It felt like a sort of spiritual manicure.

Chapter 15: November, 1976

It came as something of a surprise when Phoebe realized it was November. The only way to tell the seasons out here was by whether it was raining or not. Apparently, it could rain between Thanksgiving and Passover—a sort of twist on Camelot, where it could only rain after sunset. In a daring exception, the weather actually changed the week *before* Thanksgiving, when Phoebe and Ruth awoke to a torrential downpour. Everything was bigger out here, even raindrops.

Phoebe was feeling pretty good about things in general. Once or twice a week, she and Ruth made their little pilgrimage up to Sonoma County, where Mathieu lived. The actual schedule depended on whether she had a lesson that week or not. The Celestial Choir rehearsals took place every Sunday morning. Phoebe, Micah, and Ruth shared a ride with a few other singers to get there. But to get to the lessons, Phoebe needed a car. She borrowed money from Micah to buy a well-used Volkswagen bug. Her heart was in her mouth each time she drove up north, wondering which bit of the car might rattle off of it in transit, but so far it had hung together.

She was reluctant to borrow the money, but Micah had confided to her that he had a trust fund from a rather large fortune—some grandparent who had started a large grocery chain and then sold it for a lot of money—a fact he avoided telling people in general. With typical generosity, he had told her not to worry about the car loan, but she was determined to keep things formal. There were enough people taking advantage of Micah and besides…

And there it was—the issue she kept avoiding: her relationship with Micah. On the one hand, he was her closest and most trusted friend out here in California. On the other, it was clear he was hoping to be more than that. How she wished she could talk this all over with Abby. But Abby, although back from her travels and seemingly at peace with all their drama, was in law school and pretty much unreachable.

There was absolutely nothing wrong with Micah. He had two adorable children, whose ages bracketed Ruth's. The three children played together peacefully when Micah had them for the weekend or a holiday, and every visit was just another excuse for them to all hang out together. He thought nothing of getting tickets for all of them to a circus or a museum, and waved off her protests about the expense of these outings with a smile and a deaf ear. And so far, so good, she kept telling herself.

She should have been feeling more secure by the day—a reliable job, a lovely place to live, a good and protective friend, a happy child—but somehow she wasn't. She told herself that it was because her real life was on hold. Because, while she had wonderful music in her life, she wasn't writing. And she was slowly realizing that writing was the essence of who she was. Perhaps as a result, she encountered a bout of insomnia.

Each night, when everyone else had retired, she would wrap herself in a bathrobe and hole up on the couch, watching reruns of MASH and staying up through Johnny Carson. She became intrigued with Carson, whom she'd always associated with her parents and had paid little attention to. Now she found herself dissecting his monologues, observing his gracious style. She admired the way he treated guests ranging from the mildly interesting to the truly bizarre, giving each one his respect and attention. She wondered if she could become a comedy writer. Surely Mr. Carson didn't write a monologue every day? People like that had a staff of clever writers. She was certain she could do at least as well.

She began taking notes, jotting down punchlines and finding better ones, selecting topics and finding clever segues to other topics. It was like doing a difficult crossword puzzle—challenging and yet soothing in some odd way. The only problem was that she was burning the candle at both ends. After spending the late night with Johnny, she got up at 6:30 to spend a little extra time with Ruth. There were some weekends when she could barely get out of bed. But, in general, it did make her feel better.

"I guess writing is a low-cost alternative to therapy," she told one of her mom friends at Brilliant Babies. But in her heart, she knew that this wasn't quite true. She was writing like a stand-up comic—a series of jokes on a related topic and then an abrupt switch to a different topic. It felt a bit flat to her, as if she was wearing someone else's personality, like putting on a red clown nose every time she sat down to write. Maybe she wasn't quite prepared to take up her own writing personality again, whatever that might be.

And, as if the rain heralded the official time for existential issues to arise, it was Thanksgiving when the unexamined issues in her life collided—and from more directions than she could have anticipated.

"You haven't said what you're doing for the holiday," Micah said at breakfast, the morning of the first downpour.

"I don't think we're doing much of anything," Phoebe said. "I'm certainly not in a position to go back East."

"I could…"

"No," Phoebe said firmly, before he could offer a plane ticket, or whatever he was thinking of. "Really. No."

Micah was silent for a moment. Phoebe was about to apologize for her tone when he spoke.

"Would you consider coming to my parents' house? It would be a huge favor to me."

"A favor? In what way?"

"Let's just say I have a similar relationship with my parents as you do with yours, just without the disowning part."

Phoebe was astonished. "You never said!"

"Yeah. Well, it's not something I like to talk about much."

"They don't—what—approve of you?"

"Well, you can see their point," Micah said, staring down at his cereal bowl. "It's not like I've accomplished much of anything."

"You're a good person!" Phoebe said. "I hardly know anyone who's as kind as you are. Or as generous."

"Yeah," Micah said again. "That's not real high on their list of accomplishments. They got me into all these fancy schools and I just about squeaked by. They gave me all these jobs to do and I pretty much made a mess of all of them. Let's just say they prefer my brother. Harvard Business, CEO of his own company, on his third trophy wife."

"Lovely," Phoebe murmured, thinking how jolly Thanksgiving was likely to be at Micah's parents' house.

"The holidays are always hard. If you and Ruth were there, it would be easier. But I understand if it doesn't sound all that appealing."

"Of course we'll come," Phoebe said warmly. It was really the least she could do. And that's how she and Ruth ended up heading out the door with Micah, just as Raphael was walking up the front steps.

* * *

At first glance, Raphael appeared to be in an appeasing mood. He was carrying flowers, although they looked suspiciously like the autumn roses and yellow daisies she'd seen in a neighbor's yard down the block. He was wearing an exquisite suit—where had that come from? And how could he afford a suit like that and still need to steal flowers? Whatever the story was, he was certainly looking quite pleased with himself as he sauntered up the walk. But when he caught sight of Micah, Phoebe could see the storm clouds gather.

Of course, he *would* arrive on Thanksgiving, looking prosperous and rather stylish, while Phoebe's little group looked like ragamuffins. Examining herself with an outsider's eye, Phoebe saw a hippie who hadn't figured out that she—and the decade—had outgrown thrift store chic. Little Ruth had on an unlikely-looking dress made entirely of ruffles that a well-meaning friend had sent on from Spirit Mountain. Micah wore some sort of Indian shirt over fancy yoga pants. Phoebe could have told him that this would only annoy his parents. Had they been further along in their relationship, she *would* have told him. But technically, they weren't in a relationship yet—a nuance that was clearly lost on Raphael.

Ruth took one look at her father and squeaked with delight, dropping Rabbit and leaping into Rafe's unready arms. He dropped the flowers and scrambled to keep from dropping her. Phoebe took advantage of the moment to take a few steps away from Micah, but he closed the distance just as quickly. She looked at him helplessly. No time to explain.

"Daddy, daddy, daddy!" Ruth was babbling happily, while Rafe hugged her and glared at Phoebe.

"We weren't expecting you," Phoebe said.

"Obviously."

"Well, it *is* Thanksgiving, Rafe. You might have figured that we'd have plans."

"Yes. I can see you have plans," he practically spat at her.

Micah cut in, his voice low and calm. "Hi," he said. "I'm Phoebe's housemate. We're headed to my parents' house for Thanksgiving dinner. I'm afraid we really need to get going. I'd invite you to come along, but I really can't bring an extra guest on such short notice. Why don't you make yourself comfortable here?" He pointed inside the house through the still-open door.

"Housemate," Rafe snarled, with obvious sarcasm. "Right."

"Exactly," Micah said smoothly. "You might run into our other housemates while you're here—Bonnie and Joel. Just tell them you're a friend of Phoebe's and we said it was fine for you to hang out." He took Phoebe's elbow and steered her around Rafe.

"Mama!" Ruth cried.

"Yes, honey," Phoebe said, taking her cue from Micah and keeping her voice steady. "Time to go. We'll see daddy when we get back."

Ruth took Rafe's face between her two small hands and kissed his nose. "Wait right here, daddy," she told him. "You can have Rabbit if you want."

She climbed down, picked up the well-worn Rabbit, and handed it solemnly to Raphael, who took it absently, never taking his eyes of Micah.

"If Ruth wasn't here," he growled menacingly. "I'd..."

"If Ruth wasn't here, you'd have no reason to visit," Phoebe said. "Why don't you accept Micah's generous offer and make yourself comfortable? We'll be a while. You can help yourself to anything in the fridge that has my name on it, but don't eat my housemates' food."

She took Ruth's hand and willed herself to stop shaking. Ruth waved goodbye and trotted down the path to the car, turning around several times to wave some more. When they were inside the car, Phoebe strapped Ruth into her car seat. Frankly, she was amazed that her daughter had come so willingly.

"I think Daddy will be here when we get back," she told Ruth, feeling guilty. After all, the child hadn't seen her father in two months. Ruth was rubbing her little arms.

"Something wrong, honey?"

"Daddy squoze me a little," Ruth said.

"He's probably just excited to see you," Phebe said, but Ruth didn't look convinced.

"Were you expecting him?" Micah asked, looking a bit shaken.

"No, of course not," Phoebe replied.

"Will daddy stay here now?" Ruth asked.

"I don't think so, sweetie," Phoebe said.

"Where will he go?"

"Not sure"

"But then he'll come back?"

"Probably."

"Will Micah stay here?"

"You can ask Micah yourself," Phoebe said.

"Will you?"

"Yes, Ruthie. I'll be here. I live here."

"Where does daddy live?"

"Not sure, honey. Oh, look, Christmas lights!"

"Pretty!"

Micah reached across and took Phoebe's hand. Okay, so maybe they were in a relationship. It just didn't have a name yet.

* * *

Micah's parents seemed nice enough, in a rich people kind of way. The house was large, luxurious, and tasteful, although the taste didn't reveal much about its inhabitants. Phoebe suspected a designer had been hired. Micah's father led them to a comfortable but enormous family room, where leather couches were grouped around a fireplace. He stooped to add firewood to an already roaring fire. Micah's mother displayed her elegant posture in a leather armchair, wearing something that looked like cashmere in shades of beige and white. Phoebe assumed that rich people chose these colors to show that they could afford the dry cleaning. And to go with their blonde hair, a genetic disposition they all seemed to possess. Or purchase.

Phoebe sat as far out of the way as possible. She kept thinking that Abby would have been right at home in this environment, so similar to her own childhood home. She would have known just what to say and everyone would have been eating out of her hand within minutes. Phoebe missed her suddenly with a physical pang. It had been so long since she'd heard from Abby, aside from Ruth's annual birthday card and invariably appropriate present. She wondered what Abby would make of Rafe's appearance on their doorstep. Maybe she should try calling to talk it over? She was amazed at how alien that thought was. Abby had disappeared from her life—something she couldn't have imagined even a year ago. She realized that she wasn't even sure of Abby's current phone number. How was that possible?

The doorbell rang, and she heard Micah's ex dropping off the children. Ruth heard them too, and ran to find them. Micah's children clearly knew their way around the house and they took Ruth off to play with them. Phoebe glanced around the room and inadvertently caught the eye of Micah's mom. She glanced in Phoebe's direction, and Phoebe prepared to be interrogated. But her glance slid off Phoebe as if the chair had been empty, and Phoebe decided that her dearest childhood wish had been granted and she had become invisible. Give thanks like no one is watching? Because they're not? She decided to see this as a good thing and took advantage of her apparent transparency to examine the rest of Micah's family.

The successful brother sprawled expansively on one leather couch, taking up the space of two people. Trophy wife number three sat on a little hassock at his feet. An empty glass of wine sat on a little glass table nearby, and Phoebe saw her look longingly at it. Micah's mother looked barely older than her newest daughter-in-law, but her face had a taut look that screamed plastic surgery. And, of course, they were both blonde.

Phoebe's eyes moved on to Micah's father. He was a surprise. Phoebe had assumed he would be arrogant, aloof, and somewhat judgmental. But he seemed, if anything, eager to please. He was talkative and quick to laugh, and kept hopping up to refresh a drink or squeeze a shoulder affectionately. He had left the room to check on the children and returned with a tray of snacks. Seeing her off by herself, he passed her a bowl of nuts.

"Sweets to the sweet?" she asked. He laughed, and she felt herself smiling with genuine warmth. So what was the problem here? She glanced over at Micah, only to see his face twisted with pain. Phoebe had assumed she had the most complicated story in the room, but now she sensed competition. Clearly this story had its own plot twist.

* * *

The afternoon passed, as all afternoons eventually do. Phoebe felt that this one took its own sweet time, but then she was not in any tearing rush to return home either. She limited herself to two glasses of wine, spoke when spoken to, and did her best to sound intelligent when she did. She had the satisfaction of seeing Micah's brother—Malcolm, as it turned out—looking at her with interest and was warmed to see Micah's mother turn to her husband with real affection after he said a grace thanking God for his wonderful family. Ruth behaved reasonably well. When she got cranky, she provided an excellent excuse for leaving.

Micah's father sent them off with little packets of turkey, stuffing, and pie, declaring that the best thing about

Thanksgiving was the leftovers the following day. When Phoebe thanked him, he gave her a little hug and told her he hoped they'd see more of her. She smiled, but made no promises. Micah carried Ruth to the car, where she promptly fell asleep, and they drove home in silence, like an old married couple.

** * **

In the car, Phoebe stared out the window and thought about the ordeal she still had to face when they got home. Did she really think Raphael was going to let her run off with their daughter without putting up a fight? Look at it from his point of view, she told herself. I leave to study music and he arrives to find me all dolled up, going off to a family dinner with some guy he knew nothing about.

Well, yes, her feistier self retorted. But what earthly business of his was it whom she celebrated Thanksgiving with? She had made her separation from him clear, whether he chose to accept it or not. If he couldn't keep his manhood in his pants, what did he expect? He didn't get to be some sort of paterfamilias by declaring his commitment in the face of overwhelming evidence to the contrary.

She looked down to see her right hand balled into a fist. Apparently she was spoiling for a fight. That wasn't going to work. She spent the rest of the drive calming herself down, forcing herself to wait and see, and not jump to conclusions. She knew she should talk to Micah, find out what was causing him such pain, but she felt that she was pretty much at her limit as it was. Micah's difficulties would just have to wait. She went back to worrying about Rafe.

As it turned out, the most extreme conclusions she had anticipated didn't prepare her for the ones Rafe had come up with. She walked in the door to her home to find him taking photographs of her messy room—she and Ruth had dressed in a hurry.

"What are you doing?" she asked him.

"Documenting your lamentable environment," he told her.

Phoebe looked around at the tidy kitchen, the generous backyard, the comfortable living room.

"Lamentable?"

"That's how I see it," he said, snapping another shot of her wet towel on the bathroom floor.

"That's ridiculous, and you know it." She was having trouble controlling her anger.

"But a judge will not find it so ridiculous," he said smugly. "When I file for custody back in New York, this will be all the evidence I need. That, plus your pathetic salary at that little school will persuade any judge that I am a better choice for a father than you are for a mother."

"That can't happen," Phoebe said, thinking that no one would take a child from her mother and give it to this crazy person based on a few snapshots.

"Money is a powerful thing," said Rafe. "Watch." And all of a sudden she couldn't help believing him.

Chapter 16: Late November, 1976 – June, 1977

Micah stroked Phoebe's hair as she sobbed into her folded arms at the dining room table. She had managed to keep it together long enough to get Ruth settled for the night, but now she was too overwhelmed to evaluate whether it was fair to allow Micah to comfort her.

"He can do it," she choked out, for the twentieth time at least. "He can take her away from me in an eye blink. Some judge in New York will look at his borrowed suit and his photographs of my messy bedroom and just sign her over to him, figuring to give us all a better situation. And I'll lose her! I'll lose her forever!"

Phoebe had no doubt that lawyers would soon be involved. However he'd managed to acquire that spiffy suit (and lawyers, if he was to be believed), it was clear that Rafe had managed to make some money and was prepared to use it to get what he wanted—Phoebe and Ruth or, failing that, just Ruth.

Micah was silent. There was no point in arguing. What Phoebe was saying was true. He thought about her situation, comparing it to his own struggles with his ex-wife and his disappointed family. He and his ex had been officially married, so they didn't argue about money. There were lots of laws that took care of that. He supported her royally, and she got to call all the shots. If it hadn't been for his trust fund, he might not have had access to his two kids at all. His parents had assumed that the marriage failed due to Micah's behavior and attitude. He couldn't bring himself to tell them about the other men in his ex-wife's life, because he was afraid it might get back to the children. It was important to him that they trust both their parents and believe that they were loved unconditionally by their grandparents. He knew his parents' limitations, but he believed they were good people and he loved them. It all resulted in his feeling miserable while all the other players in his particular drama got to feel self-righteous. He sighed. It was no time to rehash that old, old story. He could do the most good now by trying to assess the situation from Phoebe's point of view.

In the space left by Micah's silence, Phoebe thought about Ruth. She'd been devastated when she woke up to find Rafe gone.

"Where is daddy?" she'd asked, over and over, looking under sofa cushions and opening closet doors as if he might be playing an elaborate game of hide and seek. But all she found was Rabbit, tossed in a corner of the sofa like a long-eared pillow.

"Daddy had to go," Phoebe said, trying to think of an excuse that would let Ruth relax a little. "Um—he had to do some work."

"You don't have to work at night," Ruth pointed out.

"That's right," Phoebe said, seeing an out. "And I don't have to work tomorrow either because it's Thanksgiving weekend. So we can go into Golden Gate Park and ride on the carousel. And maybe even get a little boat." Ruth loved the paddleboats in Stowe Lake. As Phoebe had hoped, she perked up a bit.

"Will daddy come on the boat?"

"Not sure, honey," Phoebe said. "How about we get into pajamas and see what happens tomorrow. Even if daddy can't come, mama will take you on the boat for sure."

"And I can help paddle," Micah offered.

"Bret and Belinda too?" Ruth asked. She loved Micah's children.

"Let's see what we can do about that," Micah said, moving to the phone to negotiate.

With that and a few extra bedtime stories, Ruth settled under her covers and kissed Phoebe goodnight, her world once more secure.

Phoebe tiptoed out of their room and eased the door closed. She wandered back into the dining room, trying to distract herself by planning the day in the park. Micah was waiting for her. He cleared his throat, having successfully dealt with his ex-wife and feeling bold. He had turned his attention back to the real problem and thought he'd come up with something useful.

"You need to show that you're capable of taking care of Ruth yourself," he said. "Judges are mostly interested in the money situation. You have to show that you have enough money to support her reasonably. They tend to give the mother the advantage, all other things being equal." He looked a bit bitter as he said this, but he focused on Phoebe and pushed his sadness aside.

Phoebe heard only "money," and she groaned. Her salary at Brilliant Babies was barely enough for rent.

"How did you support yourself before Spirit Mountain?" Micah asked. There was still so much he didn't know about her.

"Well, I was a musician and a songwriter for a while," Phoebe said. "I still get some royalties from a couple of songs I wrote. It isn't much."

"Could you do more of that? You're studying music. Maybe now you could write even better songs."

Phoebe thought about Robin and her own revelations about the music business—not to mention the burned bridges of her past. "No," she said.

Micah sighed. This woman was such a mystery. "What else?"

"I won a writing contest and I was working at a literary magazine in New York," she said. "But…"

"But?"

"That sort of fell apart. It wasn't my fault."

"But you must have been a pretty good writer," Micah said.

"I guess. It's been a while. I went from there to Spirit Mountain, and then out here…" Her voice faded away as she thought of what a long, strange trip it had been. If there was a career ladder for freelance writers, she had fallen off it long ago. She missed writing dreadfully, but she no longer ran home to compose essays or letters or even journal entries. She barely knew her own voice.

"I don't think you lose your ability to write," Micah said. "Although you might want to write about different things now."

Phoebe sighed. It wasn't just her conflicted feelings about writing. It was also a question of practicality. "Even if I was any good, how much could I possibly make as a writer?"

"You don't know until you try."

Desperate times call for desperate measures. She could continue working at Brilliant Babies and try writing on the side, without making any drastic changes. The end result couldn't be any less than she was already earning. And if she gave up Johnny Carson and concentrated on her own work, she could make time for it without collapsing. Maybe. So Phoebe decided to try.

* * *

There was a certain amount of down time at Brilliant Babies, and Phoebe used it to understand the current state of the local writing scene. She checked out a wide variety of magazines from the library and started asking the moms she was friendliest with to bring in old issues of periodicals they liked. She piled the donated publications in the little lobby area, ostensibly for prospective parents to peruse, but she picked one up any time she was free and did her research.

The magazines ranged widely in subject, from decorating and homemaking to humor and literature. She read and took notes, and after a while she noticed a pattern. There were a handful of humor writers who showed up in a lot of the local magazines—most of them, in fact, except maybe the decorating ones. Apparently, decorators did not have a sense of humor.

All the local humor writers were men, and they had an oddly similar style. Turning to the backs of the magazines, she found thumbnail biographies of the contributors and one day a surprised mom walked into the office to find Phoebe slapping her forehead and blurting out "They are all the same guy!"

"Honey?" The surprised mom was Ginger—a particular friend of Phoebe's. She was funny and a little loud (a former New Yorker, Phoebe had discovered) and always easy to talk to.

"These humor columns—they're in a bunch of different magazines and they're written under different names, but it's the same guy writing them."

"And? This is important why?"

So Phoebe gave her the short and somewhat sanitized story: she had been a writer in New York and was thinking of trying it again out here. In her spare time, she hastened to add. In the Bay Area, no one had to explain that they were "really" something other than what they were paid to do. Most people had aspirations of teaching yoga or getting trained in massage, but there were plenty of closet writers too.

"So, clearly, the guy is using a pseudonym. Not a bad idea," Ginger mused.

"Why do you say that?"

"Well, if you're writing humor, you're bound to step on some toes. If everyone knows it's you and you step on the toes that you know...oh, dear. I'm beginning to sound like Dr. Seuss!"

Yes. Now that Phoebe thought about it, she wasn't sure she wanted anyone to know she was pursuing a writing career. She certainly didn't want to pick a fight with some defensive mother. Or boss. And if she was going to write humorous columns about something she was familiar with ("Write what you know"), then children, parents, and bosses were bound to come up.

"Good point," she told Ginger. "Having a pseudonym leaves me free to write almost anything. In fact, why not give each pseudonym a different specialty?"

"Excellent," Ginger said.

"But…" Phoebe sighed.

"Problem?" Ginger asked.

"When I get paid—if I get paid—won't they make the checks out to the pseudonym?"

"Not a problem," Ginger told her airily. "You just file a DBA." Seeing Phoebe's puzzled expression, she clarified. "Doing Business As," she clarified. "It's a legal sort of arrangement that says that the pseudonym is you, and the checks can be deposited into your bank account as if they were made out to you. Or you can open a bank account for the pseudonym. Either way." She told Phoebe it was a simple process of filing a form at the Civic Center, smiled, gave Phoebe a friendly little finger wave, and left to pick up her toddler son.

That night, Phoebe wrapped one of Ruth's dress-up scarves around her head like a turban and draped a fancy shawl over her shoulders. Making a dramatic entrance, she introduced herself to her bemused housemates as Scarlet Rose, romantic advisor.

"Now, Bonnie," she said, in her deep Scarlet voice. "I understand you have been, shall we say, disappointed in love?"

"Yes," sighed Bonnie, enjoying this game. "I do like to flirt with the bad boys, but then my heart is broken when they refuse to replace their motorcycle jackets with a nice polyester-blend shirt for a visit with my parents."

"Excellent," Phoebe said, breaking character and scurrying back to her room to write a humorous romantic advice column that she tentatively titled "Scarlet Letters."

Dear Scarlet: I like the bad boys, and they like me! But my suburban heart wants to dress them up in Brooks Brothers now and then. Okay, you caught me—it's when I visit my folks. My leather-clad Lotharios won't cooperate! Whatever shall I do? – Playing Dress-up in Terra Linda

Dear Dress-Up: Even if you *could* fasten the top collar button around that manly throat, your parents would not be fooled. Mama can spot a tattoo under a yard of high-end shirting. What you need is a platonic guy friend with office clothes and a hankering for home cooking. Present him proudly to the parental units and spend the rest of the week with your hair flying in the breeze behind a hunk on a Harley. Hmm. On second thought, make that a helmeted hunk, and get one of your own, but you get my drift. And don't be surprised if your bad boy has a similar arrangement when he goes home for Sunday dinner in El Cerrito.

Phoebe dashed off a half dozen examples in the same style and sent them to a local women's magazine. She got a promising letter in return—they weren't mad to publish these right now, but if she could work up twenty or so with a Bay Area bent, they might consider two or three at a time as a once-a-month feature. Encouraged, she sent a few to some other magazines.

She created a few more personae: a twenty-something making pithy observations at her first job; a working mom juggling her various responsibilities; and a column that purported to be written by a toddler. This last one was the surprise success. Two local parenting magazines wanted *The View from Down Here* right away. And just as she started on those, she heard back from the women's magazine with a request for eight *Scarlet Letters* columns at twenty-five dollars a pop!

A month went by, then two months, then three. No word from any lawyers. Phoebe didn't think the issue would go away, but she was grateful for the chance to build her writing income. She collected her clippings and made copies of the checks she received, along with her paystubs and royalty checks.

When she'd moved in with Micah and the others, she'd applied for food stamps and WIC benefits. Even living communally, she had trouble feeding and clothing herself and Ruth. But by buying all the dairy products for the household with her WIC coupons and providing other essentials with her food stamps, she could guiltlessly share in the communal meals and all the food they bought as a group.

It worked out okay, but being on food stamps was not going to help her convince a judge that she could support a child. With her heart in her mouth, she resigned from the food stamp and WIC programs, praying that her writing income would make up the difference.

By the time she got a letter of inquiry from a New York court in June, she was able to show that she was no longer receiving social services and had supplemented her monthly salary with significant writing proceeds. With Micah's help, she was able to make a convincing case for her and Ruth's financial well-being.

At Micah's suggestion, she included some letters from her boss and friends, attesting to her impeccable mothering skills. She herself wrote a letter stating that she and Rafe had never been married, although she did not dispute that he was Ruth's father. She pointed out that she had never denied him visitation rights, although so far he had come to see his daughter only once, and had never called or sent letters to Ruth. Neither had he offered any child support, though she certainly wasn't asking for any. She told the court that she did not know how Rafe earned his money now, but in the five years she'd known him he had never, as far as she could tell, held a steady job. She shared her concerns that he might not always be able to support Ruth, even if he could right now.

She sent the whole lot off to the court and waited for the next round. She was pretty sure Rafe wouldn't leave it at that.

Chapter 17: August, 1977 – October, 1977

Phoebe used a post office box for her writing business, and she checked it a few times a week. One day, as she opened the box, she found a letter from a magazine she hadn't heard of before. When she opened it and read it, she realized it was just starting up and the editor was looking for some content. He couldn't promise full-time work, but a once- or twice-a-month column might be of interest. She examined the envelope more closely and found it addressed to the pseudonym she used for her romantic advice column. The return address was in San Francisco.

Well, here was a new development. So far, all the inquiry letters had gone in the opposite direction, with Phoebe begging for work. Here was someone contacting her. She smiled with satisfaction.

That night, she composed a careful reply, stating that she was interested but wondering what the pay rate was and whether the editor expected exclusive rights to the column. She signed it using the pseudonym she'd invented for *Scarlet Letters*. When she began addressing the envelope, she looked at the masthead on the editor's letter for the appropriate person to address it to. Her heart assumed its panic position. The name of the executive editor was Garth Earlham.

Honestly, Phoebe thought angrily. You move three thousand miles across the country and your worst nemesis follows, holding an offer you can't resist in one hand and your best-kept secret in the other. She could keep up the pseudonym as long as they were in contact by mail, but as soon as he wanted to meet—or even talk on the phone—the jig would be up. When she glanced at the clock, she realized she'd been holding the unsealed letter in her hand for half an hour. With a resigned sigh, she licked the envelope, attached a stamp, and put it in her purse with a determined little shove. The writing world was small and Garth was sure to figure out who she was at some point. Maybe she could get a few dollars out of him first.

* * *

"Wow," Micah said, with a startled expression on his face. "That's different."

It was. Phoebe had gone from brunette to a sort of reddish chestnut overnight. Literally. She was anxiously awaiting Ruth's reaction. It was a Saturday morning, and she'd let the little girl sleep in.

"Why…?" Micah asked, still staring. This was one of the things he simply could not fathom about women, this need to constantly change themselves. Phoebe was fine the way she was, and certainly must know that? If he squinted a bit, he could imagine her as someone he didn't know, and he admitted that she still looked quite attractive with the reddish hair. It just seemed so unnecessary. And so unlike Phoebe, who always seemed oblivious to her outward appearance. To be honest, it was one of the things he enjoyed about her.

"I know," Phoebe said, ruffling her hair uncomfortably. "And it's only going to get worse."

"Worse?"

"I'm going to get a haircut later. I need to look different."

"And I ask again…"

"Because I need a disguise."

Micah was immediately alarmed. "What is going on? Is this something to do with Rafe? Has he threatened you in some way?" Although he couldn't imagine how changing one's hairstyle could address such a situation.

"No," Phoebe sighed. "It's nothing to do with Rafe. I have to meet with the editor of a new magazine."

"Okay," Micah said cautiously, thinking perhaps it was a fashion magazine…or…?

"He's someone I used to know. He's the reason I lost my job back in New York. If he recognizes me, he might not give me any work." Or he might make my real identity public, she thought. So much for the pseudonyms.

"I'm not sure that changing your hair is going to fool him," Micah said.

"I know," Phoebe said. "I was thinking maybe glasses."

"Glasses might help but—if he knew you pretty well in New York, he's probably going to know you now. The whole disguise thing could backfire, actually."

"You may be right," Phoebe admitted. "But I think it's worth a try. Anyway, right now the one I'm worried about is Ruth. Do you think this is going to freak her out?"

"Let's make it a dress-up adventure to the Discovery Museum," Micah said. "I have a fake mustache left over from last Halloween. And I'm sure Bret and Belinda would be delighted to wear costumes."

"That's a great idea!" Phoebe said, with relief. Micah called his ex-wife and told her the plan and she agreed to send some costume stuff over with the kids. Anything for a Saturday off. When Ruth woke up, Phoebe told her the plan before she really had time to take in her mother's strange appearance, and off they went, giggling, in their fancy disguises.

* * *

A few days later, Phoebe sat in the magazine's waiting room, fidgeting with her purse and trying to resist the impulse to check her appearance in her pocket mirror. She had spent several hours at Goodwill, trying to put together an outfit as completely unlike her usual manner of dress as possible. She settled for a suit with a straight brown skirt and a tight-fitting jacket. Under it, she wore a peach-colored blouse—a color she generally shunned. Plus it was polyester. She had to purchase pantyhose at a nearby drugstore because she didn't own a single pair. And she hoped she'd be able to navigate convincingly in the heels she found at a consignment store, without wobbling or—perish the thought!—falling down altogether. She had practiced walking in them to Ruth's unrestrained hilarity. Topping the whole thing off was a stylish felt hat she'd borrowed from Ginger and large, slightly-tinted glasses. And a lot of makeup. Phoebe felt like she was wearing a face-shaped rubber glove.

When the receptionist called her name, Phoebe gathered her briefcase (actually Micah's briefcase) and her purse and made her way fairly steadily down the hall to the door the receptionist indicated. Sure enough, there sat Garth. He was a few years older (naturally) and a few pounds heavier. He was examining some papers and did not look up right away, but gestured to the chair across from his rather massive desk. It didn't seem as though he'd suffered much from his New York dismissal.

Phoebe took a moment to inspect the office for clues. Prominently displayed in a silver frame was a photograph of an attractive man. He didn't have his arm around Garth's shoulders, and if pressed Garth could probably pass him off as a cousin or close friend. But this was San Francisco, and the literary scene at that, so perhaps he was allowed to speak his love's name. And if that were true, Phoebe speculated, perhaps he'd moved to San Francisco for romance? If so, it was good to know he was capable of love. Perhaps it had changed him, made him more compassionate? Somehow she doubted that.

"So, Miss Anderson," Garth said, his eyes still on the mysterious papers. "We meet at last." Phoebe glanced around involuntarily, and had to remind herself that she was Susan Anderson—her pseudonym for the *Scarlet Letters* column.

"Mr. Earlham. A pleasure," Phoebe said, in her carefree, slightly affected Susan Anderson voice. Was it her imagination, or did Garth start a bit? At any rate, he looked up finally, and his eyes narrowed just a little. But he didn't react with anything she could call recognition.

"I've shared your samples with my editing staff and they are interested in your work. We particularly like the *Scarlet Letters* and *View from Down Here* columns.

"I'm delighted to hear it."

"Our immediate interest is a one-month trial of each column, running weekly. I assume that will not be a problem?"

"Well, we need to discuss the terms, but I can't imagine it will be too troublesome."

"We would need the content for our columns to be proprietary, but not the columns themselves. That is to say, we need the content of each *Scarlet Letters* column to be unique to our magazine, but you are free to publish *Scarlet Letter* columns with different content in other publications. And the same for the *View Down Here* columns. Savvy?"

"That's not an issue. In fact, if your staff could give me some general themes they prefer, I can tailor the content to your audience."

"Excellent." Garth was silent for a moment. "You appear to have done quite well for yourself, Phoebe. Why the Susan Anderson nonsense?"

"I have my reasons," said Phoebe, without hesitating.

Garth gave a short snort of laughter. "Oh, honestly, darling. You'd never make it as a drag queen. Go big or go home is their motto."

He leaned back in his chair and examined her more closely. "Interesting. It appears I have a bit more power in this situation than I thought."

"Meaning?"

"If you feel the need for a disguise, then you can't afford to make your true identity public. Assuming for the moment that you are not a super-hero, that means there are people here you would prefer to remain ignorant about your writing career. Well, I have no objections to keeping your little secret. Of course, I expect something in return. I don't mind telling you, it's early days for this magazine. We have to conserve funds when we can. I know I mentioned a figure in our previous conversation, but…"

"Oh, let's not go there, Garth," Phoebe sighed. "Plagiarism is such an ugly thing for advertisers to find out about an executive editor."

Garth looked startled, and then angry. "Who told you?"

"Kent. But frankly, it's common knowledge back at the old office. I have an actual letter of apology, if you want proof. Or if someone else does." She had the satisfaction of seeing him flinch.

"And if that photo represents an actual relationship," she continued, "it would be so sad to know that you moved all the way across the continent to find love and success only to have those nearest and dearest learn of your rather questionable past."

"You've grown up a bit," Garth said, but he didn't look pleased about it.

"I'm afraid we all do, at some point. And as to my being Susan Anderson, it isn't a major issue for me. I have a day job and I prefer to keep that and my writing work separate. I do it with all my clients. There's no real danger to me if you make that knowledge public—at worst a minor inconvenience. And if you don't like my new 'look,' well that's your problem. I find that my clients take me more seriously when my appearance is more in line with my subject matter."

Garth appeared dubious, looking her over as though he was sorting through a set of catty remarks to make about all the polyester, or the unhappy decision to go with peach rather than scarlet. Either none of the remarks was sufficiently cutting, or for some other reason, he seemed to decide against using any of them.

"Here's what I'm prepared to do," he said after a moment. "I'll pay what I agreed to for the first set of columns. After that, we'll see. And I don't want you to get your hopes up about becoming a staff member. I do the hiring and firing here, and let's just say it ain't gonna happen."

"Your loss," Phoebe said, without heat. She gathered her things and prepared to rise.

"Perhaps," Garth said. "But I know what I can and cannot do, and working with you is definitely on the "cannot do" list. But I won't harass you, and I hope you won't, er, bother me either."

"Pax," said Phoebe, holding out her hand. He took it and gave it a half-hearted shake.

"Pax, indeed," he said. "For the time being, anyway."

Phoebe smiled with her mouth and left.

* * *

The next morning, Phoebe got up early and began making lists. Lists were her new favorite thing. They were therapeutic and useful at the same time. Having a list was like sweeping, only you were sweeping your brain instead of your room, and you didn't need a dustpan.

He started by listing all the things she needed to get done this week for work. She'd taken off the previous morning for her interview and needed to be sure she wasn't short-changing Brilliant Babies. After that, she listed a random bunch of things she could write about.

"I need to set myself apart in the humor world," she had confided to Ginger, who was enjoying being part of Phoebe's secret adventures as a writer.

"Well, if what you say about all the successful ones being the same guy, what's the problem? Anything you write about women is bound to be different from his stuff, right?"

"If I want to really go somewhere with this writing thing, I need to be better than that," Phoebe said. "The *View from Down Here* thing is good, but it's a little cutesy. If I could find a way to make it sharper…"

"Well, it's interesting you should say so," Ginger said slowly. "We had the Todds and the Morehams over for dinner last weekend—you know, Simon and Emily's parents and Morgan and Nicole's parents—and the women ended up out on the deck talking about how sick and tired we are of all the comedies on television these days. So safe and so phony. Why does no one on these shows ever have issues with head lice or potty training?"

Phoebe laughed. "Well, because the writers of the sitcoms have wives to deal with those things!"

"Exactly!" Ginger agreed.

"Can you imagine?" Phoebe snickered. "'Marketing says the female audience wants something on head lice!' says one writer. 'Ick!' cries his partner! 'Let them eat chocolate cake—

except the wife puts in soy sauce instead of chocolate—we can get lots of yuks out of that.' 'Head lice! No way!' And off they go for a manly beer."

"The people who make sitcoms seem to think that the minute a woman gets married she turns into Lucille Ball."

"And if she's not married, she must be Suzanne Somers!"

Their laughter faded as they considered this. It was depressing, actually.

"Head lice might be ick," Ginger said. "But they also might be funny. And a little...how you say? Sharp?"

Phoebe was nodding and scribbling things on her list. By Friday, she had four columns to show Ginger: moms dealing with potty training, head lice, school lunches, and little girls with firm ideas about their wardrobes. Ginger agreed to pass them around to some of the other moms and get back to Phoebe on Monday.

As it turned out, it didn't take that long. On Saturday morning, as Ruth was playing with her Fisher-Price people and Phoebe was lingering over coffee, the phone rang.

"For you," Micah said.

"Phoebe!" said Ginger's enthusiastic voice. "What are you doing for dinner?"

"Nothing," Phoebe said, picturing the empty squares on her calendar that represented weekend evenings.

"Why don't you and Ruth come over? Say six o'clock? I've got three moms lined up. We are forming the Phoebe Hirsch Support Group and Wine Drinkers Consortium. The boys have agreed to take the kids out for pizza."

* * *

To say that Garth hated the new direction was something of an understatement. He flatly refused to publish any of the new columns and demanded something more like what she'd published in other magazines. Phoebe had anticipated this and, before he could work himself into a complete tirade, handed over her backup columns. She could almost see his ruffled feathers subside, and she had a sudden image of him as a startled, overweight cockatoo, which she tried desperately to replace with a portrait of Sherlock Holmes. She couldn't possibly explain why, but somehow the pipe thing was calming. But sometimes, she sternly reminded herself, a pipe is just a pipe. At which point she was on the verge of giggles again. Luckily, Garth finished his examination of her work at that point and glanced up, giving Phoebe just enough time to place a look of boredom firmly on her face.

"This is more like it," he said. He had skimmed the first *View From Down Here* column, in which Phoebe's fictional toddler, Annabel, shared her impressions of mama's interactions with her cookbook and a large glass of wine. Phoebe was pretty sure he'd like the second one too, in which she displayed the new vocabulary she'd learned from hanging out with daddy while he watched a football game. A lot of the words, Annabel noticed, got cut off after one or two letters and seemed to turn into something else when daddy glanced at her. For example, he seemed to talk about sugar and fudge a lot for someone who was not watching a cooking show.

Phoebe pasted a modest smile on her face, thinking how tired she was of all those coy little-kid jokes, and how unlike actual little kids they were. But she'd given Garth a shot at the new material, he'd loudly turned it down, and she'd provided what he ordered with barely a breath in between. It seemed like something she could keep up for quite a while without Garth noticing or caring that she was making her other columns far sharper and more contemporary.

* * *

Phoebe knew her support moms only slightly, and only as moms. She knew — in some corner of her brain — that they held high-powered jobs in the city. Otherwise, they would not have needed Brilliant Babies. But she'd always been rather hazy on what, exactly, they did.

As it turned out, Simon and Emily's mom — Annie — was an entertainment lawyer. Her husband, Al, was a freelance writer for a sitcom in Los Angeles. Morgan and Nicole's mom — Sue — was a producer for a local television news show. Ginger — whose husband, Frank, worked with Sue — was not working at the moment, which is why little Otto was enrolled only part-time. But Ginger had been the production manager for a local children's show before she got pregnant, and had friends in the industry. Ginger seemed to specialize in having friends.

All of the women had had a similar reaction to Phoebe's new, "sharper" columns — they were terrific, but they were never going to make Phoebe a decent living. She needed to transition to writing for television. That's where the money was.

There were plenty of TV shows about families with children. Some were heart-warming and some were cynical, but almost none of them had anything to do with real life. The columns that Garth had rejected had become a kind of audition for whether Phoebe could come up with sitcom ideas that appealed to real moms—that is, the moms in her new support group. And apparently she had passed the audition. The only problem was, she had to work one of them up into a real script, and she wasn't sure she had enough material for that so far. Not to mention that she'd never written a script in her life. But before she could point that out, Annie handed her a book on scriptwriting and Ginger made a date for one week from that night to review the first draft. Phoebe gathered up sleepy Ruth and went home in a daze.

Chapter 18: October, 1977 – January, 1978

On Monday, Phoebe was updating the Brilliant Babies contact list when she got a call from Belinda's second-grade classroom. Miss Laura wanted to speak to her. Right now. It did not sound good.

"Why are you calling me?" Phoebe asked. "If there's a problem, you should contact Micah or Belinda's mom."

"I am unable to reach either of them and the matter is urgent. Micah gave your name as an emergency contact."

"Oh, God! Is Belinda all right?"

"*Belinda* is fine. Please come down and we can go over the entire matter."

When Phoebe arrived, breathless and terrified, the other children were on the playground with Miss Susan and Belinda was sitting at the back of the empty classroom. Her little chin jutted out and she looked like she was trying not to cry. When Phoebe started toward her, she turned away. Phoebe went up to the teacher's desk instead.

"What's the problem?" Phoebe asked in what she hoped was a reasonable tone.

"I'm afraid Belinda has…well, Belinda, why don't you tell Phoebe what happened?"

But Belinda could not. Phoebe couldn't bear to look at her. She turned away so Belinda would be spared whatever reaction Phoebe failed to hide and said, "I think it would be easier on all of us if you just tell me yourself."

Miss Laura swallowed and looked down at her desk. It was one thing to deal with the parent of a "problem child," but Phoebe was part of the Brilliant Babies family. Not to mention a favorite of Lilith's. Not to mention goodness only knew what relationship to Micah, who was a Very Important Parent. And, she had to admit, Belinda was not generally a problem child.

"Very well," she said. "But…"

"Please," Phoebe said, losing patience. "Just tell me."

"Belinda stole Maya's lunchbox and threw it in the trash."

Phoebe wasn't sure what she had been expecting but this was definitely not it, and she was too floored to react. The idea of Belinda stealing anything was so unlikely, she couldn't take it in. If Belinda had hit Maya, it would have been easier to understand. She did have something of a temper.

Phoebe mastered her face and went over to Belinda, putting her hand on the little girl's shoulder and hunkering down next to her. Belinda shrank away. Phoebe was flummoxed. She had a good relationship with Belinda, but she wasn't the child's mother. How was she supposed to deal with this situation?

"Is this true, honey?"

"Yes." Her voice was barely audible.

"And you threw it in the trash?"

"Yes."

Phoebe stood up and faced Miss Laura. "What would you like us to do?" she asked. "Should I get Maya a new lunchbox, or…?"

"I think an apology would be the first step," said Miss Laura in a shocked voice.

"Ah. Well. Of course," Phoebe stammered, feeling more annoyed with Miss Laura by the minute.

"Sorry," said Belinda, and the dam broke. Tears streamed down her face.

Phoebe could never remember what she said to Miss Laura or how she and Belinda got from the classroom to the car, but when they were both inside, she turned the key. But her energy drained from her at that point and she just sat there while Belinda buckled herself into her car seat. Phoebe stared out at the playground with unseeing eyes until Belinda turned to her, her eyes blazing with anger and accusation.

"Aren't you going to ask me why?" she said, and then began sobbing again.

Phoebe turned off the car, feeling like an idiot. She unbuckled her own seatbelt and Belinda's and pulled the little girl awkwardly onto her lap.

"You are so right. Let's start over. Tell me why. I'm listening and there's no hurry. It's okay."

"It's not okay," Belinda shouted, and then buried her head in Phoebe's shoulder.

Phoebe stroked her hair and they sat for a while, waiting for the sobs to subside. Finally, Belinda climbed back into her seat, hunching her little shoulders and staring straight ahead. Phoebe waited.

"It was Aria's idea," the little girl finally said. "She told me that if I wanted to be friends with her and Nicole and Elena, I had to do it."

"So you did it."

"Yes." She looked up at Phoebe, her broken little heart in her eyes. "I do want to be friends with them. If they don't like you, you can't play any of the games."

"I understand," Phoebe said, and she did. "But here's the thing. If they know they can get you to do what they want one time, then they're going to tell you what to do another time. And another. There's not going to be an end to it. And it's always going to be something bad. And you're always going to be the one who gets the blame."

"But what can I do?" Belinda wailed. They sat for a bit, while Phoebe thought this over. The silence was broken only by an occasional sniff or sob from Belinda. And then Phoebe began to get an idea.

* * *

She had to tell Micah the whole story because Belinda was, after all, his child. Belinda had begged her not to, but Phoebe talked to both of them at the same time and turned the conversation into a strategy session. Micah was amazingly restrained, and Phoebe was proud of him. When she got to the solution, she hesitated a bit, but Belinda chimed in and Micah proclaimed it an excellent idea. Phoebe felt herself glow a little bit. Maybe it would actually work.

Sure enough, a few days later, Micah got a phone call from Miss Laura. But this time, she was the one doing the apologizing. Because, of course, it did happen again. But this time Belinda was prepared. After Aria whispered her demand, Belinda turned to her and shouted loud enough for the entire classroom to hear.

"No, Aria, I will not do that. If you want to steal Nicole's backpack, you're going to have to take it yourself."

Miss Laura could only stare as Nicole gasped and ran at Aria like a very small bull, wiping the smug look off Aria's pretty face. Belinda just walked away as Miss Laura descended, doubly angry to see the bad behavior in action and to learn how she'd been taken in. She extricated Aria from Nicole's angry little fists and placed her in a time-out at the front of the room. Belinda told Phoebe later that Aria's face had turned the color of a tomato.

At recess Aria, practically hissing with frustration and anger, found Belinda. Her young henchmen stood in front like angry little chess pawns, arms crossed and faces frowning.

"You'll never be in our group now," Aria told her triumphantly, having restored order among her followers. "*We* don't like you."

"What do you mean, *we*?" Belinda asked innocently. "I'm not sure anybody really likes *you* any more. Nicole told me she thinks you're dumb. And Maya says you smell. Elena didn't actually say anything, but she held her nose."

"I don't smell!" Aria said, shocked. "And they never said that."

"Well, you don't always know what your so-called friends will say about you when you're not there," Belinda said with a shrug. "You just can't trust some people." She walked away as each of the girls protested loudly that they had never, ever said those things and Aria glared at them with flinty little question marks in her eyes.

Belinda related the confrontation with great dramatic flair. She told Phoebe and Micah that Aria had kept her eyes glued on her little group for the rest of the day. Any time Elena turned toward Nicole, Aria sidled between them. When Miss Laura, sighing with frustration, separated them into different groups for a project, Aria swiveled around so much to keep them under surveillance that Belinda thought her head might separate itself from her shoulders and spin off like a top.

"Nice touch," Phoebe said, admiringly. "The whole smelling thing."

"What's a nice smelling touch, mama?" Ruth asked, wandering into the room.

"You'll see," Belinda told her with a world-weary sigh. "But when it happens to you, just talk to your mom. She'll know what to do."

Phoebe hugged Ruth, hoping against hope that it wouldn't be necessary, but understanding that it pretty much happened to every little girl at some point. Well, that's that she thought. And then she sat up so abruptly that Micah thought she'd been stung by a yellow jacket. But Phoebe had been stung by an idea. A pretty good idea… for a television script.

* * *

At her next meeting with the support group, Phoebe passed around a two-page outline of her script idea. The moms had decided that Phoebe's best hope for getting her foot in the television door was to submit a script for the sitcom that Annie's husband, Al, wrote for. Phoebe had watched the most recent episode and studied a few old scripts that Annie had given her. Al had even provided a video cassette of some old episodes he'd worked on. Thanks to Micah, Phoebe's household had a video cassette player, and Phoebe had watched the recordings over and over again.

There was a typical sitcom child in the cast—she was about nine years old and her main purpose in the show seemed to be to provide moments when the women in the audience said "Awww! Isn't that just adorable!"

Phoebe had her doubts about whether the people who ran the show would want anything more from the child, and just how much the young actress was capable of. The new script was quite a stretch from the current demands on the little girl. Still, nine was a perfect age for this sort of confrontation to take place. "All in the Family" was quite popular, and her episode would have been appropriate for that show—if it only had a child, and if only she had a contact there. Would a mainstream sitcom be interested?

"Absolutely," Annie said. "I talked it over with Al and he's intrigued. Ginger mentioned it to Frank and he says it has possibilities. Of course, they don't know the details. Where on earth did you get such a fantastic idea?"

"Let's just say real life provides endless examples of real life," Phoebe said.

The women laughed and passed the bottle. Phoebe abstained. She needed her wits—and her driving abilities—unimpaired. When things settled down a little, she interrupted the laughter with her first question.

"That little girl..." Phoebe began.

"Lucie?" Annie filled in, using the actress' name.

"Is that the one who plays Angela?"

"Yes."

"Can she handle a part like this?"

"Oh, she'd be thrilled. And the thing is, the audience loves how innocent she is and they just eat her up. They are going to be on her side from the get-go."

"What do you think of my outline?"

"I think the sooner you turn it into a script, the better."

So the conversation, amply lubricated by now, turned to the script. The women argued back and forth and Phoebe took frantic notes. By the time she left for home, the script was practically written—in her head at least.

* * *

It took Phoebe several weeks to move the script from her head to actual paper. She'd never written one before, and she was determined to turn in something that looked professional, so that took some time. She created lots of drafts, dating each one and filing it an ever-expanding folder. It didn't help that, at the same time, she had to respond to Rafe's lawyers. They had apparently spent a lot of time reviewing her letter to the court and were now planning a full frontal assault.

"I'm at my wits' end," she told Micah. "I don't have the money to hire any lawyers."

"I could…" Micah began, but Phoebe cut him off with a look. "Please, Micah. This is my problem to solve. Silly me, I forgot to go to law school. And I don't know any lawyers." And then she stopped.

"Well, none of us managed to do the law school thing," Micah began, but he stopped when he realized she wasn't listening and was looking at her curiously.

"You know what?" Phoebe asked rhetorically. "I do know a lawyer."

After an hour or so on the phone, Phoebe had tracked Abby down to an apartment in Manhattan. She didn't even allow herself a moment to reflect on the unbelievable fact that she did not already know where Abby was. She took a deep breath and dialed the number. It was something of an anti-climax to get an answering machine.

"Hi. This is Abby Klein. Leave me a message and I'll get back to you."

Well, at least she had the right number.

"Abby. This is Phoebe. I need to talk to you. Please, please call me as soon as you get this." And she left a number and sat staring at the phone, willing it to ring.

* * *

Working on the script was an excellent way to take her mind off her problems because the task seemed completely overwhelming and impossible. She leafed through the scriptwriting book, but the pages were a blur of unfamiliar terms and advice that seemed to be aimed at someone smarter and more experienced. She had to give herself a major pep talk to just sit down and start writing.

Micah took the children to the neighborhood park, and then out for ice cream. When they got back, Phoebe had an outline for the episode. She was afraid to talk about it out loud, but after dinner, she disappeared onto their back deck and worked some more. A lined yellow pad with many cross-outs and exclamation points was on her lap and a half-dozen yellow pages floated around her feet. She was just beginning to see how to put the various scenes together when Micah called her to the phone.

"Tell them to call back," Phoebe said crossly, without even looking up.

"It's Abby," Micah said.

"Oh." Phoebe jumped up, scattering papers, and ran into the house, leaving Micah to pick them up. He tried not to look at them, knowing how secretive she felt about the project, but he couldn't help himself. Hey. It wasn't bad. In fact, though he was no expert, it really seemed pretty good. He sat down in the chair Phoebe had abandoned and, under the pretext of putting the pages back in order, began reading in earnest.

"Abby!" Phoebe nearly shouted into the phone.

"Oh, Phoebe," Abby's voice came back, sounding close to tears.

"How did this even happen?"

"It's crazy. I miss you so much. You sounded really upset in your message. What's going on?"

"Do you have a minute?"

"All the time you want."

So Phoebe told her about Rafe and the lawyers. When she was done, there was silence at the other end.

"Are you still there?" Phoebe asked.

"Yes. Yes. I'm trying to take this all in. I'm trying to imagine a nameless father instead of Rafe because when I picture Rafe… Anyway. What's the next step? Is there a court hearing? Is it out there or in New York?"

Phoebe looked at the letter again. She had blocked out everything after the demand for full custody from Rafe.

"It's out here. In two weeks."

"Okay. I can be there on Sunday."

"Here? You can come here?"

"Looks like I'll have to. I don't know anyone I can really trust out there to take it for me. There's one woman I can work with—I need to contact her right away and see if she'll partner with me on this. I'm not licensed in California."

"Oh, God, Abby. Are you sure you can do this? You won't get into trouble?"

Abby laughed. "Who would I get into trouble with? The principal?"

"Well," Phoebe began, and then realized she had no idea where Abby worked or what exactly she did.

"I'm working for my dad's firm and I'm on track to make partner in a year or two," Abby said, as if this meant something to Phoebe. "I can do what I want as long as I bring in some billable hours."

"Oh, Ab, that's the thing. I don't have any money. I mean not your kind of money. Not lawyer money."

"Not a problem. Trust me. If we win this thing, I might even be able to get some damages for wasting the court's time. If not, I can just put off my vacation time and catch up on hours—in any case, not your problem. Can I stay with you?"

"Of course!"

"Okay. I'll call when I know my flight information and stuff. Hang in there. Nothing is going to happen before Sunday. Listen—I need to go, but we'll catch up when I get there."

"Okay. I love you."

"Bye, sweetie."

And that was that. Phoebe stared at the phone, wondering if she had dreamed the entire thing. Abby sounded like a completely different person. A good person. Just…a grownup.

* * *

With a Herculean effort, Phoebe pushed the entire legal situation into a back room in her head, a dusty psychological attic where she kept the guilty feelings she had for not calling her parents more often and her memories of her betrayal of Robin and the folk crowd. She spent the rest of the week turning her outline into a script. It wasn't really that different from writing a column. You just turned everything into dialog and camera directions. The folder of drafts was stuffed so full it looked like a Thanksgiving turkey made of paper.

She knew from her analysis of previous episodes that there needed to be two or three storylines. For sheer convenience, she decided to bring back a situation from an episode a few weeks earlier. It involved a plumber and a lost check. She remembered thinking that it could have used a slightly funnier twist, so she added one, hoping the actor who made a guest appearance as the plumber would still be available. She hadn't seen any other examples of reviving previous story lines, but instinctively she liked the idea.

She resurrected the lost check and plumbing issues, playing off some of the original dialog. That felt right—almost like an in joke that those who followed the show would recognize. She worked that into a brief scene that showed the mom dealing with the lost check problem when the phone call came from Angela's school. The mom had to put aside her problem and deal with the lunch box crisis. Then she could put the mom back into the plumbing crisis when Angela returned to school the next day and had her confrontation with her little friends. Then mom picks up Angela, learns how she dealt with the problem, and they congratulate each other on being the smartest girls ever. And then dad comes home to find that the sink still doesn't work and the lost check was at the bottom of mom's overcrowded purse all along. She hated making the mom responsible for such a dumb mistake, but it was the easiest solution. Oh, well, thought Phoebe. Pure and total feminism will have to take one for the team.

She brought her first draft to the moms' support meeting (now a regular weekly event) and the women each took a copy and marked it up. While she, of course, wanted to hear nothing but awestruck praise, she found herself genuinely interested in the feedback—not all of which was positive.

"Why does the dad get to win at the end?" was the most common complaint. "I thought they were the smartest girls ever?"

"I know," Phoebe admitted. "I hated that too. But I thought maybe the producers would want a guy to win at the end."

"I've got it!" said Annie. "What if the dad comes in and adjusts the plumbing—not realizing that the mom has had it taken care of—and totally screws it up?"

"Yes!" Phoebe said. "And then the mom and Angela can exchange knowing looks and re-repair it behind his back."

"No—not behind his back," Annie said firmly. "The mom gets to win this round."

"I can't believe I'm arguing with that," Phoebe said, laughing. "Of course! And the check?"

"Why can't it be in his overcrowded jacket pocket?" said Ginger. "He magnanimously agrees to treat his wife and daughter to dinner and pulls out a twenty—only to find the check flutter out with it."

"Absolutely!" Phoebe said, scribbling furiously.

By the end of their session, Phoebe had plenty of notes but the moms assured her she was well on the way to having something she could submit. Ginger and Annie held onto their copies, saying they wanted to sleep on it and see if they had further suggestions. Phoebe felt uneasy, although she couldn't say exactly why.

"Are you afraid word will get out and you won't have the element of surprise on your side?" Annie asked.

"Yeah, maybe," Phoebe said. "Something like that."

"We'll just give the guys an overview. No need to show them the actual drafts. But we need the drafts so we can give your feedback," Ginger explained.

"Sure," Phoebe said. How could she argue with these women, who had been so amazingly supportive?

"We'll have the comments back to you in the next day or two," Annie assured her, as she stuffed her copy of the script into her capacious bag.

* * *

Phoebe and Ruth stood at the gate, waiting for the passengers to come off the plane. Phoebe had shown Ruth lots of pictures of Abby, but she wasn't sure that she herself would recognize her best friend at this point. She needn't have worried. No one else had that smile.

They hugged so long that they formed a little island in the stream of deplaning passengers, although most of them smiled at the happy little group. Finally Phoebe broke away and led Abby and Ruth over to some seats.

"Do you have any luggage?"

"Naturally," Abby laughed. "I can't go into court in these jeans, even as a friend of the defense."

Ruth took Abby's hand as though she'd known her all her life and they made their way downstairs to the baggage claim.

"What do you think my chances are?" Phoebe asked nervously.

"Well, I looked over the materials you included in your response, and I think they're all helpful." Abby smiled at Ruth and then returned to scanning the luggage carousel.

"And?"

"And, it's still going to be a battle."

"I thought courts favored the mother?"

"They do, but Rafe has inexplicably become rather wealthy. And he seems to have used that wealth to gain influence with some powerful people."

"How? I mean, how did he become wealthy and how does he get influence just from being wealthy?"

"Those are good questions. I have some people working on answering them, but they haven't turned up anything useful yet."

"You have people? Who work on stuff?"

"Yes. I have lots to tell you."

"Mutual."

Chapter 19: March – April, 1978

Phoebe was typing like a madwoman. She had to stay late to use the Selectric they had at work—she couldn't afford her own typewriter and all her notes were in her own patented (that is to say, illegible) handwriting. She'd typed up the first formal draft of the script on her lunch hours—knowing the moms wouldn't be able to read the longhand version—but now she had to retype the entire thing to incorporate all the changes. Al and Frank had urged speed—the producers were looking at new script ideas this week.

Abby was home with Ruth, who was enchanted by her new "aunt." She was on her best behavior, agreeing to a bath and bedtime with an alacrity that made Phoebe quite jealous when she heard about it. When the little girl was tucked in, Abby hit the books and reviewed the materials that had been overnighted by her researchers.

By midnight, Phoebe had a relatively error-free script and Abby had a plan. They exchanged exhausted hugs and fell into bed. The next day, Ginger photocopied the script and held an emergency review meeting with the moms. They pronounced it ready, and Annie delivered it with great ceremony to her husband for submission to the powers-that-be. Now all they could do was wait.

* * *

"I have news," Ginger said portentously, as she swept into the Brilliant Babies office a few days later.

"Oh, please say it's good news," Phoebe said. "I could use a little good news about now."

"It is not good news," Ginger said, with a sad frown. Phoebe stared at her, frozen with shock. She really hadn't expected this. She was about to give in to despair and acknowledge that she'd been crazy to think she could do something like write a television script when Ginger's face split into a blinding grin.

"It's not good news—it's great news!" she crowed.

"How could you do that to me?" Phoebe moaned.

"Oh, the look on your face was worth it. Anyway, the writers love it! And they almost never love anything they didn't write themselves."

"That's great," Phoebe said, still in shock.

"They can see all kinds of possibilities going forward. Their only complaint is that they didn't think of it themselves. They're even talking about using you as a consultant on the episode."

"What does that mean?" Phoebe felt a little nervous about this. Handing in a script was scary enough, but being a consultant in an area she knew nothing about was terrifying.

"I think you'll love it. You get to watch them filming the scenes and make suggestions about interpretation and camera angles and stuff. Anyway, it's a chance to meet everybody on the show—they might want more work from you!"

"But I'd have to go down to L.A., right?"

"I'm sure we can arrange all that. These people are made out of money. Oh—that's the other thing. They have to run it by the sponsors. But that's mostly a technicality."

"What does that mean—run it by the sponsors?"

"You know those annoying things between the scenes of a show? Commercials, they call them?"

"Oh. Those sponsors. Would they have a problem with the script?"

"Hopefully not. I mean, none of them manufacture lunch boxes or anything." Ginger's big laugh rang out as she waved goodbye and swept out the door, headed to her son's classroom.

Phoebe sat staring at the door, her mind racing. Her whole life could change. Would it be better? Would she have to live in L.A.? She shuddered. Perish the thought. But Annie's husband didn't live there and he was a writer. She'd have to ask him how he managed that. Then she realized that she didn't even know for sure if they'd use this episode, much less any future ones. She had never paid any attention to the commercials when she was watching the episodes of the sitcom. How naïve could you get? Obviously, someone was paying for that show and they'd want it to be a certain way. Maybe they wouldn't like this development.

Oh, good. Something else to worry about.

* * *

Abby told Phoebe that she had some promising leads. She felt that the big question was how Rafe had suddenly acquired all this money. Was he involved in something shady? Even if he wasn't, was there any guarantee that he had a steady source of financial support? Nothing in his past suggested this.

She had dug into his family history, thinking perhaps his parents were bankrolling him and had an interest in their grandchild. But it turned out that his parents had died in a car crash when Rafe was ten years old and he'd been raised by a grandmother, now deceased. He'd gone to Antioch on a scholarship, which he'd lost when he dropped out to live at Spirit Mountain. His activities since he left the community were hard to trace.

Phoebe had received almost no communication from Rafe since she moved to California. He sent one letter early on, postmarked from Manhattan. But Abby could find no address for him there. He must have been staying with friends. They both racked their brains for any memory of a friend he'd mentioned in New York, but neither of them could remember him talking about anyone there. Abby had written to some old Antioch friends to see if they knew anything, but so far no one had anything useful to add.

"You've been living in Manhattan for a few years now," Phoebe said. "It's funny that he wouldn't contact you."

"Well, after everything that happened, it isn't that surprising," Abby said. "And New York, need I point out, is a big place."

"What about his lawyers? Do you know any of them? Their firm is listed on some of those papers, even some of their names."

"Yes, good thought—I'm looking into that. I found someone at my firm who knows some people there. All I can find out so far is that they are a very well-respected firm and they have a big family law department. And when Rafe is mentioned, the contact for him is a post office box."

"A big family law department," Phoebe murmured. "That's bad for us, right?"

"Well, it means he's serious. He's willing to spend big bucks to get what he wants."

Phoebe was silent, thinking dark thoughts.

"Money doesn't buy everything, Phoebe—even in New York. I think we have the law on our side. But I'd love to know about the money—where did it come from? He never finished his degree. What kind of job could he get that would pay like that?"

"Well, you don't have to have a degree to be a drug dealer," Phoebe joked. And then stopped. "Wait a minute," she said.

"Something?"

"What if that's it? What if he's dealing drugs?"

"I thought of that, but how would we know?"

"Well, there was this one time, we went to Boston to see this old friend of his…"

"Tracy?"

"Yes! You knew him too?"

"Oh yes. And he was a druggie for sure. And a distributor, I'm pretty sure. I can't believe he's still alive, to tell you the truth."

"He's definitely a distributor. Some customers came by when we were there. It was the only time in my entire life that someone who wasn't on a television set pulled out a gun in the same room I was in. What if Rafe is working for Tracy? Expanding the operation to New York?"

"Well, it would be insane for one thing. Can you imagine what the established distribution people in New York would do to someone who horned in on their territory?"

"Yes. But I got the impression that Tracy was a risk taker. Especially if he could delegate some of the risk."

"You may have something there," Abby said slowly.

"Do you have a way to get hold of Tracy?"

"Well, I stayed in touch with his old girlfriend. I could start with her." And Abby trotted off to get her files and work the phone.

All Phoebe could think about was what would happen to Ruth if Rafe was dealing drugs and somehow managed to get full custody.

Oh, good. Something else to worry about.

* * *

A week went by with no word from the sitcom people or Rafe's lawyers. Abby had gotten several phone numbers from Tracy's old girlfriend, Liz, and was getting closer to some information about Rafe. It seemed as though the drug-dealing was a definite possibility. Liz had talked to Tracy a few months earlier and he mentioned Rafe because Liz knew him back in the day. He hadn't specifically said that Rafe was working for him, but he told her Rafe was a dad and was trying to get custody of his little girl.

Liz had a few numbers for some New York friends who knew Tracy. Abby called, saying she was trying to get back in touch with Tracy. One of the friends suggested calling Rafe, who—he said—was doing some work for Tracy. Abby said she knew Rafe from Antioch and asked what kind of work he was doing. The friend assumed she was looking for a drug connection. "He's kind of an advance man," the friend joked. "He might be able to help you—depends on what you want. But prepared for a long phone call. The guy can sure talk!" Abby agreed. She managed to get a phone number for Rafe and used her connections to get access to a reverse directory that gave her an address. Calling her "people" back in New York, she had a private detective keep an eye on the place, which was in a rather sketchy neighborhood in the East Village.

All of this took several days, and then she had to wait for the report from the private detective. Finally, she got the confirmation she was looking for, but she didn't look happy about it.

"Look, Phoebe," she said that night, after they'd tucked Ruth and Rabbit into bed. "I don't think we should use this drug thing, even if we can prove it."

"I wasn't feeling great about it myself," Phoebe said.

"It's not just uncomfortable—there are legal issues. I'm an officer of the court, and so is my partner on this case. So are Rafe's lawyers. If we know of illegal activity, we're required to report it. Once I present this evidence, Rafe will end up in jail. There's no getting around it."

She paced the living room. "I don't have a license to practice in California, and I guess I can just ignore the fax. It doesn't actually prove anything one way or the other—but I have a strong feeling that if we followed up on it as a lead, it could easily lead to hard evidence. On its own, it's not enough to arrest him on—just enough to make him an unfit father. I think we've got to find another way to show that."

Phoebe felt oddly relieved. She didn't like the idea of Ruth's dad being in prison or living the rest of his life with a drug-dealing charge hanging over his head. But now what?

Abby stopped pacing and turned back to Phoebe, her face looking lighter. "Actually, I might have a way."

"Okay. Good. What is it?"

"I think I'd rather not say right now." So Phoebe had to live with that. Meanwhile, Abby was on the phone a lot, which made Phoebe nervous—what if the sitcom people were trying to reach her right now? But when she got word it was through Ginger, as usual.

"They want a meeting," Ginger announced as she burst through the office door.

"In L.A.?" Phoebe asked, panicking.

"No. Al told them it was better to have it here so he could attend too. A couple of the sponsors are based in San Francisco, and they agreed. It'll be in the city. Next Tuesday."

"Next Tuesday? Omigod. That's so soon!"

"Well, they're looking at filming in two weeks, so they need to get it nailed down."

"Who will be at the meeting?"

"The sponsors, a couple of the writers, the show-runner, and…you."

Phoebe could feel her heart about to take a dive off the high board.

"So—this means the sponsors have reservations about the whole story line, right?"

"Well…" Ginger found a sudden need to dig through her purse.

"A simple yes will suffice."

"Okay. Yes." She held up a small mirror, apparently her excuse for the purse distraction.

"Because it's a big departure? Because it's a little too serious for their taste?"

"Yes and yes." Ginger was suddenly engrossed in checking her makeup.

"What does Al think?" Surely he had some idea of how this would all go.

"He's hopeful," Ginger said, still busy with her mirror. She glanced up at Phoebe and smiled reassuringly. "But more than that, he's willing to fight for the idea. So are the other writers. They really like it."

Phoebe smiled. She'd never even met these people, and they were already on her side. That felt so good.

"Well, me too," she declared. And her heart backed away from the edge of the diving board and started down the ladder. She didn't notice Ginger's nervous fingers drop the mirror into her purse, and Ginger managed to turn towards the door before Phoebe could see the worry on her face.

* * *

When Phoebe and Ruth got home, Abby waved a fax page at her.

"Got it." she said.

"What did you get?" Ruth asked.

"Something I think might be good."

"Ice cream?"

"Almost. Tell you what—if you draw me a beautiful picture of an ice cream cone, maybe I'll take us out for ice cream after dinner. How would that be?"

"Okay!" Ruth said, rushing off to find her crayons.

"This thing you found… you still can't tell me about it?"

"I think it's better if I don't."

"But maybe we can head off the hearing entirely by telling Rafe and his lawyers. Maybe Rafe would back down." Phoebe was trying to be hopeful

"Maybe," Abby murmured.

"Could we hold this as a last resort? Go to the hearing, make our case without this information, and if it looks like we might lose, bring it out. Is that reasonable?"

"Might be. Might be." Abby crouched down by Phoebe's chair and put her arms around her friend. "You are the best, you know that?"

"Oh, Ab. In the dictionary, "best" has your picture next to it."

A shadow passed across Abby's face. "Let's wait until after the custody hearing before you make a final decision about that."

Phoebe wanted to ask more questions, but decided that right now she didn't want to know.

* * *

Phoebe was preparing a defense of her script for the sponsors' meeting when the phone rang. She jotted down a few key words so she wouldn't totally lose her train of thought and picked up on the third ring.

"Hello, this is Phoebe," she said.

The voice on the other end sounded slightly bored and extremely officious. It informed her that a date had been set for her custody hearing. It was next Tuesday.

"Tuesday?" Phoebe said, horrified. "But I can't be at a hearing on Tuesday! I have a very important meeting in San Francisco that day!"

"Well, the hearing is also in San Francisco, so that shouldn't be a problem. And I'm sure nothing is more important than the custody of your daughter."

Now the voice sounded officious and judgmental.

"Of course not. It's just—people are flying in from out of town..."

"As they are for this hearing."

"Yes. I understand. Of course, I'll be there. What time and what's the address?"

She took down the information in a daze. The hearing was at 1:00. Her script meeting was scheduled for ten in the morning. Maybe she could actually make this work?

She called an emergency meeting of the moms' support group. They figured that the meeting would end at lunchtime, allowing Phoebe at least half an hour to get to the hearing. They went over her defense strategy and each of them gave her a big hug.

"We will be waiting by the phone," Annie told her. "And Al will be there to back you up. Don't worry!"

"Right," said Phoebe. "Deny me the one thing I'm good at."

* * *

The sponsors were already seated around a big table when Phoebe arrived, Micah's briefcase in hand. Al motioned her over to an empty chair next to his. Phoebe started to tell him she'd had a new idea for the script defense, but he motioned her to wait. In a tense voice, he whispered, "Try not to look surprised. I've got a plan." Before Phoebe could respond, the little buzz of conversation that had accompanied Phoebe's entrance died down and Al spoke.

"Everyone, this is Phoebe—my personal assistant. She'll be taking notes for us at this meeting. Phoebe, these are our sponsors." He went around the table, giving names and company affiliations. As each man nodded and smiled, Phoebe was struggling not to go into shock. Personal assistant? What was all this about? Why hadn't Annie warned her? Her hands went through the motions of writing down names and company affiliations while her mind reeled. Personal assistant?!

"Well, gentlemen," Al said. "Why don't you tell me your thoughts about the script?" Phoebe just stared at him. He was acting like it was his script. Why did this feel so familiar somehow?

An older gentleman, who'd been introduced as Mortimer Goodman from a large cereal manufacturer, glanced around the room as though to establish that he would be the spokesman. "Well, Al, let me start by saying that the script is very clever and extremely well-constructed. You are definitely profiting from having a personal assistant. Bet she keeps you focused, hey Phoebe?"

Phoebe ignored this. She'd figure out the personal assistant thing later. She was thinking, "There is a big but coming after that, and it isn't the one he's sitting on."

"But," said the gentleman, as though on cue. "It is a definite departure for our little show."

Al cleared his throat and went through the points Phoebe had so carefully assembled and shared with the moms. Her sense of betrayal grew, but she forced herself to stay focused and see what Mr. Goodman's reactions were. He was clearly not impressed. Al's mechanical delivery wasn't helping. Phoebe could feel the script's future melting away, and with it went her best hope of gaining full legal custody of Ruth.

"Yes, yes," Mr. Goodman said with an icy smile. "I'm sure these are all good points, but I'm afraid…"

Phoebe dropped all pretense of taking notes and, feeling she was stepping off a cliff, decided to take matters into her own hands.

"I think I might be able to help here," she interjected. "Let me ask you a few questions, Mr. Goodman." Mr. Goodman smiled at her indulgently, and Phoebe figured he was impressed that she'd remembered his name. Before he could say something chivalrous and sexist to shut her up, she went on.

"Who is your target audience?"

Phoebe had a strong feeling that she knew where Mr. Goodman's real interests lay. She felt icy and strong. Where was this calm, collected, somewhat controlling personality coming from? Phoebe forced down a momentary panic that she had been possessed by some far more aggressive scriptwriting ghost.

"That's an excellent question," he said, glancing curiously at Al, who had gone rather pale. "We tend to appeal to women between the ages of 40 and 60. The second largest target is kids aged nine to twelve—especially if we feed lots of photos and personal stories about the younger cast members to the teeny-bopper magazines. But once they hit the true teen-age level we tend to lose them to the rock 'n roll shows and some of the evening soaps."

"Well, I've been doing some independent research of my own," Phoebe told him. "Nothing formal, you understand, just anecdotal observation and a survey of popular magazines and such. What I've found is that mothers of young children feel frustrated with the current crop of family-friendly sitcoms. They want something they can watch with their kids—even their husbands in some cases, although not if there's a football game that night, of course!"

She paused for a light wave of laughter. They were surprised at her participation, but she had their attention. She saw the other sponsors glance at Mr. Goodman for direction, but he seemed to be genuinely interested in what she had to say, so they arranged their faces to reflect his.

"To be honest, the current choices in the sitcom genre leave their children and husbands bored stiff. And as for the moms..."

She paused and sipped some water from the glass in front of her. No one jumped in to interrupt. She felt encouraged.

"As I say, they are frustrated. Now, you might wonder where the frustration is coming from. After all, there are plenty of family sitcoms out there—something for everyone, you'd think. But here's what I'm hearing: The current crop of sitcoms seem to be unaware of the real problems these moms are facing every day. The assumption seems to be that nothing has changed for mothers in this country since 1955. Gentlemen, while not all these moms would describe themselves as 'liberated,' they would definitely describe themselves as career women. They are the generation that wants it all—family, career, the whole nine yards. I know you understand this because several of the characters in your sitcom are working mothers, and we can find many examples in rival shows. Yet the working moms on TV seem to have it pretty darned easy. For example, every one of them has children who are perfectly angelic, or whose biggest problems are which attractive suitor to choose for the prom."

Phoebe looked around the room and she could see she had impressed them, but they did not necessarily agree. Yet. They were comfortable with their safe suburban TV world and didn't like the idea of challenging it.

"I think there are two ways to address this issue, and both of them involve the same kind of gentle humor that your show is so very good at."

Al cleared his throat again, as though to indicate that he was ready to take control again. Phoebe focused on the approving smile from Mr. Goodman and plunged on before Al could get a word in.

"No one wants lectures or lessons when they watch a comedy. But they do want to see their own life reflected back to them—with a generous helping of happy endings and even—dare I say it—a bit of light revenge. They want to picture themselves making the clever retort they might have made in a similar situation if they had only thought of it in time—and had the nerve. What the French call 'staircase thoughts.'"

She paused to glance around the room. They were definitely interested.

"Now what this episode does is create a potentially humiliating situation for a very nice, well-meaning mom and her normally well-behaved child. Something every mom can relate to. But instead of suffering humiliation, or being saved by some cool-headed male, the mom and daughter work together to turn the situation around. And they both learn a little something in the process."

Mr. Goodman was quiet for a moment. "You said there were two ways," he said.

"I'm glad you were paying such close attention," Phoebe joked. "Let's hope I can remember the second one!"

Another round of laughter, but it felt warmer this time.

"I want to introduce the idea of bringing back themes and characters from previous episodes. It's rarely done on today's shows, but I think it builds audience loyalty and a sense of being in on the joke. The audience sees the plumber from last month and immediately thinks—oh, I remember him! I know him! I know him because I'm part of this show's extended family. I'm in on the joke. He repeats something he said in his previous appearance, and they laugh automatically because it's familiar—the way you might laugh at your old Uncle Bob when he says 'This is good, but it needs a little salt,' the way he always does."

A younger man on the other side of the table whose face had been carefully blank all this time suddenly nodded enthusiastically. "Yes!" he said. "Well said."

And Phoebe was pretty sure she had them. Mr. Goodman looked at Al, who was trying to project a smug smile and a somewhat paternalistic pride in his little protégé. Goodman looked as though he might not be buying it. His glance moved back to Phoebe.

"This is all quite interesting. I didn't realize personal assistants provided the kinds of research and thought you've put into this project—not to mention your familiarity with the script."

Al's pale face regained its color and then some—it was now a faintly glowing crimson and purple was not out of the question. But Phoebe had no sympathy for him. She was remembering Hudson and Garth and the way Garth had managed to convince Hudson so easily that Phoebe's column was his work. Well, that time she wasn't able to defend herself. But no one was going to steal her work again if she had anything to do with it.

Al attempted a smile and an ambiguous shrug. Maybe he was going for an air of detached indulgence, but Phoebe thought he looked like a late-night habitué at a Los Vegas casino who'd lost more than he could afford to bet.

Mr. Goodman had been addressing Phoebe, but now he turned his attention to Al.

"Mr. Moreham, is there anything you'd like to add? About the script? Or anything else that you think we need to hear?"

Al stared at the table for a moment and then apparently decided he had nothing further to lose.

"As you know," he began, "I have been looking for ways to expand our show and explore new areas ever since I began writing for you three years ago. The stress of writing a weekly show can be enormous, as we try to balance the ratings from the previous episode with our arc and vision for the season. I felt that, at my own expense, I needed some help with the research and planning aspects."

"At your own expense?" Mr. Goodman asked.

"Well, I couldn't ask the network to take on extra personnel of my own choosing, after all."

Mr. Goodman turned to Phoebe. "So Mr. Moreham has been paying you for your, er, research?"

Phoebe ignored the sharp kick under the table and glanced at Al, then back at Mr. Goodman. "I'm sorry sir, and I don't want to cause any problems, but I really have to be honest. No one has paid me for anything I've done so far. I certainly was not offered a position as a personal assistant. In fact, I have a full-time job at the school that my daughter attends and between working, parenting, and writing, I can't see how I could possibly accept another position without giving up the one I already have."

"You have a young child?"

"Yes sir, and I am a single mother. So parenting is a big part of my life. Well, I guess it would be for anyone with children," Phoebe said, knowing full well that Al did virtually no parenting himself.

"Mr. Moreham, we seem to have two very different versions of your relationship with Ms. Hirsch. I think I have to ask you outright: did you or did you not write this script yourself?"

Al's face darkened again. "I had a great deal to do with the script, Mr. Goodman. My input…"

"But did you write it?"

"I can show you the drafts," Al said, managing to convey sarcasm and feigned disbelief in six words.

"Phoebe? Do you have anything to say to that?"

As was often the case, Phoebe's anger generated cold, rather than heat. The more furious she was, the more careful her speech became, as though formulating perfect sentences for each point in her arguments would make them more effective. As though her words were tiny weapons against the object of her wrath. She kept her gaze firmly on Mr. Goodman, feeling vaguely that even glancing at Al at this point would make both of them explode.

"I wrote all the drafts of the script." Phoebe said.

"Can you elaborate a bit," asked Mr. Goodman.

Phoebe took a deep breath.

"A small group of women whose children attend the school where I work had expressed interest in my writing career when I shared my magazine columns with them. They urged me to consider writing for television. One of the women is Al's wife. I gave her and the other mothers two drafts to review. It would have been perfectly understandable if they shared those drafts with Al. I was told that he was aware that I was working on the script, and that he and some other writers were supportive of the direction I was taking. For my part, I am certainly appreciative of the support and input I received from the women, whether it came just from them or was partially contributed by the writers. But I wrote the script. Every single draft of it. . There were five, not counting re-writes of individual scenes. I have them all. Since I passed along only two for review, I suspect those are the two that Al can produce. But I have the other three at home, as well as all my handwritten notes."

Al began to sputter. His own anger seemed to make him slightly incoherent. Phoebe went on.

"I've watched dozens of episodes of your show, and I've made pages of notes on possible future episodes. I have so many ideas. I love the show and I'd love to work on it. But if that doesn't suit you, or if you simply don't believe I'm capable of it, then I will accept that and take my work to another show or another network. I know I'm something of an unknown quantity, but this exercise has convinced me that I'm good at scriptwriting. Really good. If you don't agree, let's part as friends and I'll move on."

She glanced at her watch.

"And now, I'm terribly sorry gentlemen, but I have to leave. Due to circumstances beyond my control, I must attend another meeting—I was unable to reschedule it. I will leave my contact information with the receptionist."

And leaving Al in the glare of the sponsors' accusing eyes, she gathered her things and left the room.

As she closed the meeting room door, she heard Mr. Goodman ask Al to wait outside while he and the other sponsors "discussed a few things." She wrote out her contact information on a memo pad at the receptionist's desk, and was gathering her things when Al emerged and grabbed her shoulder, spinning her around.

"You ungrateful little bitch," he said in an angry whisper. She looked at him calmly, but her heart was racing. What a day, she thought. One for the books.

"Clearly you were hoping to grab credit for my work before I could react," she said. "Hoping I would be too cowed by the sponsors? Well, it didn't work, and they all know it." She paused, focusing on controlling her breath. Al was silent, his chest heaving with anger and desperation.

"Why are all you men so short-sighted? What were you going to do after this episode?" she asked him. "You know as well as I do that there was no way on earth you could have written what I wrote. What were you planning to do for an encore?"

He had an answer for this one. "I figured you needed money," he said, and Phoebe caught a glimpse of an Al who was a bit sly and very cynical. Phoebe wondered if Annie had ever seen this side of him.

"I was willing to pay you for your work. I can find a way to add you to the writing staff. These people have tons of money, and I'd have no problem getting some for you. More than you've ever been paid before, I imagine."

He glanced at her face and switched gears. "You could really benefit from being my ghostwriter, you know," he said, replacing the sly look with his usual kindly, slightly daydreaming expression. "You may be creative, but there's a lot you don't know about this business. I could mentor you..."

Now that really sounded familiar. Phoebe could practically see Garth perching on a nearby desk.

"I prefer to choose my own mentors," Phoebe told him. "And anyone who thinks he can steal credit for my work and put one over on me by failing to mention his 'personal assistant' plan until we are in a roomful of decision-makers is not the sort of person I want teaching me anything."

Before he could react, she changed the subject. "Did Ginger and Annie know about this?"

"No," Al said, startled, which banished any remaining doubts Phoebe had about his motives and actions. She wasn't sure she believed him, but she had neither the time nor the psychic energy to think about that right now. She glanced at her watch.

"I really need to get going," Phoebe said.

"Aren't you going to wait to see what the sponsors have to say?" Al asked, puzzled.

"No. And if you tell them any more lies, I'll contact Mr. Goodman directly and see that you lose your job altogether. Believe me, I'd love to wait and see how this all plays out. But the meeting I've got to get to is important. Very important."

Her heart hammering, Phoebe fled. She got to the courtroom with only moments to spare. Abby was pacing the sidewalk. They hurried inside, Phoebe sharing the news and Abby squeezing her arm in mute support, but looking worried. They'd been hoping to present Phoebe's future scriptwriter/consultant work as a fait accompli. Without a contract, or even a memo of intent from Mr. Goodman about using her script or giving her a position on the show, they were being forced into using backup arguments. Phoebe felt panicky. If they had to use the drug activity, there could be all sorts of repercussions.

She looked around the courtroom as they walked in. Rafe wasn't even there. Both women felt a sense of relief, but also wondered why this would be true. Was he that confident of the outcome? Abby looked as though she was reviewing her backup plans. They sat at a table with a well-dressed woman named Barbara Williamson who was acting in Abby's place, since Abby couldn't argue a case in California.

The judge addressed Phoebe first.

"Ms Hirsch, let me explain how this process works."

"Thank you, your honor," Phoebe said. Despite all the preparations for this hearing, she was still a little unclear on the big picture.

"Normally, we would have both parties—the parents—present, and each one would present his or her case for custody." He consulted his notes briefly. "I understand that Ruth's father is unable to attend, due to business activities and the time and distance involved, so in this case his interests are represented by his lawyers."

Phoebe nodded her understanding and the judge went on.

"I will ask some questions of each party, and then the legal representatives for those parties will be given a chance to ask additional questions of their own."

He turned to each set of lawyers in turn. "I urge you to avoid repeating questions I've already asked. And please don't try to make points in your client's favor by framing them as questions. I've been around the block a few times and I will not look kindly on such tactics. Custody is granted according to the best interests of the child, and not by promoting or smearing one or the other of the parents."

"Now you, Phoebe, will be sworn in as a witness, just like they do on television. There is no need to swear in the lawyers since they are obligated by law to tell the whole truth and so on. They are well aware that they could be held in contempt or worse if they commit perjury or try to hide known facts from the court. For the record, I will remind all of you that you can testify only to things you have directly witnessed or experienced, or—in the case of Raphael Miranda's lawyers—things which have been told to you by your client. In the second instance, you must inform us that you know these things only because your client told you they were so."

The judge removed his glasses and rubbed his eyes. He looked tired. Phoebe thought he had an awfully difficult job. He seemed to gather his thoughts, swore Phoebe in (just like on television), and started his questioning.

"Ms Hirsch, were you ever married to the plaintiff, Mr. Raphael Miranda?"

"No."

"Do you dispute that he is the father of the child in question?"

"No."

"Have you ever asked Mr. Miranda for child support?"

"No."

"Why not?"

"I had no reason to think he could provide any. He never had any money in the time I knew him."

"Did Mr. Miranda ever offer to provide support, or send unsolicited funds to support his daughter?"

"No."

"Did he ever visit his daughter?"

"Once."

"And how long did that visit last?"

"He was at our house for several hours, but since he arrived unannounced on Thanksgiving Day, and we'd made other plans, he spent only a few minutes with Ruth."

"A few minutes?"

"Yes."

"In the two years since he'd last seen her?"

"That is correct."

"Did he call her on the phone or send her letters or packages?"

"No."

"Now, you have been supporting your daughter for nearly five years—is that right?"

"Yes."

"As a single mother, how did you manage that?"

"Well, I've lived communally during that time, so I was able to share many expenses. And for about a year and a half I received some social services."

"But you are not receiving social services now?"

"That is correct."

"Why is that?"

"Well, I began to supplement my salary with some writing income and I felt I no longer needed the social services money."

"So, you hold a job, spend some of your free time writing, and also manage to care for your child?"

"Yes."

"I see from these notarized statements that there are quite a few people who think you are an excellent parent.

That's always nice to hear." The judge paused, checking another note.

"Now, Ms Hirsch, you have come directly here from a meeting with the sponsors of a popular television series. Is it true that your script is being considered as an episode for this season's line-up?"

"Yes."

"And that you are hoping to be hired as a script consultant?"

"Yes."

"And either or both of these options would involve generous compensation?"

"Yes."

"Very well. That concludes my questioning. Do Mr. Miranda's lawyers have any further questions?"

Rafe's lawyer rose and approached Phoebe. "Ms Hirsch, with all due respect, we all have hopes and dreams, but..." Rafe's lawyer implied with a shrug that hopes were just that—you couldn't deposit them in a bank. Phoebe did not respond. He hadn't asked a question, and Abby had coached her never to volunteer information unless directly asked. The judge noticed too.

"Did you have a question, Mr. Angelo?"

"I was just getting to that, your honor. Ms Hirsch, when will you know about this theoretical television income?"

"I hope to have a response from the show's sponsors by the end of the week," Phoebe said.

"And you can supply copies to the court at that time?"

"Yes."

"Ms Hirsch has given the court detailed information about her income," the judge said, a bit testily. "Did you have a point to make that is not covered by her report?"

"While Ms Hirsch's income has been adequate to Ruth's needs thus far, your honor, our client's income would clearly provide for a more, er, generous lifestyle."

"I thought I'd made it clear that your role is to ask questions and not to share your opinion about lifestyle choices."

Rafe's lawyer nodded, accepting defeat. He'd made his point. "Now, this communal lifestyle, er, situation in which you engage," said the lawyer, managing to imply that Phoebe lived in a house of prostitution or worse. Looking as though it pained him greatly to do so, he displayed the photos of her messy bedroom as though they were illustrations of a torture chamber.

"Are these unretouched photos of your bedroom at the commune?"

Phoebe examined the photos. "Yes," she said, and did not elaborate.

"Any further *questions*?" asked the judge.

"No, your honor."

"Very well. You may return to your seat, Ms Hirsch. Now," said the judge, turning to Rafe's lawyers. "Which of you would like to answer for Mr. Miranda?"

Mr. Angelo stood, hands joined behind his back like a schoolboy called to the principal's office.

"After making so little effort to contact his daughter for two years, why did Mr. Miranda suddenly decide that he wanted full custody?"

"When Ms Hirsch applied for social services, she set into motion a series of actions, which she may not have been aware of. In California, if you apply for food stamps and you are a single parent, the agency immediately wants to know whether the other parent is contributing to the child's welfare. And if not, why not. They contacted Mr. Miranda, demanding past, current, and future payments. Mr. Miranda felt that, if he was going to pay for Ruth's upbringing, he'd rather have complete access to her instead of virtually no access at all. He had agreed to a one-year visit to the West Coast on the part of Ms Hirsch and Ruth, and Ms Hirsch had expanded this period to double the agreed-upon time, making no attempt to contact him to arrange for this extension."

"I see," said the judge, making a note. The courtroom was silent for a moment while he finished, and Phoebe could hear her heart beating. When you put it that way, it sounded like she was the villain.

The judge looked up and continued. "According to previous testimony, Mr. Miranda did not have much money—possibly not enough to support a child. Yet you seem to be saying that, when he was contacted by social services, he had enough funds to provide past, current, and future support, or—alternatively—to raise the child himself. When did he acquire these funds?"

"Mr. Miranda did not specify," said Mr. Angelo, checking his notes.

"And did he specify *how* he had acquired these funds?"

"He did not."

"Do you have any photographs or other evidence showing the environment in which he and the child would live?"

"I do not."

"But he had enough money to afford your services?"

"Yes," Mr. Angelo said, without so much as a blush.

"And how did you verify that?"

"We contacted his bank, which assured us that he could easily afford our fees."

"Do you have a street address for Mr. Miranda that might suggest the sort of residence he could afford?"

"We do not. He used a post office box as his return address. And his telephone number is a relatively new Manhattan exchange that is not associated with a particular neighborhood."

"Did his bank provide any history for his account, for example, how long his balance had been at the level it was when you contacted them?"

"He opened the account about six months ago. There was a transfer from an offshore financial institution. We did not see any reason to investigate further."

"Do you have any affidavits or notarized statements attesting to Mr. Miranda's fitness as a parent?"

"We do not."

The judge looked over at Phoebe's table. "Any questions, Ms Williamson?"

No, your honor," said Ms Williamson, and Phoebe looked at her nervously. Why didn't she have questions? Rafe's lawyers had been so convincing. Phoebe didn't feel at all confident in the outcome.

The judge asked opposing counsel how they would like to proceed.

"While we feel we have a strong case for the father's custody plea, we would like to postpone further arguments until the report on the television income is documented and presented to court, your honor," he said. "That appears to be the only outstanding issue."

Mr. Angelo went on. "I think what we can do, to make the best use of all of our time, is to use the interim period to discuss some formal guidelines for visitation, which would apply to either of the parties who did not gain full-time custody."

"Well," said the judge. "Prepare a proposal and we can discuss that when we have the missing documentation." He glared over his glasses at Phoebe.

"Any questions from Ms Hirsch's representation?"

"We have a request for the interim period as well," said Nicole coolly, while Phoebe slid down in her seat meekly and tried not to cry. She couldn't tell whether they'd already lost, or whether that would happen at the next hearing. Nothing in the room felt like success to her. But Nicole didn't seem concerned.

"And your request is?" asked the judge.

"We would like a psychiatric evaluation of Mr. Miranda by a professional appointed by the court."

"On what basis?" asked the judge.

Nicole drew a sheaf of papers from her briefcase.

"Apparently, Mr. Miranda's behavior over the last ten years at least has been erratic and poses a potentially dangerous situation for a child. May I read from these notarized statements?"

Rafe's lawyers looked as surprised as they felt. This was the first they'd heard of this. Phoebe felt pretty much the same way, but when she glanced at Abby, she could see that it was no surprise to her friend.

And Nicole began to read.

Some letters described incidents in which Rafe had either engaged in or proposed sexual relations during Phoebe's pregnancy. Several indicated that, when told the woman was not interested, he had acted aggressively, even threateningly. And while it was painful to hear just how many women Rafe had betrayed her with, the tears that ran down her cheeks were tears of gratitude. When she'd left, she'd felt like a pariah. But now, in her darkest hour, all these women from Spirit Mountain had come forward to support her.

After reading a sampling from these letters, Nicole went on to read accounts of Rafe making wild claims that were later proven to be untrue. Several people described Rafe's erratic disappearances, from the community, leaving important tasks unfinished. His reappearances were equally unsettling. A few men testified that Rafe had demanded special treatment from the community, threatening to accuse people at Spirit Mountain of dealing drugs when they refused, despite the fact that all residents had taken an oath never to bring drugs onto the property.

When Nicole got to the seventh statement, the judge interrupted her.

"How many of those do you have?"

"Twenty-three," said Nicole. Phoebe just stared. How had she managed to collect twenty-three statements in just a few short weeks? And how had she guessed that the statements would be so universally damning? She turned to look at Abby, who had a look of grim satisfaction on her face. Oh dear God in heaven, what had she ever done to deserve a friend like Abby and how would she ever repay her?

"I am prepared to make a ruling now, without the need for any further research, evidence, or agreements," the judge said.

"But…"Rafe's lawyer began.

"No buts. Here's what I'm hearing. Mr. Miranda never sent a red dime to the mother of his child for that child's support. The mother says, rather generously, that this was because Mr. Miranda never had much money. Yet somehow, in a single year, he is able to hire some pretty high-powered lawyers and demand full custody of a child he cannot be bothered to call, write to, or visit. In fact, when he does finally make it to the West Coast, he spends only minutes with the child. This suggests to me an insufficient interest in the welfare of the child and possible illegal activity resulting in sudden wealth—unless he can prove that he won the lottery?" He glared over his glasses, but Rafe's lawyers had no answer for this.

"Meanwhile, the mother manages to convince Rafe to leave her and the child in peace for a year and works like crazy to create a good environment for the child, attested to by her employer, fellow mothers, friends, and neighbors. By contrast, the affidavits relating to Mr. Miranda document a long history of philandering and deceit. The only real accusation Mr. Miranda's lawyers can make is that Ms Hirsch failed to contact Mr. Miranda to negotiate a second year in California. But hearing the letters concerning Mr. Miranda's behavior, one can understand her desperation to have even one more year to live in peace with the daughter she so clearly loves."

The judge paused, catching his breath. He shook his head sadly. "And the court is expected to award custody to Mr. Miranda simply because Ms Hirsch couldn't face placing herself and her child at the mercy of Mr. Miranda again?"

"Ms Hirsch, I sincerely hope your pursuit of a writing career is successful. But even without that, you have demonstrated consistently that you can and will provide a good life for your daughter. The court grants you full custody. We will discuss visitation rights and child support in a separate meeting, as requested by Mr. Miranda's lawyers." He banged his gavel.

"This hearing is adjourned."

Phoebe turned to Abby. Both women were sobbing.

"Do they let you dance in the courtroom?" Phoebe managed to say.

"No one's watching," Abby replied. And as the judge and the other lawyers filed out of the room, Phoebe and her best friend waltzed around the room and out the door.

Chapter 20: June, 1978

Phoebe was at Brilliant Babies on Thursday, trying to focus on the end-of-month financial reports, when the phone rang. It sounded exactly the way it had when it rang all day yesterday, when none of the callers had been Mr. Goodman. She was trying hard not to think about that.

"Brilliant Babies," she said, as chirpily as she could. There was a short silence.

"I am trying to reach Ms Phoebe Hirsch?" said Mr. Goodman's voice. "Do I have the right number?"

Phoebe felt all the air leave her lungs at once, and wondered if this was audible over the phone. "Yes, Mr. Goodman," she said when she could speak. "This is she, I mean me."

"Ah. I didn't recognize your voice.""

"Well, I try to sound upbeat for the potential parents. This is my day job—managing a little school."

"I see. Well. I thought you might like to know the outcome of our meeting. I was surprised to find you gone when we emerged…"

"I'm so sorry about that," Phoebe said. "As I mentioned, I had another meeting that could not be postponed. I am quite anxious to know…"

"Well, I won't keep you in suspense. It became obvious to all of us that you were the actual writer of this episode. I am not sure whether it was you or Al who felt the need to present it as Al's work."

"It was not my idea," Phoebe said firmly. "I was quite surprised by the whole thing."

"I suspected as much. Well, my question for you is whether you can take a trial position with us, starting immediately. You would initially be credited as a script consultant, with the idea that you could graduate to becoming a writer if your work continues to meet our standards and requirements. You are still something of an unknown quantity. But perhaps your obligations to Brilliant Beginners…"

"Brilliant Babies," Phoebe corrected automatically. "And yes, I am quite prepared to take a trial position with you, although not quite immediately. It's something my employer and I have discussed, but I didn't know when—or whether—my obligations to you would begin, so... Anyway, I can be available during working hours by next Monday, if that's acceptable?"

"I think we can work with that."

"Excellent. But—if it's okay to ask—about Al…will he…?"

"He will remain with us as a writer for the rest of this season. After that, we'll see."

"Oh, good. I didn't want to be the cause of his losing his position."

"Ms Hirsch, you are in no way responsible. Our decision is based squarely on his own behavior."

"Well. That's a relief. So, how does this work? Do I need to relocate to Los Angeles? Because that would be a bit difficult."

"No, not at all. We would need you to come down for a day or two at a time periodically, that's all. To act as a consultant on filming and so on."

"I can do that."

"Any other questions?"

"Well, it would be very helpful to have your offer in writing. It's something I need for—personal reasons, I guess—and anyway, I think your offer should be a formal one, right?"

"Absolutely. I will fax that to you immediately, if you have a fax number?"

Phoebe supplied the Brilliant Babies number. They chatted a few more minutes and then hung up. When the offer arrived, Phoebe gasped and had to count the zeroes. Good lord. The staggering script consultant fee would seem to put an end to Phoebe's financial insecurity.

The custody battle was over, but she knew she had not heard the last of Rafe. She had no intention of allowing unsupervised visitation, and asking Rafe to come out to California every time he wanted to see Ruth seemed unfair, but she didn't have time to work out a solution at the moment. She realized that all her victories were temporary ones, however important and cherished. At least she could work out a solution with Rafe from a position of power when things calmed down a bit. She wrote a short message to Lilith requesting a meeting and placed it in her inbox. Apparently, her entire life was about to change. Again.

* * *

Ginger and Annie were horrified when they heard Phoebe's account of Al's behavior. Phoebe didn't know what to think. She didn't want anyone's marriage to founder on her account, for one thing. For another, she hated the idea of distrusting these women who had so generously befriended her. Maybe Al really had acted on his own. But in her heart, she knew that at least one of the moms had to have supplied Al with the script drafts, even if it was because she thought it was in Phoebe's best interest to get his feedback. Phoebe understood that concern, but on the other hand, they had specifically promised not to do that.

She put it out of her mind. She had more immediate issues to resolve. The moms pointed out that there was a lot riding on the response to the new episode. What if it got hate mail? What if no one even noticed the change? When Phoebe got to Annie's house, she lingered for a moment in the foyer and overheard the end of a discussion about some sort of promotional campaign.

"If each of us called ten friends and got them to call ten more…"

"That's nowhere near enough. We need magazine articles! Interviews on the morning shows!"

"How on earth can we…"

And that's when Phoebe walked in and was handed champagne and the seat of honor.

After acknowledging their victory and giving them mountains of thanks for their help, Phoebe picked up a tiny cheese knife and clinked her champagne flute for attention.

"Speech!" Ginger cried, sounding just a little drunk.

"Author! Author!" Annie chimed in.

"Ladies," Phoebe said, with a mock frown. "You are the absolute best. But let me just say, I overheard you when I got here—I can't pretend I didn't. I want to ask what I hope will be my final favor from you."

She paused and looked around the room at these faces that had become so dear to her. All she saw was curiosity and a desire to help. Her voice softened.

"Please," she said. "Don't try to promote the episode."

"What? Why?" The questions came from all sides of the room.

"It's got to stand on its own. It's got to prove itself. I've got to prove myself."

"Very noble dear, but this is the real word we're talking about."

"All the more reason. Listen, these sponsors are taking a big chance on me. I gave them some good arguments and they are big boys who can certainly make their own decisions but—if I skew the results the first time, and then the show flops a few weeks later—that's a degree of guilt I can't handle. Plus no one will ever hire me again."

She took a sip of champagne while they thought about this. She gave them some time, reminded of Spirit Mountain meetings where people took a few moments to watch their breath before speaking.

"I think she might be right," Ginger admitted, finally. "What's the point of skewing the ratings for one show if she can't sustain it? She needs to know if it's really going to work or not."

"And the thing is," Annie said thoughtfully, "If it is a real success, it'll get all the magazine articles and morning show interviews we want."

So they did the hardest thing—they waited.

* * *

Waiting was not an option for Phoebe. It was a heady and exciting time for her, but an insanely busy one.

Although she now found it surreal to deal with her office managing job, she knew it was important on every level to be responsible to her past life as well as her future one. After all, she could never have guessed that working at the little school would lead her to the current opportunities in her life. And the world she seemed to be moving into was not known for being virtuous. She had to keep from being sucked into values she didn't value.

So she discussed the situation with Lilith with great seriousness and sincere concern for the transition, even when she found it sort of funny to be working out who would give tours of the infant room while she was off giving feedback to seasoned professionals at a television studio in Los Angeles, making in two weeks as much as the entire school earned in a year. She just took a deep breath, smiled at Lilith, and figured it all out.

The two women decided that the best thing would be for Phoebe to take a leave of absence for a few months and see how things panned out. After all, the fairytale could vanish as quickly as it had appeared. It was Friday, and Lilith decided to get a temp to replace Phoebe starting on Monday. The school would muddle through. She was genuinely pleased for Phoebe, but realized how much she'd grown to depend on her. Phoebe promised to train a successor if she couldn't return, and they left it at that, with a friendly hug. As Phoebe left Lilith's office, she could hear her dialing a temp agency and knew that Lilith would handle the situation with her usual efficient cool.

Phoebe had already thought through how all this would affect Ruth. She would remain at the school no matter what. Micah was happy to take responsibility for the little girl whenever Phoebe had to be in Los Angeles, which wasn't all that often. Ruth's world would remain safe and happy. As for Lilith, she and Phoebe would see each other whenever Phoebe dropped Ruth off, and they could check in on how things were going at either end. Phoebe felt pretty good about the whole thing.

She walked out of Brilliant Babies feeling that somehow the sky was higher and the air was fresher. The world awaited! She was totally free to write full-time. Feeling crazy rich with her new contract as "story consultant," she bought her own typewriter—the very latest correcting kind. It was a shocking amount of money, but so was the advance check she'd received. In a gesture that felt both grand and a bit pretentious, she invested in a fax machine as well. Without Brilliant Babies' convenient office equipment, she needed a new way to trade drafts with the show people.

Back at home, she jotted down some ideas for the future episodes, but the show didn't need another script from her for a month. So, with a sigh, she turned back to her columns, writing a slew of new ones for each of her aliases.

It was a bit of a shock to realize that she was due to give Garth another set of columns for his magazine at the end of the week. It seemed like months since they'd had their little meeting, but it was only a few weeks. She felt as though some other person had written these columns and it was hard to fit back into that person's shoes. But when she reviewed the columns Garth had liked last time, she found it boringly easy to provide similar ones. God, she hoped the scriptwriting thing would prove to be a regular thing. She was ready to move on, and the columns were feeling increasingly phony.

Two weeks flew by and before she knew it, the new episode was scheduled to air. Naturally, the moms' group met to watch it together. Micah and Ruth came too, but Abby was already back in New York. Still, Phoebe could almost feel her watching along with them—even though the time difference meant she'd seen it three hours earlier. They had agreed not to discuss it until Phoebe had seen it herself. Phoebe closed her eyes for a moment as the opening theme song began, sending up a little prayer of gratitude to whatever powers there were that had allowed her to reconnect with her friend. With Abby at her side, even if that side was three thousand miles away most of the time, nothing seemed impossible. Micah reached over and squeezed her hand and she sent up a little prayer of gratitude for him as well.

The show began in earnest and Phoebe heard the lines she'd labored over become part of the larger reality of the television-watching world. It was a strange feeling. She leaned forward, not wanting to miss anything.

In her consultant capacity, one of the things she had suggested was to omit the laugh track. The show-runner and director felt extremely nervous about this. They finally compromised by removing it from the scenes involving the mom and child, but leaving it in for the plumber and husband scenes. The moms felt this was even more effective, because, as one mom put it, "You don't really notice the laugh track after a while when it's constant, but you really notice when it stops." And this was definitely true. Phoebe could feel the impact it had.

She enjoyed watching the actors. She knew they loved the challenge of the new episode. Little Lucie rose to it like a real champ. Phoebe thought this might be a significant boon for the kid's career. Even the smaller roles, like the teacher, were given thoughtful performances.

"Can you say Emmy?" Ginger whispered, after the scene in the classroom.

Phoebe paid more attention to the ads this time. Now, when she saw the little cartoon bears in the toilet paper commercial, she saw Mr. Avery, the young man who'd liked the idea of bringing back previous characters and themes.

And when the kids in the sparkling kitchen ate their breakfast cereal with a zeal that was a little terrifying, she smiled, thinking of good old Mr. Goodman.

There was sustained, sincere, and loud applause from her cheerleaders when the show ended. Now came the hard part. Which turned out to be waiting again—this time for the ratings.

* * *

The show-runner faxed a copy of the ratings report to Phoebe's new machine. Like many of the big moments in Phoebe's life, her first glance at the report was a bit anticlimactic. A lot of people liked it. As far as she could tell, no one was terribly offended by it, which was good, but a significant percentage did not notice any big difference between this episode and previous ones.

The surprise came from the producers. One of them called her just hours after the ratings came out to tell her that they considered the episode a smashing success.

"Really?" Phoebe blurted out. "Um, I mean, which aspects of the report are you…"

"I forget that you haven't seen previous ratings reports. This one has an entirely new category! Affluent, recently-married women under forty! In previous reports, they tune in, but leave after the first commercial break. And there were so few of them to begin with that we just assumed we'd never get a significant number of them. But with that dramatic classroom scene right before the first ad, they were captivated! We are getting calls from a whole new set of sponsors! These are proven consumers, my dear. Sponsors would kill to get their attention. You have hit the proverbial jackpot here."

Phoebe had mixed feelings about her first big success being a way to sell more stuff to young women, but she figured she should see it as a good thing. Perhaps she could somehow parlay this success into something that would actually help the world, the way Abby did.

She realized that, as she daydreamed about saving the world through sitcoms, the producer had said something she was meant to respond to.

"I'm sorry," she said. "I didn't hear that last bit."

"I said, we are faxing you a contract for three more episodes over the next season. You'll notice that it includes a clause that requires you to give interviews and provide content for network-sponsored shows and articles. I hope that won't be a problem? We want you to talk about all the things you said to us to convince us to try this new approach—the real issues of working moms, and so on."

"Well, that sounds great!" Phoebe said, feeling better already about the stuff that the sponsors were going to sell to those women. At least she could talk to them about something substantial. And this time, it would be in her own voice—not some cloying little faux toddler, or a fly-by-night advice columnist.

"Good! Glad to hear it! I'll be faxing that right over," said the jubilant producer. They said their goodbyes, and Phoebe switched the phone over to the fax machine. Then she sat and watched her future tumble out of its fancy plastic mouth.

Chapter 21: December, 1979

Phoebe was outlining a scene for a new episode, and didn't hear the phone at first. When she was writing, the rest of the world seemed to fade out. The summer had gone by like a dream from somebody else's life. She and Micah took all the kids down to L. A. when she went on one of her consultation trips and they spent a terrific week at Disneyland. She and Micah had grown closer and closer. It wasn't the sort of hypnotic feeling she'd had with Rafe, but it was real and warm and sweet, and Phoebe found herself missing him terribly when they were apart. Ruth adored him and his children. It was like a little sitcom of its own with a lot of "Awwww" in the sound track.

The phone rang on and Micah ended up answering it. Phoebe finally came out of her writing fog when he stepped into her room.

"It's for you," Micah said, holding up the phone. The cord was stretched to its limit and she had to get up and move into the living room to talk comfortably. As he passed her the phone, Micah whispered, "I think it's Rafe."

A little chill went down Phoebe's spine and she could feel her heart preparing to parachute out, but she took the phone and said hello as calmly as she could.

"How's Ruth?" Rafe asked, with no preamble. He sounded nervous, or maybe just wound up.

"She's great," Phoebe said on auto-pilot. She took a breath, reminding herself of her vow to be fair, to be kind, but also to be wary. "She got the package you sent."

"Did she like the dress?"

"She did, but it's a little small for her. She's really grown."

"Wow." There was a silence. "Listen. I want to work things out. I want to be part of her life."

"In what way?" Phoebe said, trying to remain calm.

"In the way of being her dad. Look," he quickly interjected before she could respond. "I know I'm not in a great position here. Abby told me you suspected that all that money came from drugs. Well, you might have been right. But you know I never used any of the stuff. I was just desperate. I had to make some money. It was all for Ruth—and you."

"Well, you can forget about me," Phoebe said crisply. "You have to accept it. I've moved on."

"But we…"

"There is no we," Phoebe said firmly. "I'm seeing someone else now and even if I weren't, there is zero chance that I'd get back together with you. Let's talk about Ruth. That is something that's possible."

There was a silence on the other end. "You are so different," Rafe finally said.

"I am. Or maybe I'm who I always was, but was afraid to be. I'm not afraid any more."

"Yeah. I get that."

Another silence. Phoebe was tempted to hang up, but she made herself wait.

"Here's the thing," Rafe said. "I'm out of the drug business. I can't even say it was my choice. Tracy got busted.

To be perfectly honest, I need to get out of New York. I'm moving to California."

Phoebe felt panic rise in her gut. "Where?"

"As near to you and Ruth as I can get. I have to figure out a way to support myself. But I have a few contacts from Antioch days and I think I can get something going."

"If you try to harass me…"

"No. It's not going to be like that. Phoebe, I need to be part of Ruth's life. I think about her all the time. She's my reason for going on at all. I get that you don't want to be with me right now…"

"Ever!"

"Okay, ever. I can deal with that. But she's my daughter and you can't deny that."

"No." Phoebe had given this a lot of thought since the trial. "No, you're right about that. She needs to know her dad. But you have to become the kind of dad who is worthy of her. You can't screw up. And you can't be involved in anything illegal. I mean that, Rafe."

"I know. Believe me. I'm working on it."

"Okay. Well, let me know your plans when you have some."

"I will. And Phoebe…"

"What?"

"Thanks."

They said goodbye and Phoebe hung up the phone.

"So?" Micah asked.

Phoebe rolled her eyes.

"He really wants to be part of Ruth's life. He's not going to change in in any real way, but Ruth needs her dad and Rafe needs her. I think that as long as I can make sure Ruth is safe, things should be okay. Not great, but okay."

"You are a much nicer person than you actually need to be," Micah said.

"No." Phoebe grimaced. "I am a much worse person than I could be, but I'm doing the best I can." And they took a few moments in each other's arms before Phoebe sighed and went back to her writing.

* * *

With no day job to distract her, Phoebe was able to continue her columns and do the work she needed to do on the sitcom. She and Garth had worked out an uneasy truce, and she suspected that her columns were a good deal more popular than he let on. She decided early on to avoid mentioning her recent foray into television work. She wasn't quite sure why, but she had a feeling that the less Garth knew about her, the harder it was for him to find ways to take advantage of her. She had called Kent as soon as she got the good news from the sponsors and producers, but she'd asked him to keep quiet about it as well. Not that he had much contact with Garth. Kent had finally been promoted at the magazine and was plenty busy, with no time to maintain an extremely unpromising relationship with someone on the opposite coast. He wanted to tell Hudson, but Phoebe asked him not to. He agreed, but thought she was being foolish. If he'd had that kind of success, he'd have wanted to tell everyone.

It was easy to keep people ignorant of Phoebe's good fortune. Her credit as "script consultant" flashed past while the theme music played and images of the main actors filled the screen. Her own mother could be pardoned for missing it, even if she watched the show, which she didn't. Phoebe had given some talks about her new approach, but they had mostly been to film students and media-related conference-goers. The network was planning a set of magazine articles and interviews about Phoebe in the future, but they weren't quite ready to pursue that yet.

Phoebe noticed the first indication of the network's plans in a People Magazine article on the upcoming television season. It was nearly New Year's, and all the magazines were talking about the end of the seventies and what to expect in the eighties.

In this particular article, Phoebe's show was featured as a trending, must-watch series. She read the article with interest, noting the focus on the very changes she had initiated, but with no mention of her personally. The producers faxed her copies of similar articles from smaller magazines and newspapers. She made some notes on things she'd discuss if asked to do an interview.

She was due to submit a new batch of columns to Garth within the coming week. She always made a point of doing so in person. Again, she couldn't say why this was so, but the phrase "keep your friends close and your enemies closer" came to mind.

She had been slowly and subtly inching the columns more in the direction of her sitcom work. The toddler was now commenting on the day his mom absent-mindedly put her portable tape player in his lunchbox instead of a sandwich because she was worried about a meeting she had that day. The advice column was often addressed to working mothers with parenting issues—one even dared to mention toilet training—albeit in a coy, double-entendre sort of way.

A day before her scheduled meeting with Garth, a letter arrived from his office. It seemed to be a copy of a memo he'd sent to his superior, in which he noted several complaints that he linked to her columns. He mentioned only two such complaints, and they were fairly general—the basic gist was, "Why such an emphasis on parenting all of a sudden?" Checking her copies of recent issues of the magazine, Phoebe found several long articles on parenting, so it was hard to take this complaint personally. The whole world of young couples was becoming obsessed with parenting, and it wasn't surprising that the magazine had jumped on that particular bandwagon.

Phoebe checked the letters to the editor and couldn't find any letters making those complaints. Perhaps the magazine thought it better not to publish them. Perhaps the comments had been made by phone. Perhaps they had been made by Garth. Perhaps they hadn't been made at all.

Garth's memo also spoke darkly of declining readership that he "suspected" was the "silent majority" of readers voting with their feet, so to speak. He implied that the magazine's editors might want to reconsider these humor columns which, he felt, were driving readers away. It looked to Phoebe like a strategic move in a smear campaign that had probably started months earlier around the water cooler.

The memo failed to raise Phoebe's blood pressure. Her heart beat contentedly in her chest and did not seem to be inclined to leap to its death on the floor. Garth was advancing his armies into a war that didn't exist anymore. Her forces had moved into another country entirely.

She was getting tired of the columns anyway. They were now a negligible part of her income and an inconvenient demand on her time. Of course, Garth didn't know that.

* * *

She dressed carefully for her meeting, as she always did when dealing with Garth. She had a private ritual of stopping into the ladies' room on her way to his office and giving her reflection a silent little pep talk and a nod of approval. He still had the power to get under her skin and her formal outfits and makeup were her armor. She was standing there mid-pep-talk when one of the executive secretaries walked in. Phoebe quickly pretended to check her eyeliner, which was practically non-existent.

"Phoebe?" the secretary said. "That's you, right?"

"Yes," Phoebe acknowledged. "Have we met? I've met so many new people lately…"

"Oh, no, we haven't met before, don't worry," the secretary assured her. "I've just been hearing your name a lot recently and some photos of you came across my desk. I've seen you waiting out there for Garth and I just put two and two together. You're the toddler columnist, right? And that advice thing? So funny!"

"Guilty," Phoebe smiled. "But why would you have photos of me?" Sudden memories of protest marches attended during the war sprang to mind and she wondered if people were still blacklisted. Surely not?

"The editors are planning an interview with you—haven't they contacted you yet?"

"No," Phoebe said, wondering what this could possibly be about.

"Well, I guess they have to go through the producers, huh?"

Phoebe looked blank. The only producers she knew were the television producers. She didn't realize anyone at the magazine knew she was writing for the show. The secretary didn't seem to notice her unease. She chattered on.

"It's a story about breaking the glass ceiling. All those male writers in Hollywood, and you come up with the fresh new approach that everyone's talking about..."

"They are?"

"Sure! Anyway, congratulations. You're a real hero to the women writers here, I can tell you."

"That's great," Phoebe said.

"I'm sure you'll hear from the editors soon. They're definitely going to need new pictures, for one thing. The ones I saw looked like your driver's license photo! Anyhow, I don't think anyone but me has figured out that you are the same person who writes for television and who writes those columns! Isn't that a hoot? I feel like a little Ms Sherlock Holmes."

"Yeah. Wow. Well, they're bound to figure it out at some point. Let's see how long it takes them—don't give it away."

"Oh, fun! Okay—I'll let you know just how far ahead I was when they finally figure it out."

"Yes—I'd love to know."

* * *

Phoebe made her way to the waiting room, wondering if Garth was as sharp as the secretary. He had always been so good at keeping his ear attuned to office gossip. It was hard to imagine he hadn't taken the same two and two and added them up, but perhaps he hadn't seen the photos. Maybe he wasn't involved in planning the interview, either. Hmm. Maybe he wasn't as in with the in crowd here as he implied.

As she was working through these thoughts, Garth appeared in the doorway and summoned her with a peremptory little gesture. He looked like the queen greeting the crowd at Buckingham Palace. Keeping a straight face, Phoebe gathered her things and followed him into his office, taking her usual seat across from his desk. She clasped her hands in her lap and smiled, waiting for Garth to begin.

Garth did not sit at his desk, but began pacing behind it, which was not easy considering the size of the office versus Garth's girth. Say that three time fast, Phoebe thought.

"Well, Phoebe, I'm afraid I have some difficult news."

"Ah?" Phoebe said. "Well, give it to me straight. I can take it."

"I tried to counsel you," he said, in his most paternalistic voice. "I told you—more than once, I believe—that this little feminist niche you've chosen for yourself is a dead end. Humor—true humor—is timeless. It does not limit itself to the passing fads of a few self-absorbed young ladies who want to jump on the minority rights bandwagon. Our readers are more sophisticated than that. They expect more from us."

He paused, grimacing and shaking his head like a disappointed grade-school teacher.

"The fact is, I can't cover for you any longer. Whether you believe it or not, I have been your staunch defender here, but my own job could be in jeopardy if I continue to try to make a case for your relevance in the face of all the evidence to the contrary. I know you're struggling and have a little girl to support, but I fear this is not the way to accomplish that. I hate to sound like a cliché but my advice to you is—don't quit your day job."

Phoebe listened without comment. When it was clear that he had finished, she stood and told him, "I understand. I assume you don't want these then?" She held up her little sheaf of new columns.

"I'm sorry but—no, I don't. I can't"

Phoebe smiled sadly. She stuffed the columns back into her briefcase and held out her hand. After a moment, he took it and shook it. It seemed to require something of an effort on his part, and he broke contact almost immediately. "Thanks for giving me a chance," Phoebe said. "I mean it."

She left his office, but she didn't leave the building. She found the secretary she'd spoken to in the ladies' room and asked if she could have a moment with the editor who was planning the interview. It was several hours before she left for home.

* * *

The next issue of the magazine came out a few weeks later. There, on the cover, was a lovely photo of Phoebe. She was glad she'd dressed so carefully.

In the course of the interview, she revealed her "double life" as the column writer and sitcom consultant. She was gracious in her comments about the so-called "boy's club," expressing gratitude for the support of the other writers on the show, while making it clear that they were all men, as were the producers and sponsors. She managed to use words that suggested older brothers, while clearly delineating the advantages of having a woman in the writing room. She made sure to have some interesting statistics to throw in — increased viewership and sponsorship, decline of people checking out after the first commercial, and so on. She radiated humility and gratefulness but, with genuine enthusiasm, she encouraged women writers everywhere to submit their work and not get discouraged. Getting the heads-up from the secretary had been a godsend.

The interview generated an avalanche of mail. Readers expressed their special delight to learn that Phoebe had been the author of the columns that they'd enjoyed so much over the last few months. Many asked if she could possibly continue them, now that she'd moved on to the "big time." She wondered what that conversation with Garth would be like and she grimaced. It sounded rather painful, frankly. Turning to the front of the magazine on a hunch, she saw that Garth's name no longer appeared on the masthead. So, no need to worry about that painful conversation. Oh, well. He had only himself to blame.

With a mixture of guilt and relish, she responded with her own letter, expressing her sincere gratitude to her "old friend" Garth, who'd helped her so much in her career. She said she hoped, at some point, to have time to provide some more of the columns he'd "nurtured so lovingly" and that she hoped she could continue evolving them, even in his absence.

Epilogue: December, 1982

Phoebe tipped the limo driver and let him carry her suitcase to the door. Sometimes even feminists get tired. It had been a tense couple of days in Los Angeles and she was looking forward to seeing Ruth and Micah and sitting on the back deck with a glass of wine.

Gosh, there were a lot of cars on the street. One of the neighbors must be having a holiday party. Maybe more than one, judging by the number of cars. She hoped Micah hadn't promised that they would attend. She was dog-tired.

The limo driver hurried back to his double-parked Cadillac and took off. Phoebe picked up her suitcase with one hand and fumbled in her purse for her keys with the other. But the door swung inward when she leaned on it, before she had a chance to fit the key in the lock. Immediately, scenes of television crime shows in which unlocked doors led to grisly scenes jumped into her brain and she pushed the door open all the way, peering in with a worried expression. The front room was empty.

"Micah?" she called, but not very loudly. What if the perp was still in the house? Her voice was shaking ever so slightly. "Ruth?"

"Surprise!" came the answer, from what sounded like a hundred Micahs and Ruths.

"Oh for Crissakes," Phoebe muttered, dropping the suitcase. "It's my birthday."

* * *

Some blessed individual pressed a cold glass of white wine into her hand and relieved her of her purse and suitcase. Micah was beaming with the success of pulling off a true surprise and gave her a quick hug, stepping back to make way for all the other well-wishers. Ruth came rushing forward with a rather wilted bouquet that she had clearly been holding in readiness for some time.

"They're beautiful, honey!" Phoebe told her. She longed to scoop Ruth up in a big, slightly grubby armful, but her little girl was getting too big for that. She grabbed the flowers instead and, with a loving arm around Ruth's skinny shoulders, went in search of a vase. From the kitchen, she could perceive a change in the soundscape—there were a lot of whispers all of a sudden and a scraping of chairs. Apparently something was about to happen. Trust Micah to have a plan. He hated leaving anything—even a party—to chance. She played along, watching Ruth's determined dawdling in the kitchen and putting the flowers in water. The conversation in the living room was definitely in an anticipatory whisper mode when Micah wandered casually into the kitchen and said (in a transparently stagey voice, Phoebe thought), "Well, Ruth, I think it's time for a little music, don't you?" And Ruth, looking a bit like a trained seal, nodded her head vigorously. She took Phoebe's face in her hands, looking a little like she had at age three, and smiled.

"Mom, I picked out this music just for you!"

"Well, that sounds like a great present," Phoebe said. "I'm always up for a little music." She grinned at Micah.

"What do you have up your sleeve this time? As if the party wasn't enough?"

"Live and learn," Micah said, leading his two ladies back into the living room.

In front of the sliding glass door to the deck, two microphones and a big speaker had materialized. Two guitar stands stood nearby and one of them looked very familiar.

"Isn't that my guitar?" said Phoebe, with a sinking feeling. "You want me to sing? Now?"

"Oh, don't worry," Micah told her. "You'll have help."

The sliding door opened and in walked Robin and Abby.

"You didn't think I'd miss your thirtieth birthday, did you?" Abby asked with a smile.

"*I* didn't think I'd miss *you*," said Robin. "But I do. Come to mama. All is forgiven."

It was hard to remember exactly what followed because when you cry a lot, things get kind of blurry. But like the witches in Oz, there are good tears and bad tears, and one thing Phoebe knew was that these were the good ones. The Glindas of the tear world.

"But I haven't played in years," she protested. "I can't remember..."

"It'll all come back to ya," Robin said confidently.

As it turned out, they were both right. There was a lot of starting and stopping, but they did get through some songs, and they had a very sympathetic and tolerant audience.

"Your voice sounds great," Robin said.

"Yeah. I've been taking lessons," Phoebe said.

"Voice lessons?"

"Mmm. Yeah. But not the kind you're thinking of."

"Whatever they are, it's working for me," Robin laughed, and the sound of that laugh was so good.

So they sang a little more, and somehow Robin knew just the point when they were running out of steam and goodwill. She smiled and took over effortlessly, like the seasoned performer she'd become. She had the crowd dancing and clapping in no time. Phoebe's choir friends had been told to bring instruments and there were plenty of drums and guitars and the occasional flute. No one was going to offer this group a national tour any time soon, but they sounded mighty good to Phoebe, and she ceded the microphone to a choir soloist and slid the guitar strap off her own shoulder.

As she insinuated herself into the audience, Abby took the guitar out of Phoebe's hands and placed it back in its stand. She put her arms gently around her oldest friend. "Welcome home," she said.

"Home," Phoebe said. "Yeah. Look at me. I'm a girl with a home."

She blew a kiss to Micah, who was leading the kids—and some childlike adults—in a snaking dance around the edge of the room. Oddly—and yet completely naturally—Rafe brought up the rear of the snake, with Ruth riding on his shoulders. She had to duck under the ceiling beams, and Phoebe got a lump in her throat, realizing that her little girl was growing up

She took a deep breath and let it all in. And then she smiled at Abby and they danced together the way they used to in eighth grade—like no one was watching.

Acknowledgments

My heartfelt thanks to Joan Robins, for allowing me to use her wonderful photograph on the cover. You can see more of Joan's amazing nature and wildlife photographs at www.joanrobins.com.

Thanks to my amazing writing group for their warmth, encouragement, and awesome talent. Thanks, Marlene Cullen and Susan Bono, for leading it. To experience some of the writing, go to http://thewritespot.us/marlenecullenblog/.

Thanks to my early readers: Joan Robins, Steve Evangelou, Gabriel Grace Solmer, Melanie Allen, Ann Reichsman, Lynn Levy, Mary Regan, Kristi Jacobs, and Clarice Stasz. Your gracious and deeply thoughtful comments made everything better.

Thanks to Clarice Stasz, Tom Hyma, and Peter Manuelian for helping me with the technical aspects of making this book available to the public.

Thanks to the Abode of the Message in New Lebanon, NY for providing the inspiration for Spirit Mountain. Readers should understand that the episodes in this book that take place at that location are entirely fictional. Well—pretty much everything in the book is entirely fictional.

Loving thanks to my supportive and tolerant husband of twenty years, Kim, who exercised superhuman restraint in giving me space and time to write. And there are simply not enough thanks on this planet for Tom and Melanie and Anna for being the best friends possible.

Special thanks to my oncologist, Krista Muirhead, for keeping me alive against all odds. Among other things, she enabled me to finish this book and plan a sequel. Here's hoping.

About the book

Voice Lessons is the story of Phoebe Hirsch, an aimless young woman who comes of age in the turbulent nineteen sixties, pursues art, music, and communal life in the seventies, and finally finds her voice as a writer as the eighties begin.

Along the way, she falls in and out of love, discovers the mystical world of the Sufis, learns to be a good mother, and finds the courage to stand up for herself, her child, and her work. Most importantly, she learns how to be herself.